Killer Rayne

Also By Alanna J. Faison

The Rayne Whitmore Series

The Unmaking

Killer Rayne

The Rayne Whitmore Series

Book II

Alanna J. Faison

Killer Rayne

Alanna J. Faison

Published 2015

ISBN-13 978-0692423417

ISBN-10 0692423419

Cover Art by Alanna J. Faison

Cover Model: Brittiney Faison

Published through www.Createspace.com

To any LGBT individual that has been demeaned, bullied, threatened, or pushed to the point of no return: You are **not** the problem. Hate and ignorance is the problem. The solution is to live, to thrive in spite of it all. It truly does get better. Don't allow anyone to erase the beautiful story of your life that you create every day, with every smile, with every mountain you climb.

Acknowledgements

I may not have a team of professional editors, a large publishing company backing me, or an agent to help me through this journey;

(Not yet, at least)

But, what I do have is a group of people that believe in me, that encourage me, that get excited when I tell them that I'm working diligently on my books. I have people that don't ask for anything in return when I ask them to go through every page and help me make my book as error free as possible. They know who they are and I hope that they know that I am eternally grateful for everything.

It is humbling to hear how much The Rayne Whitmore Series (RWS) is loved by this growing group of followers that I have been blessed with.

For all of the readers that have adopted my books, keep reading. I won't let you down.

Chapter One

I fight as hard as I can, but he pushes into me with all of his weight. Hand over my mouth; I struggle to breathe as his gray eyes give me a window into hell. They seem to suck me in like a black hole. I kick, I flail, but nothing works. Panic sets in and when I reach for my power, nothing inside me answers the call.

"Rayne, I'm inside your head. I have a first-hand view into your deepest fears and do you know what I've discovered? Me." He laughs in delight.

"You fear me. I consume your entire world and I have the key to destroy you. You won't rest without me invading your dreams. Every time you gaze over your shoulder, you will wonder if I am far behind."

His voice becomes lower, deadly as he promises me no peace. I turn away from his stare, afraid of what else he'll see in my own eyes. Then, there is nothing holding me down.

I immediately wake and jerk myself upright in the dark room and reach for Selene, but she's not here, hasn't been around for three days. My heart is hurting from the loss, but it's her fault. She lied to me and I'm not ready to forgive her. I can't even look her in the eyes.

Instead I call for Zara who is in the next room. Dammit Namen, what did you do to me?

Zara wastes no time in coming to my side. Although I am grateful to her for allowing me to hide out in her home, I can't help but be afraid that we could end up getting too close. We already have this bond, but I can sense the small hints of attraction that flow between us. The last thing I need is for me to crawl into her arms because I'm hurting.

That's not who I am and Selene deserves better than that. Zara hasn't even tried to make that kind of move on me. I don't think either one of us would be surprised if one of us tried to ignite that tiny spark. I really want Zara as a friend, just a friend. Yet, for the past two nights in her presence, the power that she represents has called to some of my deeper urges.

Diana was definitely right. She told me that I would seek power, crave it. Ever since my power grew, it seems to be seeking something dangerous and darker. It's actually scaring me, if I'm being completely honest with myself. I don't want to be a power hungry person nor do I want to have an awkward relationship with a friend.

Zara is funny, dangerous, and charismatic. She's also determined to get her soul mate back. I want that for her as well. Because of her blood that flows through me, I also want her to take me there,

Alanna J. Faison   Killer Rayne

to rip me open while she ravishes my body in ways that I've never imagined.

Selene is too good, too nice to do to me what this power inside me is urging, and I don't like it at all. Now, with Namen invading my dreams, it's only adding to this stress. I need to be honest with Zara and ask her about this bond and if there's a way to dampen its effects on me.

This ought to be embarrassing.

When Zara pushes open the bedroom door, she hesitates in the doorway as if reading my energy and wondering if this is a good idea. She's tried not to read my thoughts without just cause and based on her expression, is trying to decide if that link should be open right now. It would be extremely easy to just show her what I'm feeling, but I enjoy the privacy of being the only one to access my mind. Namen is trying to take that away too.

I kick the covers from off my legs and sit up straighter in bed so that I won't look as though I'm trying to seduce her. Immediately, relief is in her expression. I almost get offended at that. Geeze, would that be so terrible if I were?

Ugh. Okay, I'm completely not myself right now.

I tug at the bottom of the long black t-shirt that I'm wearing to make sure that I'm not showing any underwear or extra leg, and then I pat the bed beside me needing her to have a seat. I can't have her hovering over me. It just doesn't feel right. She strides confidently over to sit next to me in her brown thermal, scarf, loose fitting blue jeans, and brown Polo boots. I've never seen her dress this well and I smile.

"Hey, what's wrong? I was just getting ready to head out," she says, pointing back out the door. "The dogs are all sleep in the living room."

Zara has three dogs, one Doberman Pinscher named Nova and two German Shepherds named Tank and Camo. Two girls, one boy. They are big brats with their own room full of toys and a queen size bed. Absolutely ridiculous. When she said that she was a dog lover, she wasn't playing.

"I won't take up your time, we can figure this out later. I forgot that you said that you were going to hunt," I respond, feeling bad for holding her up from feeding. Maybe that's why she was hesitant to come in the room, she didn't want to have the urge to bite me.

"I can wait a few more minutes. It's not like my prey is scarce. There are humans everywhere. If something is bothering you, I want to know about it, Rayne." Zara's face is etched with concern.

I sigh. "Namen is invading my dreams. I'm afraid to go to sleep because I feel like he can hurt me somehow. It's just like when I thought he took my arm. I don't know what's real or fake and I don't know how he's doing it. But, if I can't rest, I can't fight and he knows it," I tell Zara, not wanting to admit that I'm feeling vulnerable.

Zara ponders my predicament and runs a hand through her braided hair that is still in singles, hanging down to her shoulders. "If I feed you more of my blood, then that should help because you'll be more anchored to me, but it's a temporary fix. You're going to need Selene to work a spell to break it. It seems like you're almost under a type of compulsion. When he touched you, he marked you somehow. I don't know. He's coming after you hard and I want to find out why."

"Okay, first, I don't think I should have any more of your blood in my system if I can help it. I don't know if it's too much too fast, but you're making me crazy Zara. It's making me... want you," I admit sheepishly. I almost want to run out of the room. So not me.

Zara looks at me sideways and then smiles like a lion that just cornered her prey. My heart pounds in fear and anticipation. Zara shakes her head as if trying to come back to her senses. She then slowly gets up and then leans against the far wall.

"Stop that," she demands.

"Stop what?" I ask, extremely lost as to what it is that I'm supposedly doing.

"You're reaching for the predator in me. Control your thoughts and slow your heart rate. You're making yourself so vulnerable right now that I can't help but feel you through the bond," she says as if it isn't rocket science.

"Zara, I don't even know what the hell you're talking about, let alone how to not do it. All I know is that you or your aura is calling my power and it wants to reach out and meet it, physically," I tell her. As if to drive the point home, a throbbing down below begins.

Zara groans and crosses her arms.

"Why am I feeling like this? I like you Zara, as a friend, maybe a best friend one day, but I can't do this if my body is going to keep wanting you," I admit, feeling foolish.

"I apologize, Rayne; this is all my fault. It has been so long, since Sage, that I've formed a bond. I've forgotten how powerful my pure blood is. It didn't occur to me that your own power would seek mine this way. It is controlling your carnal urges. My blood inside you is telling you to be all that I may need you to be. A donor, a lover, whatever. And your own power wants to dominate me, consume me."

"But why?" I ask.

"It is how we purebloods make those we bond with loyal. For us, bonds are for life. I've never bonded with someone who wasn't my lover, so I never thought it would affect you because we haven't been intimate. Plus, you were with Selene so it wasn't an issue."

"And now?"

"Now, with your anger at her, mixed with the growth of your power, your chakra is seeking something else to feed on because of my blood. Powerful beings seek other powerful beings and your body is craving me in the most basic way," she explains, making it almost make sense to me.

"So, this is all because of vampire blood? And you're telling me that you really didn't know this would happen?" I cross my arms, skeptical at her obliviousness.

"I can't say that it's all because of the blood that there's an attraction. You had to feel some kind of way toward me, Rayne for it to have erupted like this. I can feel your want as well as my own. As I said before, you are incredibly attractive. I definitely can't say that I would mind if we went there, even if it were just once."

She shrugs casually as if we are talking about what to eat for lunch. I put my hands up in surrender.

"Whoa whoa there, please don't go there. I can't deal, man."

Zara laughs and walks back to where I'm sitting. I nearly gulp as I become all too aware of just how much she definitely would not mind.

"Listen, Rayne, I am a vampire. I told you already that blood and sex go hand in hand. I've taken your blood and so much of mine is flowing through you. I can't help but want to do both with you. That doesn't mean that I will push you, when you so obviously want nothing to do with that scenario. Your emotions are just heightened right now. Once you work things out with Selene, which better be sooner than later, and once you get used to this power, you'll be fine," Zara promises.

"I want to be your equal, Zara, not your food source or lover," I tell her honestly.

She bows in her formal vampire way and smiles at me. "I want you to be my equal as well, Rayne. But, I'm just telling you what is in my nature. I've never really had a friend that I could confide in. I want you to be that. Without sex. You are beautiful, but I have my mate as do you. I still need your help bringing her back by my side."

I sigh again. "Okay. We'll figure this thing out. For now though, I think you should definitely go feed, far away from here. Tomorrow we need to speak with Jaxson."

I know how angry he is with me, but I can't say that I blame him. I brought Anubis into something that he wanted no part of, and then I killed him.

"I agree. Now, try to meditate before you fall asleep. Maybe if you keep your mind clear, Namen will not be able to enter your dreams. We will find a way to rid you of his invasion. Good night, Rayne."

"Night," I whisper as Zara gently closes the door behind her, leaving only her scent of cinnamon and mint.

Chapter Two

When I told Jaxson what I had done, he tried to kill me. Zara had to throttle him in order to get him to calm down. She then promised him that she'd kill him as well as any remaining pack members if a hair on my head was harmed. That was yesterday, once he finally healed. I know that I have no right trying to face him today, but there is still too much work to do. I want to truly apologize for my failure. I know that I can never make up for the life of his alpha, but I want to stay committed to finding justice.

As I get dressed in a dark blue romper and brown open toed sandals, I begin to shudder at the thought of being face to face with Jaxson. I may be stronger than him, but I don't have the rage that he has. Right now, I simply feel defeated. A look in the mirror and a tiny pep talk later, I walk outside to the car to wait for Zara.

Zara has a red Dodge Challenger with twenty inch rims and a stereo system that you can hear two blocks away. She likes to drive fast. For her to be three hundred something years old, she sure acts like a teenager. As I lean on her car, she comes out the house in sunglasses, a fresh white t-shirt, cargo shorts, and white shoes. I shake my head.

The days are warm, but the nights are cold. Spring is still here and by this evening, I'll have to be in jeans and a jacket.

"What?" she asks, noticing my head shake as she unlocks the car door with a remote.

"Nothing at all," I respond, sliding into the car.

"Whatever," she says, buckling up. "Don't you think we should find Selene first? I mean, we're going to need her help. You might as well get this all settled with her and apologize for telling her you'll kill her brother."

"I won't apologize for that. I meant it."

"You may not have to."

"And why do you say that?" I ask, turning toward her as she pulls onto the road.

"Because, I'll do it for you. That way, she can hate me instead."

◊◊◊

Forty minutes later, we are pulling up at the pack's estate. There are ten cars either in the driveway or on the street. This is all that's left of Anubis's pack, Jaxson's pack. My heart starts to beat quickly and Zara reaches to grab my hand in reassurance. She gazes at me through her sunglasses and smiles, fangs showing. She's ready if there's a fight. I left Katsu at Zara's in hopes of appearing diplomatic, but now, I'm wondering if that was a good idea.

I feel like I'm walking the plank as I make my way to the front door. The pack's compound-like house is huge. Two homes were combined after Anubis purchased all the properties on the block in order to make plenty of space for the pack to be able to shift and learn the ways of werewolves. High walls and expertly placed trees create a perimeter and a means to maintain privacy. Many pack members choose to live here and roam the woods behind the home.

Before I can even knock, a wolf that I've never seen before pulls it open. He's average height, only looming over me by two inches and his hair is cropped closely to his head. He seems ex-military to me. A growl forms in the back of his throat and his eyes are ringed yellow in anger. I can feel it coming off of him in waves. My tattoo responds to his challenge.

"You don't want to go there," Zara warns, voice as cold as death.

Her energy gives my resolve a boost. It slips into my own with such ease, awakening power inside of me. "I'm here to make peace, but if you test me, I will defend myself," I promise. I finally start to feel like myself again. "Now, move aside."

Alanna J. Faison   Killer Rayne

The wolf looks back as if listening to orders that I can't hear and then slides out of our way. I still get a push from behind for my trouble. I ignore it as I wind my way into the meeting area where we just planned to go after the lamia. It seems like so long ago that our plans were ruined and I was forced to kill a good man.

All the wolves in the room stand up and flank Jaxson who is standing at the head of the table, facing us, rock solid arms folded across his massive chest, face turned down in a frown. He has on a black t-shirt and jeans, reminding me of when I first saw him as a bouncer. There are twelve wolves in total in the massive room. Four females and eight males, all of various ethnicities and heights.

They look like the mafia as they make no effort to hide their anger toward me. Some of their faces show hints of weariness, sorrow, and anger. Most of the werewolves look to be about my age with a few exceptions here and there. More than a few have seen battle, by the energy they project.

The room temperature drops a few degrees and I force my feet forward, focused on the task at hand.

I keep my gaze down and motion for Zara to stay where she is. Then, I walk slowly to meet Jaxson. Once he's towering over me, wordlessly, I lift my head so that my neck is exposed in submission.

I am definitely not a submissive person but in this situation, I will do what I must to make peace. Jaxson reaches out with lightning speed and grips my neck tightly, only giving me a slight ability to breathe. I don't move as I allow Jaxson to make a choice. It seems like minutes that he holds me firmly before forcing me to lock eyes with him, shaking me. I refuse to turn away from his prying stare as he seeks whatever it is he's looking for.

Finally, he lets me go, defeated, and less angry. There are tears in his dark eyes but he blinks them away quickly, refusing to show that kind of weakness. I grab my neck and cough as he turns away. Still, I refrain from backing down from his muscled form.

"We shall keep Anubis's word as his last request. You are pack. No harm shall come to you," Jaxson declares.

Half of the werewolves in the room cry out in rage. Their human voices turn to growls and whimpers. The other half remain silent, fearful of backlash. Jaxson turns on all of them and roars. "It is done!"

I back away as one tall wolf with short, dark hair and eyes steps forward. He looks to be at least half Hispanic with a very light, olive skin tone. He's dressed in an expensive navy business suit and is sporting a no nonsense look. "Nothing is done. By pack law you must earn your title as alpha, even if you were the second. Just because you can follow orders doesn't mean that you can give them. Until you win, I do not recognize you as my alpha."

Jaxson stares at each of his pack members one by one until he stops at a man that seems to be in his early seventies. The man nods his agreement with the man in the business suit. Jaxson then throws up his arms as if he can't believe this is happening. He steals a glance at me and Zara before puffing up his chest, poised to speak.

"Are you formally challenging me Christopher, to a battle for alpha?" Jaxson asks humorously. I don't blame him. He doesn't look like much, but I know how much looks can be deceiving.

Christopher takes another step forward and raises his voice more for show than to be heard. "Jaxson Kellog, I, Christopher Hughes, herby contest your claim for alpha through battle."

"I accept your challenge and declare that everyone within the sound of my voice bear witness to this fight," Jaxson growls.

He'd just given Zara and me front row seats to this drama. I wouldn't have it any other way. I have a stake in Jaxson winning this after all. Next, the old man that Jaxson had an unspoken conversation with stands up. All eyes fall on him.

"Tomorrow night, this shall be settled. Today is a day for mourning. There will be no more interruptions this day. Rayne Whitmore, if there is something that you'd like to state, please do so and leave quietly. Until this is settled, we will not recognize you here," the old man states. His hair is gray on the sides, hinting at his age, but his body is solid as he stands proudly, commanding everyone's attention. There is no hatred in his voice, simply a matter of fact.

It's okay, Rayne. Just let them know how you feel and be done with it. They will either accept you or they won't, Zara tells me through our blood-link that was created when she gave me her blood for the third time after feeding from me too.

I give her a mental nod, and then speak up. "I failed. My failure has forever changed all of your lives. Anubis believed in me and I not only let him down, but myself. Please understand, I made a decision to protect our secrets and innocents from getting slaughtered. He killed one pack member and nearly killed Jaxson as well. If he would have gotten away in the city, the outcome would have been dire. I did what needed to be done in the time that I had. It is what a leader is supposed to do. So, if you never trust me and I have to walk alone because I had to make an impossible choice, then you all are fooling yourselves. Anubis knew how it would turn out and he asked me to stop him. I came here to make peace with his people because he was becoming my friend."

Tears fill my eyes and I allow them to fall. I don't care if they feel that I'm showing weakness. I hated what I had to do. Some of the pack remains unconvinced, but that's just as well. Anubis must have been a great alpha.

"She's right. It is not just Anubis that we must mourn, but half of our pack. That is not her fault. We should have protected our own as well. We are all failures because of this. Look into yourselves. I had to realize this too. You know we can detect lies and you know there was none spoken by Rayne. Namen Young is the enemy," Jaxson tells his pack members. Some of them hold their head down in shame as they realize how true his words are.

Jaxson then walks back to me, places a hand on my shoulder and ushers me to the door.

"I will speak to you outside," he tells me.

Once the door shuts behind us, Zara stands with her back to the door and gives us room to talk. I think she also wants to listen to any conversation they may be having inside. I turn to face Jaxson and before I can even think about it, pull him into a

Alanna J. Faison   Killer Rayne

hug. He's hesitant to return it at first, but when I don't let up, pulls a massive arm around me tightly. Finally, I release him.

"How are you healing?" I ask concerned. He had a lot of damage and I know that he's not getting any rest. There's too much to handle with his pack.

"I will be fine. My anger will keep me on my feet, trust me," Jaxson responds. Anubis had attacked him once he lost control and Jaxson's stomach wound had looked pretty bad.

The sun beams down on us and suddenly I long for a long beach vacation. I haven't been down to the Bahamas in a while. Maybe I should just move there when this is all over and live out my days. In the distance, cars zoom by. It all seems so normal compared to the problems we're dealing with.

"So, who is this Christopher character?" I inquire.

"Christopher Hughes, or Chris, is the pack attorney and handler of all our major accounts. He takes business trips on behalf of the pack. He also has degrees in accounting, finance, and communications which make him perfect for the job. I don't know too many people smarter than him. Chris was also Anubis's mate's cousin. He is also our most skilled tracker and often trains new pack members that show skill in tracking. He's also the fastest wolf we have," Jaxson admits.

"Damn. That is quite an impressive record. Can you beat him?"

"Absolutely. He doesn't have the fighting experience that I do. Plus, I am the pack enforcer for a reason. For all of his brain power, he has yet to even master the second shift. It's because he thinks too logically about things. He's too afraid to lose control and not be able to change back. He also doesn't understand the sacrifice needed to be a great alpha."

The second shift as Jaxson called it, or the man-beast form is a pack gift that Anubis bestowed upon them. He taught them to control their beast and shift certain parts of their body so that they could use the best of man and wolf in battle. It is a scary sight. I think about Jaxson's massive chestnut wolf self and shudder. Again, I'm glad that he's my ally. Then, I think of Taryn, another wolf that was lost because of Namen's existence and I shake my head. They definitely do not need pack in-fighting right now.

"So then, if you are so confident in this fight, what is the next step?" Zara speaks up.

"Tomorrow night, in the woods behind the grounds, all of us werewolves will shift. Then, we shall battle it out while you all surround us. No one

Alanna J. Faison   Killer Rayne

is allowed to stop the fight and the winner of the battle is to decide the punishment for the loser. It can be either simple defeat and submission or death. Both are fair and recognized by pack law."

"Which will you choose?" I ask as a soft breeze blows by, carrying my words, making the silence seem even more suspenseful.

"I will decide during the battle. My wolf will tell me which one he deserves," Jaxson explains.

Zara nods. "So is there something that you need from us, a reason why you want us there?"

"Rayne is pack to me, as declared by Anubis. You are an ally," he looks Zara in the eyes with a serious gaze.

In other words, Jaxson wants as many people on his side as he can get.

"Good enough for me," Zara says. With that, she walks back to the car and climbs in, waiting for me to say my goodbyes until tomorrow night.

"Jaxson, you will be a fine alpha. I know the circumstances freaking suck, but you can lead, I know you can. I stand by you. Not just because we need your help but because I already view you as a friend. I did the minute that I saw you at Obsession that day," I tell him honestly.

Obsession is a wolf club that I met Anubis at. He had given me Namen's identity and also warned me to stay away from anything involving him. Obviously, I didn't listen. I'm stubborn that way. Or it could be that Namen murdered my family and deserves to have his head savagely ripped from his neck.

Jaxson grunts and pushes me away. "Just be here at nightfall. I don't want the party to start without you."

"It ain't a party 'till I walk in, believe that," I joke.

He snorts in response and I glance back to catch a thin smile on his lips. His nose ring's glistening in the sun. Then, I walk to the car and hop in, stealing one last glance at the werewolf as his large body slips back into the house. Zara speeds away before I finish buckling up.

Chapter Three

"Buckling up comes first, then driving," I tell her sternly. I'm a safety freak. Accidents like car ejections are preventable and people still refuse to buckle up.

"Yeah, yeah, my bad," she responds. "Hey, how did you end up sleeping after I left?"

My temper flares as I remember the invasion of my dreams and my inability to do anything about it. It gives me another reason to despise Namen. That list is getting pretty long. My temper is growing shorter.

"I took your advice and meditated. It worked. Well, at least I think that it's because of that. For all I know, Namen simply got bored."

"Yeah, well, your lover is a witch, this can all be settled if you just... Never mind, the look on your face says it all. Not yet, you're not ready, blah blah blah."

I punch her and she swerves in and out of the congested lanes as if I hurt her. Horns blare as she pretends to lose control of the wheel before smoothly slipping safely back into traffic. It scares me half to death and she laughs.

"Not funny at all you ass; you could've caused accidents. And this is a serious situation between me and Selene. She lied to me-,"

"Didn't tell you, there's a difference," Zara interrupts.

"Sin of omission. Basically lying. She lied about searching for her long lost brother in the club that night when I almost got captured. You saved me because she was too busy looking for him."

"And you met me because of that. Silver lining, Rayne."

Zara speeds up to beat the light and then cuts in front of two cars that are going too slow for her liking. I clutch the seatbelt tighter. Lord please let me survive her driving. I liked fast, just not fast and dangerous.

"Look Zara, you can't honestly say that you would be okay with everything if you were in my shoes. I have every right to be angry. I don't know if Santos had something to do with my family or even the pack's deaths. He's obviously been involved with Namen for a while and Selene had to know something about her twin," I reason.

We turn a corner, in front of a semi. I close my eyes and count to ten.

"And until you hear her out, you'll never know the truth, will you?"

Alanna J. Faison   Killer Rayne

Ugh. She makes it sound so easy, but it isn't. To me, this is like a betrayal and I can't get over that in two days. Even if that means that I'm going to have to deal with Namen in my head for a couple more nights. Zara looks at me and frowns. She's probably rolling her eyes under the sunglasses.

I search for something to change the subject about. Zara isn't really on my side about this. Or, she probably does understand, but just wants us to reconcile quickly. I look at her full sleeve tattoo covering her left arm. "So, what exactly does the tattoo say?" I have been meaning to ask.

"Fine, I'll play along with this subject change, for now. First, the words are in an ancient vampire language. It is part of a prophesy."

"And what is this prophesy that it's so important that you decided to get it marked on your body?" I ask, even more interested now.

She's hesitant to answer, but then sighs and says, "It says that the Blade's sword will bathe the world in blood and that the blood spilled will bring about unrest. A storm will then come that will cause the land to be divided. The Blade must then become a bridge for those that seek safe passage. A shadow. For shadows cannot lead. But, they can only complete their task when the sun shines bright. As a shadow, the Blade must protect the light."

"Um," I begin as the words sink in. Zara is the blade and she is not meant to lead. That much I got. "That's pretty deep, and some of it is beyond me," I admit.

"Yeah well, I'm still trying to accept it. That's why I force myself to look at it every day. My entire life I was groomed to become the leader of the nine, but apparently, my cousin Apollo is meant to earn that title. He's named after the god, Apollo, the god of the sun. There is no brighter light than that. Not only that, but I think there is someone else that I'm meant to protect. It could be you, Rayne, you could be the storm."

Zara pulls up in front of her house but we remain in the car as I unbuckle. I need some things answered first. "How long have you known of this prophesy?"

"I went to the seer when I was nineteen. For sixty years, I rejected those words. I didn't even tell my grandmother what the seer revealed and I kept pushing forward as if I had never known."

"Okay, so when were you going to tell me about this?"

"It doesn't matter yet, Rayne. I mean yes, all these things seem to be adding up, but it doesn't change anything with you. Our prophesies are our own. This is my cross to bear, not yours." Zara takes off her sunglasses and turns to face me. Her eyes are rimmed in red. She's sensitive about her role in this world.

"I started this with Sage when I became known as the Crimson Princess. The only thing is, I can't help but feel deep in my heart that Namen was either the cause of the Dark Days or is finishing the work of whomever started it. Anubis going feral is not a coincidence; it's too similar to that time. His death made me realize that and I was going to share my suspicions with you and Selene together."

I rub my eyes and lean my head all the way back to the headrest. This is absolutely amazing. Not. How long has this man been wreaking havoc? "The sooner we kill him, the better," is all I manage to say.

"You're telling me. We need to hit him and hit him hard. Now, as for the rest of my tattoo, I have tiny blades and tribal designs. I also have the crest of my family covering my back."

Wow. Now, I want to see her back tattoo. "Let's go inside so you can show me," I demand. I've always wanted one, but I have no clue what to get. Well, I guess I have a magical, circular tribal one, but it's not something that I can show the world.

"Sure, bossy lady," Zara responds, hopping out of the car and then sliding across the hood like a teenager.

She unlocks a few of the six locks (overkill much) and is greeted by three furry monsters. They jump all over her, licking and whining as she wrestles with them for a few minutes. Then, she lets them out to go use the restroom. I can't help but smile at her affection for her pets.

Zara has at least four safe houses around the city and a condo downtown, but this is the place that she actually calls home. There is little in the way of furnishings other than the bare minimum, but it still manages to be cozy. The house isn't too large for a three bedroom, but it has a big backyard for her dogs to run and play. I think if it wasn't for them, she'd not even bother to stay here at all.

Zara's favorite color is obviously purple because she wears it all the time and her room is painted a plum color with gold trim along the wood. The small kitchen has a hickory colored table to sit and eat at, with only two matching chairs and a microwave that sits on the counter. This area seems to have been designed for basic use. There are no modern, updated items to be found.

The living room's sofa and chaise lounge are red with black pillows. The rug covering the hardwood floor is black as well. There are no pictures on the walls, no art, and no sense of personality. It's good for her if she needs to leave in a hurry and not leave much of a trace. I'm surprised that her spare room even has a bed.

I guess when you are constantly hopping from house to house, trying to save the world; you just don't care about that kind of stuff. Maybe there was a time that she did care. She has to have her valuables, her treasures, stored somewhere. At least the house is clean and her dogs are well taken care of.

"Okay, let me see it," I say to her as she comes back into the living room after washing her hands.

"Alright, hold up." Zara grabs the bottom of her white shirt and pulls the fabric free of her toned, brown skinned body. Then, she undoes the wrap binding that covers her breasts as she turns her back toward me.

The cloth binding falls to the floor softly as my eyes linger over her muscular shoulders and arms. The desire to touch her flares to life. She feels it too as she stops breathing for a couple seconds. Her strength seeks out my own as I force the feeling back down. It isn't real. It's just our blood-link seeking more than I'm willing to give.

"It's okay Zara," I promise her. "I'm in control."

Zara begins to breathe again, her relief obvious.

Finally, I focus on her family crest that she has imprinted into her skin. The details are so beautifully intricate that I can't help myself from stepping closer and touching her. She jumps at the touch of my warm hand, but quickly catches her composure. Unmoving, like a statue, Zara allows my hand to explore the art on her skin.

"Tell me about Sage," I say as I look over the dragon that is bathed in fire on her back. The purple and gold scales seem incredibly realistic as well as the blazing red eyes.

"Hmm. Where should I start?" she asks, relaxing since I've given her something to focus on.

Her lover, her mate that she has been separated from for over one hundred years.

Zara murdered an immortal and their punishment was to take Sage away from her, locked in a magical sleep for one thousand years. The punishment the immortals chose, equal to the age Blake was when he was killed.

"Tell me about who she was before she was marked. What made her so special?"

I touch the crimson and orange flames surrounding the dragon almost like a blanket of protection.

Alanna J. Faison   Killer Rayne

"She was born in Japan, but moved to Europe when she was young. Her father was one of the few white men at the time that truly respected Asian culture and martial arts enough to study it. He met Sage's mother and fell in love, but her family didn't know about them. After she had the baby, they made him take her and leave. He made her study her culture trained her from a young age and she excelled as if she was born to fight," Zara tells me with a deep longing in her voice.

I touch the claws of the dragon, reaching out as if they are trying to grab its prey. Then, I step back once again to admire the entire piece of art as a whole. It is beautiful and deadly all at once. Just like Zara.

"She was exceptional at everything that she tried, as if she were meant to be awakened. Powerful, alluring, and so damn beautiful." Zara turns toward me, as if she doesn't realize that she's topless. Yet, I don't even attempt for my gaze to trail over her body. Our eyes lock as she speaks of the woman that she so desperately wants to touch again.

"I've always thought that she had some fae blood in her because she was born with hair as white as a ghost. That is a trait that elves are known for. It would also explain why she was so powerful as a human," Zara tells me, finally

Alanna J. Faison   Killer Rayne

reaching to re-wrap her chest. A bra would be much easier, but hey, we all have our habits.

"So, you've never even tried to confirm it?" I ask.

"No. I mean it doesn't really matter. She is who she is. When she got marked, she was riding through a nearby village. There was a fire in a cottage and she rushed inside to save three children while the parents looked on. She told me that there was an old healer in the village that saw the whole thing. Apparently, Sage's aura was glowing and once the man saw that, he knew what he was supposed to do. That man used the last of his strength to call the immortals. Diana and another immortal showed up and marked and took Sage the same day. She was only fifteen."

"Wow. It's amazing how life sometimes works isn't it."

"Yes. At that time, there was a little more knowledge of awakeneds and for someone like Sage, it was much easier to believe than it would be for someone like you."

"I can understand that. So, where do you come in?" I inquire, taking a seat as I hear a soft bark from outside. The dogs are ready to come in. Zara goes to let them in the house before coming back with two glasses of water and sitting beside me. The dogs run playfully through the house as she begins again.

"Sage was notorious for handling rogue supernaturals. Even the ones that weren't all that dangerous began to fear her. Word got around and a request was sent to my family for me to handle her before she became a problem for us. I was in Eqypt at the time training with a half-demon friend of mine named Mikhail. I accepted the mission because I was curious about how a human could create so much fear in our community."

Tank bounds into the room, jumps between us and down quickly before Zara can swat him on the butt. She can't help but smile.

Then, she continues, "I followed her for weeks, studying her fighting skills and habits. I hated to admit it, but she was nearly as strong as me. Definitely even smarter. I had to test her. I needed to feel her energy through battle. That's when she truly came alive. Her aura sang with a need to fight someone worthy. When we fought, I knew there was no way I'd be able to end an angel like her. I fell in love with her before I even knew what hit me."

Zara leans back and I can feel the sorrow of her loss.

"Let me see, Zara," I tell her.

She understands what I mean as she opens up our link and lets me view the woman behind her affections. I see glimpses of hair so white that it looks like freshly fallen snow. I glimpse eyes that are so gray they almost look silver. I see love, a first kiss, hesitant, fearful even, then desire-filled. I see a battle. Zara and Sage are surrounded by nearly twenty wolves, but they fight so beautifully together it can only be art. I see a fallen Sage, the beautiful gray of her eyes fading into nothing and then I see the change as she becomes vampire. Last, I see a tall, dark-haired, glowing Immortal that looks nearly identical to Lawrence standing over Zara. It can only be Blake, the one that Zara killed and fed Sage his blood.

Zara's anger surges around me so strongly that it coats the back of my tongue. She evicts me from her mind and I am left gasping from the magnitude of the hate. I thought that I hated Namen more than a person can hate anyone, but I was wrong. Zara's rage has been festering a long, long time and in this moment, I am more afraid of her than I've ever been of anything. Now, I understand why even Diana was so hesitant to make a move against her that day at Anubis's house. She feels almost demonic to me right now.

Before I can contain my thoughts, Zara growls at me in rage, slamming me against the wall. Her eyes are redder than I've ever seen them. There is no black visible. It's absolutely creepy.

"You smell like them," she snaps. "Are you one of them?"

Oh shit. She's completely lost it by allowing me to access that part of her. I try to swallow my terror, but it's very hard right now. Her body is pressed firmly against me. A few feet away, I can hear the dogs whining, unsure of what to do.

"Listen Zara," I say, much more calmly than I feel. "I'm not them, I didn't take her away. I'm like Sage okay. We were marked by the immortals. I'm your friend."

"Liar!" she screams. "You've come for me haven't you. I'll kill you." Without hesitation, she finds my neck and buries her fangs into me.

I struggle against her, my hands try to pry her off of me, my power tries to trump hers, but her hold becomes stronger as my strength wanes. The sound of her sucking my life force from me makes me sick as she doesn't even attempt to make the bite less painful. It burns and feels as if my artery has been ripped completely from my neck. She pulls back so that I can see the pleasure in her eyes, my blood dripping from her mouth. Then, she attacks again. I scream.

Chapter Four

"No!" I yell loudly, pushing away at... air.

Zara looks at me from the couch as if I am a mental patient. "Uh, what the hell, Rayne?" she asks, disturbed by my behavior.

"I, I. You were biting me. You lost control," I say, sounding crazed.

I look at her eyes and she returns the gaze with wonder. Her eyes are normal, dark, and concerned. There is no blood on her mouth, no rage to be felt. How is that so? Why did it feel so real? I touch my neck and shiver. Namen.

I feel even more violated and betrayed by my own mind. I couldn't even tell that it wasn't real. Is this how schizophrenics feel? That was terrifying. I put my arms around my middle and try to keep from shaking.

"Rayne," Zara starts, reaching for me. I pull away. "It's okay." She tries to give me a reassuring look.

"No, it's not," I respond, tears filling my eyes. "I need some air," I mumble before I get up and jog for the door.

When I get outside, I lean against the house and force myself to breathe slowly. My body trembles as I realize just how afraid I was. How afraid I am. I force myself not to cry. I tell myself that it was never real, that Zara would never attack me like that. Still, I had felt her rage; that much was true. But, when did reality shift? What did Namen Young do to me?

I sit outside for half an hour, more so embarrassed that I had let myself lose it like that. Zara keeps her distance, thank God. When I return inside, she's not even in the living room like I expected. I search for her until I find her in the basement, doing pull-ups with a bar that's attached to the back wall.

"Can I join you?" I ask shyly.

"Sure," she responds as if nothing even happened. I appreciate that, but I also know that I can't run from my issues.

I sit on the yoga mat and stretch. "Thank you," I tell Zara.

"For what?" she asks, pausing from her routine.

"For giving me space until I'm ready to tell you what happened. For allowing me to hide out here."

"Oh," Zara says. She looks at me and smiles. "I'm here whenever you need me. I made you a promise. Whatever you can't handle, I'll protect you from."

"I don't understand why. Despite the past, you barely know me now. Yet, you're so confident." My expression is puzzled, but Zara returns my look like a patient parent.

"Rayne. I can feel you. I see you for what you are and you're special. There are no doubts."

"Zara, I'm going to help you get Sage back," I tell her suddenly, not even realizing why I said that right now.

Zara smiles. "Thank you, Rayne."

I smile back. How in the hell am I going to do that is the question.

◊◊◊

Zara and I sit on the basement floor as I tell her everything that I felt when I thought that she had attacked me. She questions me about every single detail, hoping to be able to unlock the puzzle of my manipulated mind. We come up with nothing.

"It's like a super glamour. Even if I tried to negate it with my own, I don't think it would work because he seems to be deep within your subconscious. Namen wouldn't go through all this work if he wasn't concerned about your power. He knows something that we don't," Zara decides. I agree with her. "I can help you meditate, but you have to relax."

"Well, he's making me feel crazy. Try to search my thoughts and see if you can find something I'm missing," I tell her as I pull her closer to me, wishing her proximity would just negate his invasion of my mind.

"Okay, look directly into my eyes," Zara whispers as I breathe in her scent.

She smells sweet like freshly baked cake, inviting, warm. The pheromones she's kicking out make me want to taste her. This may not be a good idea after all. I pull back hesitantly, thinking about the intimacy between us, but Zara grabs my hand firmly.

"Don't run. Strengthen your will. We are bonded, but I don't have to affect you so. Breathe in my scent, recognize it, and then push it away. I'm your friend remember," Zara coaxes.

I shake my head and then look into her eyes once more. She closes hers, remaining completely still as I reach a decision. I take a slow, deep calming breath and breathe her in completely. Her sent is layered, a hint of sweat under the sweet smell. It sends tingles into my core and I try to push the feeling away. I lean in closer, instinctively as my body craves to be pressed against her.

I tell my mind firmly that that will not happen, but my body, my blood, now laced with hers is responding to her call. Still, Zara remains unmoved as I battle these urges. I recognize her warmth and her need to protect me. I reach for that and pull it into me, accepting her nature. Yet, my body still craves more. My tattoo begins to glow as if it too is seeking her power.

Zara told me that the immortals had so much sex after they reached a certain maturity because they were swapping their energies in the most primal way. Sex rejuvenated them, their auras mixed, replenished one another, and their chakra flowed stronger in their bodies because of it, prolonging their life. It is just as necessary as breathing to them.

Vampires often mixed blood and sex together. It heightened the feeding, gave them something more than just the blood. Vampires crave the energy that the blood gives. Wolves often made love under the full moon, when their power was at its highest peak. Not only is it a rush, but there's something almost spiritual there for them. Selene never told me about power and sex with witches, but I've often felt her magic rise during our lovemaking, even before I knew what it was, before I knew what she was.

Alanna J. Faison   Killer Rayne

Now, I understand this loop even more. A whole new purpose that sex has when you have been awakened. Diana had tried to explain it to me and I didn't listen. If I touch Zara now, my power will rise. My body is pushing me to that and my mind is doing what it can to fight it. Zara knows and understands. That's why vampires choose to bond in the first place. Within the bond is power, love, sex, and protection. I don't want all that, but I may not win this battle.

Without much thought, I give in, allowing weakness to claim me. I open the bond between us, and call Zara's name, the voice in my head filled with need. Her eyes fly open, red rimmed and purposeful. She's suspicious of my call, observing my body language.

Please, I whisper inside my head, not completely understanding what I need, but knowing full well what I want.

"I'm sorry Rayne," she whispers, hesitating only for a second before pinning me to the floor. Her warm breath caressing my neck. Even though she's shorter than me, her body's position on top of me makes us eye level.

I turn to her at her apology. "What are you sorry about Zara?" I ask, drunk off the emotions she's feeding me. A throbbing down below, my body betraying me.

Suddenly, she lets her emotions crash into mine, leaving me gasping for air. She pushes me harder into the floor and I have to force myself not to press my body against hers. Her eyes beg for me to be the one in this situation with some self-control. My desire triggers her instinct, making her lose the battle for composure.

"It sucks when you're in love with someone who is out of your reach and you're incredibly attracted to the one in front of you. I want Sage back, Rayne, and regardless of what you're going through, I know what Selene means to you. But, I'm lonely and you're hurting. We have a bond and I feel you even when I don't want to. I wasn't going to admit it until you did. I'm a hunter and right now, you're looking like the sweetest meal I've ever had. I want to taste you, badly," Zara admits, her voice low with desire. My body becomes warm all over as I know she means those words in more ways than one.

"I can't deny anything you've said, Zara. I can feel you through this link. I don't have good judgment right now," I admit. My breath comes out raspy and I dare not move from under her, feeling like a cornered deer. It will undoubtedly set off a regrettable, albeit probably amazing set of events.

I hope that she didn't catch that last thought.

"The problem is Rayne, that mixed with our bond and sharing blood, I would never be able to let you go if we had sex. I already have a strong drive to protect you. I wouldn't be able to stand it if I wasn't allowed to touch you, even when you work things out with Selene. She would have to share you. You don't want that, Rayne. I could never give you all of me. I love Sage too much. It would destroy all four of us." She sounds broken and I'm ashamed to say that she's just fueling my inner flame.

"Zara," I start as I stare at her beautiful, full lips. My gaze reaches her eyes, red and pleading. I reach up and run my fingers through her intricate braids. She shudders and kisses the inside of my arm, purposely scraping me with her teeth. "One kiss," I whisper to her.

"What?" she asks, even though I know that she heard me.

"Just one. Kiss me," I demand despite my better judgment. I feel my power rise to meet hers in anticipation.

She groans in need and slowly falls into my body. I try to remain still. She moves her mouth closer to mine with the slowness of a baby snail. I know that her behavior is to give me plenty of time to change my mind, but I won't. I can't. A single kiss from her is my strongest desire right now. I let her see that in my mind. Believe it.

Zara locks her eyes with mine as she pauses one last time before gently colliding with my lips. With a gentleness that I didn't believe a vampire could ever possess, she kisses me. It is filled with a promise that wherever I want to go with this, she will follow. I lick her bottom lip as slowly as I can manage, tasting her and committing it to memory.

Then, I allow her razor sharp fang to draw blood from my tongue as I deepen the kiss. There is no pain, only desire. The blood sparks something within her and we both explode with deep craving, clutching each other protectively as our bodies melt into one another.

Zara pumps vamp pheromones into me through her saliva and it increases the pleasure of the kiss 100 fold. I moan and grip her tighter as she possessively sucks on my bottom lip. Our power explores each other's as I feel like I'm on the verge of an explosion. The raw desire flowing between us is a product of our need to connect, the bond pushing us together. My back arches just as...

Nothing. There is only me and an empty room. The front door closes loudly before I hear the rev of her car engine. Part of me is horrified that if it wasn't for Zara, I would have never been able to stop myself. The other part of me is angry at her for stopping at all. The latter is the part that scares me.

I've never felt anything like that before, not even with Selene.

I love Selene, deeply. But this, this is danger. Skydiving without a parachute, swimming with sharks while bleeding. I was on the edge and falling fast. Zara is a drink of water after a week of thirst. I can never, ever do that again. That woman will consume me and I will enjoy every second of it.

Diana had once told me that people believe vampires to be unemotional creatures. The truth is that they are the most emotional of all. With them, everything is heightened. Well, that's a climb to heights that I should definitely stay away from. I shudder as I press my fingers to my mouth, now scorched from her soft, pink lips. Even my power seems to hide out from the force that Zara is. I don't think that I'll have an issue with the bond anymore at least. Hell, I can't even remember what we were supposed to be doing in the first place.

Chapter Five

Zara doesn't return until the morning I'm sure that she fed well and probably did other things that I couldn't give her. The entire night I thought of her and Selene. Eventually, I'll have to talk to Selene about Zara. I won't lie to her. It's amazing that I'm thinking of this when I can't even stand to be in the same room with her right now.

This is all bullshit. That damn kiss may have just been the end of my relationship. I'm such an idiot. I had said that I wouldn't allow that to happen, but I did at the very first opportunity.

The nail in the coffin.

After I shower and throw on some of Zara's basketball shorts due to my lack of clothes, I find her out in the back with her dogs, playing fetch. Zara turns to acknowledge me but continues to play with her pets.

"I'm going to make this quick okay," I tell her, the sun beaming into my eyes.

Zara throws the yellow ball one more time as the three race to catch it. She turns to me, arms crossed, closed off. I roll my eyes at her and she smirks and uncrosses her arms.

"I'm going to be honest. That kiss was, wow. It truly opened my eyes. I've never felt something so powerful, Zara. At the same time, it scared the hell out of me. Whatever that was, I don't want that. I can't handle that. I think that I've gotten the result that I needed. You and I, we'll be friends, just friends. I think the bond will be okay now." I take a couple steps toward her and motion for her to close the gap. She does and then I embrace her.

"You are wonderful, Rayne. I'm sorry that I allowed you to betray Selene for my own needs. The priestess already thinks so low of me and I did nothing but prove her right," Zara says, pulling away.

So, that's what she's worried about huh. I smile sadly. "It takes two Zara. I will worry about telling her when the time comes. It'll be her choice what she does with the info. I just know that it can't happen again. I'm way too afraid to lose myself in you. Even my power is afraid," I tell her honestly.

"Well, trust me, you won't have to deal with me forcing the issue. I felt what could have happened. I already told you that I wouldn't be able to let you go if it went farther. I think you understand that now."

"Uh, yeah. Definitely. Thank you for understanding."

"Thank you for choosing to be my friend. I think it's what I need more than anything right now," Zara admits, pausing to throw the ball once again when Nova drops it at her feet.

"You and me both Zara. You and me both."

◊◊◊

As Zara and I get dressed to go to Anubis's house, I convince her to let me drive this time. I can't deal with her driving right now. I'm surprised that she agreed so easily. After I put on my army yoga pants and dark green v-neck sweater, I snatch the keys and wait for her by the front door to lock up with Katsu, my beautiful sword, strapped to my back.

The night air is brisk and the moon illuminates our faces. Tonight is a good night for a battle. Zara is silent as we slide in the car, connecting her phone to the Bluetooth stereo. She plays some old Nas, the rapper, and I nod my head to his smooth rhymes as I pull away. She told me that I need to check out J. Cole, so she's looking up some of his songs.

It's a fun ride back to Anubis's estate and I'm almost sad when I park. I was enjoying vibing to the list of songs that I'd have to catch up on. Jaxson is waiting for us on the sidewalk without a shirt on, the chill in the air not affecting his werewolf body chemistry. I smile at him when I shut the driver's side door. He nods at Zara and she strides to the back of the house, pulling her black hood on her head. The street is once again filled with cars and I'm sure that they're all in place and waiting on us.

Jaxson confirms it as he escorts me to the back and into a clearing with his hand on my lower back. We round a corner and there are three wolves in Zara's face, growling, still in human form. When Jaxson steps in front of me, they give him a look, and then back off. Zara snorts and leans against a tree. They obviously have no idea who she is. Maybe they weren't at the house yesterday.

"Is everyone present?" The old wolf from the other day steps into the middle of the circle and everyone turns to face him.

I look around. The group is slightly bigger than I've seen so far and as I breathe deeply, I absorb all the tension. Even with a slight breeze and the openness of this makeshift arena, it isn't hard to pick up the rage coming off of Christopher. It is painfully obvious that he blames not only Jaxson, but me and Zara for the events of late. He'll channel all of that to take out on Jaxson.

I pull Jaxson to the side quickly. "You may be stronger, but he's pissed. Be careful."

"Oh, you have no idea the rage in my own heart. I'm just much better at hiding it," Jaxson counters before stepping to join Christopher and the elder wolf in the middle.

"Everyone is accounted for," Jaxson tells him loudly.

"I think so too," Christopher adds. His voice is deep and rich, filled with confidence and excitement.

Zara puts a hand on my shoulder and I shiver. *This is going to get bloody,* I say to her through our mind-link.

Definitely, she responds.

Will you be able to handle it? I ask, suddenly remembering how she was when we found Taryn and the other bodies, the dead children we had worked so hard to rescue. She'd almost lost it. There'd been so much blood. I never asked her about her friend on the force, if he'd taken care of the bodies, Anubis's too.

There were a number of reasons why I reacted that way last time. I was already angry and let my guard down. I wasn't prepared for it. This time, I'll be fine, she promises.

I shut down the bond and turn my focus to the werewolves now spreading out, widening the circle. She and I do the same until we all are about thirty feet away from the middle of the makeshift ring. The older wolf nods and lifts his hands, acknowledging all of us.

"Very well then. This is a formal battle for Alpha. Our leader is to be decided tonight. Are there any other competitors here tonight?" he asks. A few moments pass by and no one speaks up. He continues, "Jaxson and Christopher will fight until there is a clear loser. One may either submit, be knocked unconscious, or be killed. All are justified. The victor will then decide if the loser shall be pardoned, exiled, or killed. This is pack law." His voice carries to each and every one of us. I let his words sink in.

"This is just," every pack member responds in unison causing me to jump. Creepy. Just plain creepy how they all seem to speak so robotically in unison. With that, the elder wolf steps back and finds his place within the circle.

Finally, all the werewolves begin to strip out of all of their clothes. There is no modesty here. Their naked bodies are beautiful. All are fit, some are scarred, telling their own stories of fights they've had to endure, and they all stand proud to be with their pack. It is a bond that I'll never understand. Even this close, I still feel apart.

Finally, the grunts of the change take over. I study carefully and can almost see the aura of each wolf alter along with them, the unseen wolf magic bathing them like a blanket of gentle ocean waves.

Jaxson and Christopher change the fastest and I can tell which of the group are the strongest by the speed of which they shift. Sometimes, younger, weaker weres can take ten minutes or more to transform before they master their nature. Tonight, among pack, the slowest wolf only takes three minutes to change. It is an amazing scene to watch.

The wolves shake off the pain of the change and I look at Zara, suddenly extremely glad that she's with me. Every wolf stands to at least my navel with variations in between. Sage had defeated a whole pack of wolves alone? Wow. What do you have to do to become that powerful? How intelligent do you have to be to understand the nature of battle so precisely to be able to defeat that many enemies? Zara picks up my thoughts and smiles. I shake my head at the thought of ever having to do that. Not alone.

My tattoo begins to glow, warming me as it responds to the power of the wolves. I touch my chest above my heart where it was burned into my flesh by Diana with her blood and magic. Then, my attention is brought to Christopher and Jaxson as they begin to growl at each other. They size each other up, hackles rising as they close the distance between each other, fangs gleaming in the moonlight. Before I can blink, the fight begins.

Chapter Six

Christopher strikes at Jaxson first, a blur of silver and white fur as he attempts to catch Jaxson off guard. Jaxson is nearly knocked off his feet when Christopher collides with him. They snarl and attack each other, snapping and striking with fangs and claws. Jaxson's strikes are harder, more precise, and because of his larger size, seems to do more damage. The other wolves look on, low growls in the backs of their throats. I hold my breath as I watch it all unfold.

Chris uses his superior speed to jump on Jaxson's back, biting his ear and shoulders, but Jaxson quickly bucks him off before launching an attack of his own. They crash into each other and roll in a pile of fangs, fur, and claws until they hit a wall of wolves that make the circle's barrier. The wolves snarl and snap at them until they move their fight away. Jaxson anticipates his opponent's next few moves and easily leaps over him, turning, and slicing out with his humongous paws.

His attack is met with a whine. They break apart and then Jaxson strikes again, obviously confident that he's going to gain the upper hand. He lands well placed bites that coat his opponent's fur in dark blood. Jaxson feints and then knocks Christopher down, but allows him to get back up, in no hurry to end the fight. Honestly, I think that he just wanted to feel out Chris's power or let his wolf decide what he should do once he wins. I don't think he'll be much of a threat.

Chris seems to realize that he's not in a position to win the fight and explodes. Desperation is evident in his behavior as he moves in a frenzy. He strikes and zips away. Then, he feints, slipping past Jaxson's next attack and manages to clamp down on his throat, shaking viciously and drawing blood. Yet, Jaxson uses his superior weight and falls on top of the smaller wolf, pinning him.

Chris struggles to get from under Jaxson, kicking and growling. Jaxson too growls in anger as Chris manages to slip from under him. But, Jaxson refuses to relent and catches the silver and white wolf's hind leg. Bones crunch and Christopher howls in anger. Jaxson flings him across the ground. He tries to pop up and get away, but Jaxson lands on top of him, and bites down with fury, ripping fur and drawing blood in numerous places.

My fists clench as I steal a glance at Zara. She's standing with her arms crossed, watching the fight with a cool glare. There is no hint of bloodlust in her eyes and satisfied, I turn back to the fight as it reaches its conclusion. Jaxson was just giving him a chance to show himself as a capable fighter to the pack, but Chris doesn't have what it takes. In terms of intelligence, I'm sure that he'd be a great leader, but this is a battle of strength and you need both to be a leader of a pack like this.

The rest of the pack seems to be coming to the same conclusion. They begin to step in closer, closing the battleground in for the final strike. I catch sight of one wolf as she whines quietly. Her eyes become desperate as she strides forward covered in beautiful black fur. She's obviously a supporter of Christopher's.

Jaxson has Chris between his front paws, neck exposed. One powerful paw slams down on his throat and Chris barks out a cough as his windpipe is compressed. A hush falls over the entire group, leaving only the sound of the wind through the trees as Jaxson brings his face close to Chris's. Removing his paw, he places his teeth on Christopher's neck, biting hard enough that even more blood coats his fur.

But, Jaxson releases him before he kills him once Chris makes no attempt to fight back. A sign of submission. Then, Jaxson steps backwards and changes back to human, panting from the exertion. The naked, new alpha stares at every single one of his pack as they all lay on their bellies with their tails tucked. Jaxson looks at me last, eyes still yellow from the change, blood dripping from his body, a series of cuts coating his light brown skin from Christopher's attack, before he tilts his head back in an inhuman howl. The rest of the pack sit back up and howl with him.

Oh, what will the neighbor's think?

"It is done." Jaxson points to Christopher still lying on the ground in defeat. "Come, recognize your new alpha," he demands to the group. They all step up to show their respect. Jaxson touches each wolf's shoulder. Chris is last. He limps before Jaxson, leg really injured. Since he's in werewolf form, his advanced healing has luckily already kicked in.

"I let him live because our numbers have dropped and we need a strong pack in order to stay ahead. Christopher Hughes may have been defeated this night, but he is still an asset to our pack, our family. My wolf judged him and saw him fit to live. It is done. Colin," Jaxson addresses the elder wolf.

With the strength of the pack behind him, Colin changes back into human quickly as well. "We recognize you, brother," he states, voice raspy, to Jaxson.

"Tonight, we will run in celebration. But first, I will name my second, my enforcer, my right hand," Jaxson shifts his left paw slowly back into a wolf's paw. He turns to Christopher, still in wolf form just like the rest of the pack and gives him a look until he shrinks back into the rest of the crowd. I think we all assumed it would be him in an attempt to solidify the pack. Well, you know what they say about assuming.

"I name Rayne Whitmore as my second," Jaxson's voice booms through the crowd.

I have to pick up my jaw as his words sink in. Among the werewolves are growls and whines of protest. To my left, I hear Zara snickering. At least someone thinks that Jaxson basically giving a middle finger to all of his pack and choosing me, a human that killed their alpha, to be his second is hilarious. I give her a side glance and she shuts up.

"Uh," I manage to say before Jaxson raises his hand to silence the group.

"She is my second. There is no debate," he says with finality and a threat of violence to anyone who dares to try him. His eyes shine an even brighter yellow. The alpha magic quickly embraces and recognizes Jaxson as worthy. It's like the magic agreed that he fill Anubis's shoes.

Colin speaks up, "This is the most absurd thing that I've ever heard in my time. Yet, it's absolutely brilliant. There is no pack law against it. I second that it stands. As an elder of this pack and with the respect that this title has given me, I recognize you, Rayne Whitmore. I recognize you, sister." He chuckles at Jaxson's move.

With his words, I feel a rush of pack magic reaching out to touch me. It's nothing like Selene's magic, it is wild and carefree. Wolf-like. It's almost as if it's playfully nudging me as it tries to figure out who I am. Jaxson beckons me forward and with one more glance at Zara, I step into the middle of the circle. The wolves are all silent, unsure of what to do.

Jaxson takes his clawed left hand and slices his right hand until it bleeds. Before I can protest, he does the same to my hand. Then, he shakes my bloodied palm and our blood mingles. Both of our cuts then disappear. Incredible. I look into his eyes in question.

"Pack," is all the answer I get.

He steps in front of me; chest puffed out in pride and once again addresses his pack. "There is a new dawn approaching. We shall continue on with the legacy that Anubis left us, but we shall also strive to become even stronger than before. Because of this, we must eliminate a vicious enemy known as Namen Young. No more shall we cower in the shadows. We are werewolves and we will fight this threat as pack. United. Strong."

His words coat my heart and I smile at my friend that may have done something that divided the pack even more. He did this for me and for Anubis. Jaxson is a strong man, caring on a level that I have yet to completely understand. Still, I can

Alanna J. Faison   Killer Rayne

feel it in my heart that he will be loyal beyond measure.

"Now," Jaxson begins. "Let us take to the forest and run in celebration."

A growl from behind us turns our attention. The black female wolf from before leaps at me, fangs dripping; a promise of death looms in her glowing eyes.

Chapter Seven

I feel her before I see her; she's already reacted before I can make a move. A wall of magic bats the wolf away causing her to topple over and onto the ground. I'm too dumbfounded at the quickness of Selene's reaction to move. My hand is ready to clutch my sword. Her footsteps echo through the night as she steps forward, into the circle. All of the other wolves look between her, Jaxson, and me. Zara slides back into the shadows for cover, prepared to strike if need be. I remove my hand from the blade, satisfied that there is no longer a threat.

One arm outstretched, hair flowing in a non-existent wind, Selene keeps the wolf pinned to the ground with her power. She stays focused on the black werewolf, even as she comes to stand before me. Her green eyes glow in rage and her mouth is a thin line. I notice that she's biting down on her teeth. Oh, she's angry alright and I don't think it's all toward that wolf.

"Good thing I asked you to come. Let her up," Jaxson tells Selene.

She doesn't contest it, but flicks her hand and the wolf slides further across the ground before Selene releases her. Jaxson gives her an amused look, arms crossed. She shrugs and then looks at me, head tilted slightly. "No one touches what is mine," Selene warns.

I look away and at Jaxson, not knowing what exactly is the best course of action right now.

Jaxson demands in his Alpha voice, "Change. Every single one of you."

Colin shakes his head at the female wolf that tried to attack me as the rest of the pack slips back into their human form, breathing as if they've run a marathon. The scent of fear from the pack assaults my nose and I wonder if they know what's coming next. Jaxson steps to the female wolf as she tries to cover her naked body with her long black hair and arms. He snatches her by the arm, his huge frame dwarfing her own. Then, he drags her to the center of the circle, even as she is still trying to catch her breath from the change. Her yellow wolf eyes meet mine defiantly, but then she quickly turns away before Jaxson can catch it.

Her attitude angers me and sensing it, Jaxson pushes her to her knees at my feet.

"Please Jaxson," Christopher begs from his spot in the circle. Most of his body is coated in drying blood. There are ugly puncture wounds marring his skin. His hair is matted down and he can't hold any weight on his leg yet. "She's my mate."

Jaxson turns back to me. "Rebecca, Rayne is pack. She is my second and she outranks you. What you did was a betrayal and it was cowardly. That is not the way we do things. I give you to Rayne in retribution. You will not purposely attempt to harm one of mine without consequences. Before Rayne chooses how to deal with you, you may speak so that I can understand why you would test me so." Jaxson's voice is calm and quiet though I'm sure none of the wolves have any problem hearing him.

"I, she, was given a place in the pack when she's done nothing to earn it," Rebecca cries.

Christopher begins to step forward and Selene's magic chills the air in warning. He stops immediately, but stares at me in anger, knowing her life is now mine to claim. If he intervenes, Jaxson will kill him.

"Chris has worked harder than anyone to keep the pack together and you just spit in his face by not allowing him to be your second. How could you, Jaxson? After all that he's done for us, how could you overlook him?" Sobbing, Rebecca looks at the ground, eyes closed, fists clenched.

I see her point, but Chris is not a fighter. He doesn't have what it takes to do that job. Each pack member has a role and his place is not number two, not yet at least. She loves him and her pride and affection is clouding her judgment.

Jaxson pretty much sums up what I'm thinking, saying, "Christopher is a tremendous asset to this pack. He is family, no doubt. Still, Chris has other talents that cannot be matched by anyone else. That is where I need him the most. He can't be my enforcer if he is running out of town on pack business all the time. I need someone who will be here.

"I've fought beside Rayne and also sparred with her. I know what she is capable of and believe me; she will not let any of us down. Rayne believes in family, she understands how deep that bond runs. She can do this. When I find one of you that I'm sure can be what she is now, then I will choose a new second. Until then, you can either wait, or you can choose to fight her now for that right. Prove me wrong, show me that you can do this."

I hold my breath for fifteen seconds as my tattoo begins to glow in anticipation of a possible fight. I eye each wolf, trying to make out a potential threat. This is not what I signed up for, but there's no way that I'll leave Jaxson hanging and looking like a fool. If he wants to name me his enforcer, so be it. I think that I owe him that much.

No one steps forward and satisfied, Jaxson states, "Now, Rayne, she is yours to do as you see fit. No one will interfere." His voice is deep, deadly, and daring someone to test him.

Zara flashes next to me in a sign of solidarity. I look to Selene first, Zara, then Jaxson for a sign of what I should do, even though I know what I want to do. They all wait patiently until I reach a decision.

"Stand up," I demand. "I want you to stand before me and look me in the eyes."

Rebecca snarls silently and stands. She is about my height of 5'5" and is toned nicely, her abs defined against her ivory skin. She seems to be about twenty, which means she's probably between twenty eight or thirty. Werewolves treat aging like a disease and their high metabolism seems to burn it away. Her face is blemish free as if she takes great care with maintaining it and her long black hair falls against her body like a curtain.

I lick my lips and smile as I pull Katsu, my sword given to me by Lawrence and Diana, from my back. She feels sure in my hand and I give her white blade a once-over. Then, as quickly as I can, run her tip through Rebecca's middle, until the hilt is touching her stomach. When I pull Katsu out, gleaming with blood, Rebecca gasps in pain and falls to the ground face first.

"No!" I hear Chris yell, but I tune him out, knowing that I have at least three others watching my back.

I fall to a knee and place my mouth next to Rebecca's ear. "I didn't hit any vital organs. Change and you'll heal quickly. This. This is the extent of my mercy," I whisper, my voice full of collected rage. "Never threaten me again wolf."

Chapter Eight

Jaxson orders Christopher to take Rebecca back to the house to begin her change. The run is still on tonight and she isn't allowed to be a part of it. Chris limps over to Rebecca and together they slowly make their way back to heal. Jaxson pulls me to the side to ask if I'm going to stay until it's over, but I decline. When I turn back around to look for Selene, she's gone.

"She said that you can come look for her when you're ready to listen to her side," Zara explains.

I sigh and run my fingers through my hair. Selene is undoubtedly pissed off. My heart aches at the loss of her presence, but I really don't know what I should do. She kept her brother a secret from me. He probably was in on my family's deaths. At the very least, he knows what kind of man Namen is and he chooses to follow him.

Santos.

He's a threat to me and maybe even Selene. If I want to stop Namen, I'm going to have to go through him. How do I just lay up with Selene knowing that I may have to fight and kill her brother? How can I pretend that this doesn't change us?

Alanna J. Faison   Killer Rayne

Feeling my turmoil, Zara touches my shoulder and smiles, "Hey, it'll all fall in place. I told you, she can turn that anger toward me. You won't have to do anything."

"Still, she'll know. She'll know that I would do it if I could and that we've spoken about it. It can't be the same between me and her, Zara," I sigh.

Jaxson looks on as we speak and then says to Zara, "I need to speak with you about something quickly."

Zara nods and lets go of my shoulder. Then, she walks a distance away with Jaxson. The other wolves look toward me, still unsure. I smile, trying to seem non-threatening as I walk to the group.

"I'd like to know all of your names if that's okay," I say.

I promise the wolves that I'll do my best to commit all of their names to memory right before Zara's steel grip grabs my arm and pulls me back to the car. The wolves begin to growl at the perception of aggression, but I wave them off. Soon, Jaxson takes their attention as I get pulled through the trees.

"Hey, what is the problem," I ask pulling away from her once my arm begins to throb. Then, I look into her fiery eyes and step back. "What the hell is going on?" I ask calmer now, hoping to hide my fear.

"We are going to take a ride. Give me the keys. I'll tell you on the way.

◊◊◊

Hesitantly, I let Zara drive. She zips through traffic with scowl on her face. I really don't even want to ask what in the world is going on, but I open my mouth anyway.

"So, where's the fire?" I ask, watching the scenery blur by animatedly.

"Jaxson just informed me that my contact on the police force has not released Anubis's or the other pack member's bodies through the proper channels like he was supposed to. It seems that he's gone missing," Zara growls, looking madder than a cat taking a bath.

"Oh shit," I say.

"Oh shit is right. We're headed to his place now."

I sit in silence as I go through all of the possible scenarios as to why this has happened. All roads lead back to Namen. Zara is pissed at the screw up and her bond reveals that she is definitely out for blood tonight. I don't blame her. The pack needs his body back for burial. This is the closure that they need, how could this go wrong too?

Chapter Nine

We pull up to a house on the north side of town. This neighborhood seems awfully busy, especially at ten p.m. I could never sleep with cars rolling all up and down the street at all times of the day. Zara turns left at a stop sign and then pulls up to the curb at the last house on the block. It's an old brick house that seems to be averagely maintained. Big bushes in the front block the window, but the light from the t.v. makes me think that someone's home.

Zara walks up the pathway to the house and when she reaches the porch, waits for me to meet her by the door. "I don't sense anyone, so wait outside just in case he pulls up." Without waiting for my response, she breaks the knob and steps inside.

An alarm blares, making me look around to see if we've attracted attention, but she doesn't seem to even care. In less than thirty seconds, she's out the house.

"Come on. His bags are packed. I need some information from a vampire that's on the force as a liason. I know where he'll be," Zara reveals as we get back into the car. She doesn't even care about the door being wide open, the cars driving past curiously, or the alarm screaming into the night. We pull away and hit a u-turn at the corner.

"How long have you known this person?" I ask curiously. Zara obviously doesn't take lightly to being played. I'd truly hate to be on the wrong side of her wrath. Just ask Blake.

"I've been working with him for the past five years. There's never been any issues before. He's human and a pretty decent guy, or so I thought."

Zara rubs her face and sighs. She slows down when a police cruiser turns a corner and drives on the opposite side of the median. Then, she fiddles with the music before deciding to turn it off.

"Okay, we'll figure this out together. Do you think your vampire friend will be able to give you the info you need?" I ask hopefully.

"He'd better or blood will flow tonight," Zara promises.

Shortly, we pull into the parking lot of a nightclub that I'd been into a couple times in the past. It's called *Wet*. I'd always thought it was because once you walk off that hot ass dance floor, that's how you'd leave. It was always packed with sweaty bodies. I definitely didn't expect to come here.

We park and I can hear the music bumping from here. The crowd is extremely loud as a group of about fifty wait to get inside. Purposely, Zara strides up to the front despite protests from the line dwellers. She pretends that they don't even exist.

"Move the rope," she commands, looking the bald headed bouncer in the eye, glamouring him with vampire mind control. Wordlessly, he lifts the barrier keeping us out and we stroll in. One look at the guy taking money inside and he says nothing as we walk by.

The dance floor is packed body to body, and we have to push our way through as we reach a door that I've never noticed before. Once I feel the shimmer of magic, I know that it's glamoured to anyone that isn't an awakened. She pulls the door open and a set of stairs is revealed. Down we go.

Once we reach the bottom step, the upstairs music is replaced by a calmer beat. My eyes take a second to adjust to the darkness and I begin to make out the shapes of tables, chairs, and bodies. There are people smoking cigars, drinking, and taking blood. Yet, everything stops when we step into the room. The music becomes nothing but soft background music. Zara's eyes are cold and calculating as she takes in the entire room.

"Where is Logan?" she asks in a powerful voice like the ruler of a kingdom. The sound is amplified by the room's acoustics.

The entire group stands up in unison. I sense their aggression and pull my sword. Zara's eyes turn red and she grabs the nearest vampire by the neck and snaps it. It's only a threat, not enough to kill the vamp, just knock him out. No one moves nor says a word.

"I said, where is Logan!" she roars.

Her anger blindsides our bond and my head begins to throb under the pressure. But, she doesn't relent. Some of the vamps back up but some hold firm. Finally, another door opens and a vamp comes through, an unconscious woman on one shoulder. He drops her to the floor like unneeded trash. Then, he turns to Zara.

"What do you want Zara?" The guy asks. He must be Logan.

"I need information. I'd appreciate it if the rest of you would stay out of my way," Zara responds, voice as cold as a glacier.

"No," Logan says.

"Excuse me?" Zara asks angrily. I practically see her aura dancing off of her skin as she reaches for the power of a pure blood vampire.

"I no longer will help you. We all serve Namen Young," he says confidently. The rest of the vampires seem to be proud of that statement as well. "Now, because I am kind, this will be your only chance to walk away. Now, leave."

Zara looks around at the group, then at me, still holding Katsu ready to strike. This is going to get ugly.

"Do you know who I am? Or should I give you a refresher?" She picks up the unconscious vampire off of the ground that she attacked earlier and plunges her fist through his heart. Then, she licks the blood off of her hands as the body disintegrates into nothing.

"You won't win if you do this Zara," Logan warns, seeming almost frightened and unsure.

"If I do this, I'll make sure no one ever remembers your names," Zara tells everyone in the room.

They don't say a word, just hold their ground. Stupid, stupid, stupid.

"Well," I say as my tattoo begins to glow, "This ought to be fun. Shall we?"

"After you," Zara extends her hand, pointing at the vampires. None of them are pure bloods so this may not be too hard.

I attack first, slicing and kicking, never before wanting to shed blood so much. Zara's own rage mingles with mine, strengthening me. This will

Alanna J. Faison

Killer Rayne

be for Anubis. Katsu cuts through a woman's stomach like a knife through warm butter before I twist and take the head of another. He becomes nothing but dust as I sense two more attempting to come behind me. Through our bond I realize that Zara and I can use each other as a second pair of eyes. I see what she sees and can adjust my fighting style. Jumping in the air, I plunge my katana through the head of the vampire on the left and kick the other one away.

I smile as I sense Zara attacking with the force of a raging bull. I thought that the werewolves fighting in sync was the most beautiful thing that I've ever seen, but she's had hundreds of years to perfect the art. No move is wasted. Even without a weapon, she melts in and out of the shadows, taking heads, and consuming life forces. My own power becomes excited and wants to be tested more. I oblige.

My motions become quicker as I spin on my heel and between a table hurled at me and a vamp. She tries to bite me with her knifelike fangs, but I grab a handful of her hair and ram Katsu through her. Then, I toss her to Zara who finishes her off by ripping her head from her shoulders, growling as the body turns to dust. The sheer power that it takes to accomplish that is amazing.

With only a half dozen vampires left in the room, I find Logan trying to escape. Using the blood-link, I warn Zara as I toss her my blade. She catches it just as she leaps over a vamp, spins to slice him in half, and then hurls my sword at Logan with blinding speed. He's pinned to the door that he was trying to escape from and Zara wastes no time taking him.

She rips him free of the door just as I catch a blow to the side of my head then feel teeth ripping into my shoulder. It burns like hell, but I refuse to scream as I slam the persistent vampire into the wall with my back. The rest of the group tries to overpower me while Zara is occupied. I head butt the one closest to me so hard that I see stars, but I don't care, I can't let them pin me down. She spits out teeth and rains blow after blow on my face before I manage to pull one of the other vampires into the line of fire.

Eye almost swollen shut from the attack, I begin to see red myself. Not my face; I love my face! I fight back hard as Zara joins the fray again, having knocked out Logan so that he can't escape. She slices swiftly through three vamps, severing their connection with this world. Gripping the toothless female by her neck, having finally gained the upper hand, I squeeze until I feel her trachea collapse. She slumps to the ground and Zara plunges Katsu into her chest, dispatching her as well. She hands her back to me, eyes wild, smile on her face.

Together, we attack the last two vamps, quickly and efficiently. This bond increased my skill by ten-fold, Zara's blood still running through me, making me more powerful than before. We both feel the change in me and once again, my tattoo glows and seeks out Zara's power. This time, it reaches for it and seems to remember the force that Zara is and backs down even if it does want another taste. Satisfied, Zara wipes her mouth of any remaining blood and I wipe my blade off on a table cloth before sheathing it again.

Next, I follow her to where Logan lies. She pulls him up and places him in a chair roughly. Patiently, I look around at the room, the music still a light touch to my ears. Splotches of blood coat the tables and chairs. Some of the furniture is turned over or broken and many drinks are spilled. Still, there's not a soul in this room other than Zara, Logan, the unconscious woman, and me.

Zara wakes Logan the betrayer up and he immediately bites down on his tongue so that he can't talk. He spits his severed tongue out of his mouth and at Zara, teeth bloodied and eyes filled with insanity. Pissed, she slaps him so hard that he flies from the chair before she pulls him back up. He reminds me of the other three that I fought before I officially met Zara that night in the alley. It just confirms my suspicions even more. These guys are so crazily loyal to Namen that they removed their tongues willingly. Damn.

Knowing that she isn't going to get anything from him, she resolves to finish the job, her way. "Rayne, I know that you've seen someone tortured before, but what I'm about to do, you don't want to see, ever. Go through that door and see if anyone else is hiding. I'll come back there when I'm done."

"Okay, but you know I'll just see it through the bond anyway," I tell her walking away.

"Oh, trust me, this, I will make sure I keep from you."

I look at Logan one last time and smile. He deserves everything that he's going to get. "And now, you won't even be able to beg for mercy. Goodbye Logan," I say.

His eyes are filled with terror for the first time tonight. I sense him try to make one last move against Zara, but she quickly knocks him back in the chair. Satisfied that she can handle herself against one lowly vampire, I close the door behind me.

Chapter Ten

I found three women and two men in the back rooms, all unconscious with multiple bite wounds. Zara gave them all blood to heal their bites, including the first woman, glamoured them, and sent them back upstairs to enjoy the rest of their night. In the morning they would all believe that they had a crazy drug filled orgy. Great memories to have.

When I came back into the room, there was nothing left of Logan. I didn't ask. She wouldn't tell me anyway. We went upstairs, had a couple drinks at a back table where it was dark enough to conceal any blood that we had on our clothes, and then left to go to Zara's condo downtown to clean up. She hesitantly called one of the people that works for her family to take her dogs out, semi afraid about who she could trust. Then, she called her cousin Apollo in order to let him know what was going on with the rogue vampires.

All vampires were not expected to do any and everything that a member of the nine asked, but they did have a certain level of respect for them in most cases. Namen must have offered them something pretty significant for them to go against Zara like this. You don't mess with the Drakes. So I've heard. Apollo suggested to Zara that she see her grandmother soon and that she'd better get a handle on things before he stepped in. She almost seemed afraid of that notion. I wonder if he's more powerful than her and she's just afraid to admit it.

After relaying all that to me, Zara orders some food while I shower. It's amazing feeling the heat beat against my sore muscles. Zara's blood inside me heals my swollen eye significantly and I cover my face with my hot wash cloth as I lean against the shower wall. Finally, I force myself from the shower and wrap a towel around my naked body, hesitant to be around my vampire like this after the day we had. Gratefully, she's not in sight when I tiptoe through the hall and into the bedroom.

The carpet feels like a pile of feathers under my feet and I almost find myself lying on the floor. I walk to the bed and it's just as soft and inviting. I plop down before I notice the t-shirt and boxers. Grateful, I lotion up and then pull them on. When I walk back out, there is a carton of Chinese food waiting on me. Zara is sitting outside on the balcony's railing, legs dangling dangerously over the ledge.

I scoop up the food and step into the night air, joining her as I eat.

"Isn't the night so beautiful?" she asks quietly, somehow balancing perfectly.

I look out into the night; listen to the faint sounds below, of cars honking, music playing, and stare at the beautiful city lights and smile. "It is."

"Night time has so many more secrets. It's like a completely new adventure waiting. When you're one with the night, there is no need to ever be afraid," she tells me.

"Zara?" I ask, suddenly curious. "What are you afraid of?" I inquire even though I know it is an extremely personal question to ask someone so prideful and strong.

Zara looks at me and then back into the mysterious night. She's silent for a few minutes as she contemplates my question. I'm sure someone like her rarely thinks about the things that she fears.

"I'm afraid of failing. At anything I do, I hate to lose. But, what I'm most afraid of is never seeing Sage's face again. I don't care if the entire world falls apart around me as long as I can get her back," she tells me so quietly that I have to lean forward to hear her.

"From what you've told me about Sage, she'd want you to protect this world. What if you had to choose between letting her go and saving the world?"

"I won't fail Sage again, Rayne. If nothing else, even if she chooses never to stay by my side after all that's come to pass, I'll choose her," Zara resolves.

I can't say that in her position I wouldn't do the same thing. Quietly, I stand beside her and truly take in the beauty of the darkness.

◊◊◊

Sleep was a blur other than Namen pushing himself inside my mind in order to tell me that he knows it was me that had a hand in killing his vampires. He warned that payback is coming and that he has spies everywhere. Then, he left me to the privacy of my own mind. I have to get him out of my head and in order to do that, I have to speak with Selene and get this all figured out.

Zara and I drive back to the other house so that she can take care of her dogs and so I can get dressed in the outfit that I just bought since I have no new clothes on me. Once we return to the house, I change into a red cowl top with ruffled sleeves and some black jeans that hug my hips deliciously. Then, I put on some black leather boots and fix my hair. Maybe, just maybe, I can distract Selene a little bit.

While I'm preoccupied thinking about how this is going to go, Zara comes in the room right after I text Selene to let her know that we're coming over. She has on a light gray, slim fitting short sleeved dress shirt, a gold necklace, gold earrings, light blue loose fitting jeans, and light gray Polo boots to match her shirt. Great. Now we almost look like we're going on a date. I almost ask her to change, but then decide it's too much of a waste of time.

We begin to leave, but, I go back and decide to bring Katsu, my katana, with me. Sword firmly in my hand, I walk to the car, get inside and buckle up for safety.

On the way, we pass by the mall and I almost have Zara stop so that I can go buy Selene some "I'm sorry" jewelry or something, but decide against it. It's a corny move and I know it. She'd see right through it and probably just cuss me out in the process.

After ten more minutes of driving and small talk, Zara turns off on a side road, not in the direction of my house. I begin to ask what she's doing when the car jerks forward and we blow through a stop sign. In the side mirror, I see a dark blue car behind us doing the same thing.

"How long have we been getting followed?" I ask, trying to remain calm as she turns back onto a main road.

"I just noticed it a few blocks ago, that's why I turned off to be sure," she whips another corner and the wheels squeal. "They kept coming, so I know that they're serious about this. In the daytime, no doubt."

Just then, a black Suburban switches from the incoming lane and comes right at us.

"Fuck!" Zara growls, speeding up and putting both of her hands on the steering wheel.

"What the hell are you doing?" I shriek, clutching my seatbelt tighter.

"I'm going to beat them at their own game," she growls again, knuckles turning white. I think I hear the crunch of the steering wheel under her hands.

Pulse pounding loudly in my ears, time seems to slow as I realize that neither one of them is letting up in this game of chicken and I have no doubt that I'm the only human on board. Zara is going to kill me without even thinking about it! On the driver side, the other car is attempting to speed up and block us so that we can't pass. There's a guard rail on the passenger side so there's no way to switch lanes. Zara picks up her speed, cursing.

Cars on the other side begin honking wildly, trying to stop the collision the only way they can think of. I pray out loud and Zara curses again in response, drowning out my pleas. Then, I see it, a slight chance to get out of this. Zara is too focused on the car coming at us, so confident that they'll turn at the last second that she's missing it. She's acting like a freaking implusive teenager and apparently I have to be the parent in the situation.

"Turn left," I demand.

She doesn't respond, so I slap her in the face to distract her and grab the wheel and turn as quickly as I can. The other car hits the back corner of our vehicle causing us to spin out. Then, I hear the sound of louder crash behind us. Tires screeching, Zara does her best to keep the car from losing complete control. I do my best to keep from losing my lunch. Tears fill my eyes as the world spins violently. Finally, mercifully, we stop and I begin to breathe again.

Zara slowly gets out of the car, assessing the damage before turning to the two vehicles that are crunched together. They are pushed against the guard rail, smoking. One car door opens slowly and I get out as well, making sure Katsu is still with me. There's a rev of an engine closing in on us, followed by two more. Zara flashes to my side and pulls me out of the way just as one more black truck slams into her Charger, totaling it. There's a symphony of shattering glass and crunching metal.

Suddenly, we're surrounded as men pile out of the other cars. I feel their power hit me and I stumble even after I just picked myself up off of the ground. Zara looks at me, eyes red in fury. These aren't normal supernaturals. Namen has sent two of his lieutenants for us.

I guess I should feel special.

Chapter Eleven

They step closer in unison. Two witches stand back and cast some kind of net over the area. The air around us shimmers like rippling water reflecting sunlight. Like a vacuum, the outside world is sucked away. I no longer can hear any of the outside traffic or other sounds. It even smells different inside of our mini arena. The rot of magic that I associate with Namen is here along with a hot, sweet smell almost like fresh brownies and cupcakes. Mixed together, it's nauseating.

"Dead or alive?" Zara asks, startling me. She unbuttons her shirt casually as if she's getting home from the office and drops it to the pavement, leaving only the wraps that cover her breasts. She rubs her hand down her arm tattoo as if she's cold and opens our link. *You have one job, do you understand. Take out the witches that are casting the spell. They don't want to expose themselves yet. If the net drops, they'll retreat,* she tells me in my head.

I don't respond, because I understand completely. I also come to the realization about another thing: Selene could be in danger right now and we're here. I feel my power building up inside at the thought. I allow my humanity to take a step back for a while, shedding any sense of sympathy

Alanna J. Faison   Killer Rayne

for these monsters in front of me. My job is to kill, to get to Selene. I won't fail.

"Dead," one of the lieutenants responds. He's dressed in all black, hood pulled over his face. A sword in each hand. I don't know what he is, but I guess I don't have to worry about it. The other lieutenant is eying me suspiciously. He's also dressed in black but with a ski-mask type headgear showing only his eyes. He doesn't say a word and doesn't look like he has any weapons. The quiet ones are always a problem.

Then, I feel it and Zara and I both turn to look at the quiet one. It hits me like a jolt from a taser and then seems to cling to me like a sticky spider web. His aura is nearly visible around him, dark and vicious.

"What is he?" I whisper, fearful.

"He's a demon. The more human they look, the more powerful they are. What the hell has Namen accomplished to create such a demon following?" Zara does a quick take of everyone. There are seven in all. *This changes nothing. I have a few tricks up my sleeve. Just do what I've asked. I'm trusting you.* Zara steps in front of me, a snarl deep in her throat.

I pull Katsu, purposely choking off my own fear as I let the ring of metal from my blade being released from its sheath fill my ears. Then, I let my power explode as my tattoo flares to life, brighter than ever before. For a second, I am deafened by the roar of my strength through my body. I think of my family, of Anubis, Jaxson, the pack, Selene, and of the betrayal we've all endured.

One job to do. Kill.

Zara moves, leaving dust in her wake. I follow on her heels as fast as my feet can carry me as she clears a path for me. She crouches down as I leap over her, connecting an elbow with one of the enemies. Then, I get low and flip him over my head, backwards over my shoulder. Zara catches him and I hear a crunch. I don't turn around, but through our link I know that she's broken his neck. I'm almost at the edge where the first witch is doing the spell when the hooded one slides in front of me. I continue at him, full speed as I feel Zara slipping into step behind me.

At the last second, I turn to the left as Zara meets the man head on with the sound of two pro football players colliding. Out of the corner of my eye, I notice the other one, the demon gearing up for an attack. I fight the urge to stop and help Zara, instead relaying the message through our blood bond. She does her best to anticipate the demon, but he's too fast and manages to knock her off of her feet.

I'm now eight feet away from the witch when dark shadows zoom across the pavement at me.

One catches my leg and pulls me to the ground, but I quickly break the thread with Katsu. It becomes a dance as I spin and dodge out of the way of the others, slicing and flipping. Shout out to my dance background for those moves. I analyze the situation as quickly as possible, noticing the half second delay between the next waves, the twelve or so threads before each delay and then I have my plan.

Zara's pain nearly throws me out of focus as I feel her body bounce off the pavement and a powerful foot slam down on her, breaking ribs. The muffled scream of pain and the rage that builds up as I feel her face contort into that of a true vampire whose power is on the rise, sends a jolt through me. She is being driven by instinct and a need to survive a predator that is stronger than her. I force myself not to look as I know that there is nothing human about her face right now.

She fights her way off of the ground and even though she's fighting more skilled opponents with greater numbers, I'm satisfied enough that I can kill at least this one witch. Screw her order, after this; I'm going to help her.

No! she growls through our link, obviously catching my last thought. *You have a job to do,* she tells me firmly.

Fuck you, Zara. You don't run me, I snap.

Alanna J. Faison   Killer Rayne

I allow one of the threads to wrap around my right arm, seemingly distracted. The other threads follow close by, through the air and slithering across the pavement. They all reach me at nearly the same time as I get even closer to the witch. He doesn't seem to mind the closing of the distance. With his focus and one hand working to keep the spell running, he can't seem to work out what exactly I'm doing.

The thread has gotten tighter around my arm and seems to be trying to work its way to my neck. I have seconds left before it chokes me to death. Now is the time to test my theory out. Lawrence, the immortal that created my sword, had told me that my blade will get stronger as I do. I don't exactly know what that means but I hope that she will be more aware of my intentions.

I call for Katsu to pay attention to me in my mind. The steel of the blade in my hand warms in response. I tell my sword to pull some of my chakra through me and push it out at the witch. In the time it takes to blink, it feels like there's a phantom hand digging into my stomach and pulling out my life force. I sense my energy swimming through my katana and slamming into the witch in a blast of white energy. He goes down as the threads loosen and disappear from my body. I waste no time in leaping and slamming my sword into his heart.

Exhaustion pulls me to my knees. I guess I overdid it with the chakra pull. I definitely can't do that again until I learn how. I'm just glad that I remembered that my sword was forged with magic and that I may be able to use that to my advantage. Or, maybe it's just me. Maybe one of my skills is transferring my chakra through magical objects.

The shimmer of the spell blinks out for a second and then returns, weaker than it initially was as the other witch must now pick up the slack. With any luck, he'll tire before I even have to attack. Helping Zara is my priority right now. I don't give a damn if she wants it or not.

As I stand, I turn to observe as the demon and other lieutenant are the only ones other than Zara left standing. Somehow, Zara took out all of the weaker opponents. But, the lieutenants are a challenge for Zara whose face is still morphed into a monster's; face scrunched, fangs bared, crimson eyes glowing with rage. It's a face that I never want to see focused on me.

I still can't figure out what the other man is. His eyes are red like Zara's, but they are rimmed in yellow. I think that I see claws on his dark hands. Then, I realize that it's dark fur lightly covering his hands and arms. He's ripped off the sleeves of his shirt and if I'm not mistaken, seems to have gotten taller as well. He's not wearing any shoes and as I watch, his feet begin to elongate.

Alanna J. Faison   Killer Rayne

The demon finally makes another move for Zara, disappearing in a cloud of smoke and reappearing directly in front of her. She's distracted by the leap of her other opponent over her head. I begin to race into the battle just as they both attack at once. Their combined strength and speed is too much for Zara, especially with broken ribs. She manages to block most of the assault, but is pierced between her shoulder and chest. The demon's arm extended from its socket, growing at least a foot longer before running right through her. She takes the force of the blow and slumps into the arms of the other enemy. He turns her head sideways and bites down on her neck spilling blood all over Zara and himself.

Her pain slams into me through our blood-link, and horrified, I nearly freeze. I'm so close that I can hear the long draws of blood that he takes from Zara's throat. The demon turns on me as I run forward. I push myself with a final rush of adrenaline, spin, and slice with as much power as I can muster at the very last second. His long arm grazes my face just under my eye and leaves wet blood from Zara's wound dripping down my skin.

I don't even wait to see how much damage I've caused because my next move slices through the arm of the creature that is draining Zara's life force. He howls in pain and rage as I keep running, going after the last witch, knowing that this is our only hope. There's no way in hell that I have a chance against these two.

I open the mind-link once more to check on Zara's condition. She's barely conscious and not in a good state of mind. Survival mode kicks on for her and somehow, she stands back up, swinging and snapping at the one that bit her. The demon's footsteps stop trailing behind my own and he turns to finish the job with his partner. The witch sees me coming and presses a finger to his lips, speaking quickly.

"Not today!" I yell as I throw Katsu like a javelin across the space. Time seems to slow as my blade cuts through the spell directed at me.

There is one final look of incredulousness on his face before my katana connects with his throat and ends his life. His body is hurled through the air as he comes to rest bouncing on the pavement. The net of magic drops immediately and reality snaps back into place like a rubber band. I turn back to the last of Namen's minions. They both stare me down, the vampire-like one snarling as he picks his arm off of the ground. Zara is on one knee next to them, eyes barely open. They take one more look at her, and then at the traffic that's returning this way. The demon places one hand on the other's arm and they both disappear, leaving an eerie chill in the air.

Chapter Twelve

Outside sounds return and the wind picks up as well. I glance up to the sky where dark clouds are now forming before jogging to pick my bloody blade off of the ground. All of the bodies are now evaporating and I know that this has something to do with Namen's magic. What isn't he capable of? Once I sheath Katsu, I notice that Zara isn't standing. Glancing around making sure no one is watching, I pull her up, placing her arm over my shoulder and limp to the guardrail where it meets a thicket of trees.

We'll have to worry about the car situation later. Zara's going to have to glamour some people. For now, I have to get her back to normal. I reach for my phone but it's not in my pocket. Hearing cars drive by and begin to stop, I don't have time to go back. There's no way to call Selene or Jaxson and if I bring Zara back up there, she'll probably kill all of the humans.

I pull Zara deeper into the growth until I can't hear anymore voices. Then, I push Zara down against a big oak and assess her damage. She's still bleeding out of both wounds but it's not a fast flow. Looking back to make sure that we didn't stupidly leave a trail of blood, I find that we're okay and I relax. She's not going to be able to make it anywhere without some blood, but I'm weak enough as it is. For a second, I think of calling Diana. She'd probably kill her if she saw her like this. I have no choice, her strength is more important than my weakness.

Birds chirp angrily at us invading their home, but they fly to trees farther away as others pick up their chorus. They begin to drown out the sounds of the vehicles moving on the road. I don't hear any sirens so we have some time.

Once again, I grab my katana and make a tiny slice in my wrist to get the blood flowing. I barely feel it as the adrenaline is still working inside me. Placing my wrist up to her mouth, I run my other hand through her braids. I do my best to rouse her from her half-conscious state.

"Come on Zara, snap out of it," I whisper as I push my wrist deeper into her mouth.

Her lips part and then her tongue darts out to taste me. Suddenly, her eyes flick open, but it's like no one's home as she bites down with hunger. I instinctually moan from the pleasure and pain which causes Zara to come alive even more. Before I can even register her move, Zara has me pinned against the tree and is sucking my neck with passion. She feels rock hard against me, leg in between mine rubbing me down low, taking my life force inside of her.

I tilt my head so that she can take more even though I know that she's taken enough. Her long, slow draws cause a fire to ignite between my legs. The vampire pheromones cause me to feel this pleasure even as I try to fight it.

"Zara, no," I tell her passively.

She pushes harder against me, one hand now roaming my body, touching my breasts, reaching between my legs. A trail of heat lingers from her touches. Zara pulls away, moaning quietly right before slamming her lips against mine, causing my head to spin and my world to explode. I pull her in deeper, tasting my blood and finding it a rush. Her soft tongue seeks out mine as she lifts me against the tree. It scrapes my back, lifting up my shirt and drawing blood. Zara smells it, sets me down, and turns me around before licking the blood from my back, slowly, purposefully.

Both hands against the bark, I bite my lip in delight before my senses rush back to me. Without her taking my blood, the pheromones no longer rule my mind as strongly. Mixed with the bond, I'd be helpless against her if she was still taking my blood from the vein, pumping those feelings inside me. Now, my heart and mind scream, "no" in unison and I manage to push her away.

I look at her in sorrow as her eyes still possess the blankness that is not the vampire I know. She looks at me in confusion and growls, crouching low as if threatened. I open our blood-link and call to her. My knees are weak and my heart is beating against my chest as if it is trying to break out. I touch my neck punctures and do my best to hide my fear. That total loss of control is unnerving.

Stop. Listen to me Zara, you're not hurt anymore. You're safe. I gave you my blood to heal and it's working. Look, I say showing my vampire her own image in her mind.

She looks at me sideways in confusion before touching the side of her neck where her own wound is now closing.

"Rayne," she says aloud. She begins to take a step toward me then stops as she touches her lips in rememberance and then looks at mine in horror.

Zara falls to her knees once more and says, "Oh God Rayne, I am so so fucking sorry. Oh shit, I fucked up." She pounds a fist in the ground and says something unintelligible.

I run my fingers through my hair and then wipe my mouth. "There's no time for this right now. We'll handle it later. Right now, we need to get to Selene and I don't think that I have that much in me now," I say honestly, leaning against the tree that she pinned me against.

She looks up at me once more, eyes still burning crimson and filled with honest regret. As she opens her mouth to speak, my eyes linger on her sharp fangs that just roamed my body and I shudder.

I have to tell Selene about this. I have to make sure that she's safe first.

Zara pauses to listen to the commotion back on the road right before I hear sirens in the distance. She looks farther beyond the trees then motions for me to come along.

"We have to move quickly. I didn't want to show you this just yet, but I'll do this to make up for what I've done and also to get to Selene quicker. I owe this to both of you," Zara says mysteriously.

"What are you going to do?"

"I'm about to use one of my special abilities. When I take blood from an awakened, I can use their powers. As far as I know, I'm the only vampire with this gift. It's how I was able to kill Blake," Zara reveals.

I let those words sink in. The gift of taking abilities through blood gives her the potential to have unlimited powers if she can master them. If she were someone else, someone evil, I don't think that I would want her living.

"Don't ever forget Rayne; I may not be evil, but I'm not the good guy either. I'm a vampire first. I kill with no remorse and often with a lot of satisfaction. Don't ever forget what I am; you'll be safer that way," Zara warns listening to my thoughts through our still open link.

I think about her words and nod. Selene was basically telling me the same thing. She said that vampires are always plotting and working their own angles. I should tread carefully when it comes to them. It wasn't dislike, it was just facts. Still, I can't picture Zara as a cold-blooded murderer, not in the way Namen is. Maybe they aren't so different though.

"Now, the key is to understand the power and having time to learn it. It just doesn't come immediately. I've been a werewolf, used witch magic, and even some demon magic too. Using all those different abilities has given me advantages that other awakeneds can't hope to possess. It also gives me insight about other races and their weaknesses. I took a piece of that demon during the fight, so I'll be able to transport us like he does before it wears off. Luckily it's pretty much the same as a spell that witches use and I've done it before. Let's move. Come closer," Zara beckons me.

Above us, lightning strikes and thunder cracks. It's going to be pouring any time now.

Hopefully any traces of blood will wash away. I step into Zara's arms, trying not to get too close, any more intimate than we've already been. Then, I am pulled through a void.

◊◊◊

We arrive just as the rain begins to pour. I run up to the front door prepared to break it down if I have to. I try to ignore the woozy feeling in my stomach as Zara pulls me away from the door to go around back. Something crashes through the glass just as we head around. Selene leaps through the broken window with one hand, glass cutting into her hand, brow and lip bleeding, hair wild. Electricity leaps across her skin and I follow her gaze to the monstrosity that is lying on his back in the grass.

The demon looks to be covered in stones, much less comical than the Thing from *The Fantastic Four* comics and more deadly. The Thing is a large, orange, superhero whose body is made of rocks. No, this monster is more realistic and much more intimidating. As he picks himself up off of the ground, Zara and I both rush to Selene's side. She doesn't even turn since she's focused on the enemy.

"This cadela is strong. There was one more, but she disappeared into the sky so be careful," Selene warns just as she slams a fist into the ground, causing the earth to shake.

Alanna J. Faison   Killer Rayne

I keep my balance by pushing Katsu into the dirt. The demon is wobbly on his feet and both Selene and Zara use that to their advantage and attack in unison. Rain begins to pummel the earth as Zara draws the demon's attention. Selene weaves a hand sign by quickly lacing her fingers together in a specific pattern and lashes out with a spell.

I push my wet hair from my eyes as I scan the sky for signs of the other demon. Dark clouds overhead make my vision less helpful. Instead, I close my eyes and seek the demon energy that I'm getting all too accustomed to. In the distance, I can feel the other one watching, but making no moves. There is no intent to strike there, just to observe.

Selene is knocked through the air, but Zara catches her before she hits the ground. Slipping out of the way of the next strike, the ground shakes where the demon stands. I call out, forcing him to turn his attention toward me.

"Hey!" I yell over the thunder screaming out to the sky. "Don't you want to fight a real opponent?" I tease, gesturing for the monster to attack me.

He roars in response, a sound that will definitely have the neighbors poking their heads outside any minute. Looks like we've really got to finish this quickly. Abandoning my fatigue, I stand firm on my feet, knowing that I have two capable women backing me up. I have no doubt of the outcome of this one. I search for weak points as I open my bond with Zara once more. Through her eyes, I see Selene prep a spell, slowly pulling the energy from the world around her like a vacuum. Incredible. Zara slips into the shadows and I silently ask Katsu to sharpen enough to cut through the armored body of the demon.

My sword is only as strong as its master, so I just hope that I'm powerful enough to do this. The only weak point I see is the eyes, so that'll have to do. I play it all out in my head, my analytical skills seeming to grow exponentially. Each move will be calculated and precise, there will be no strength wasted here. There's a shift in the wind as it begins to howl through the trees causing the branches to genuflect. I shift once, tattoo glowing, and take off in the direction of the demon with both hands on my katana.

Two steps slower than me to react, he clumsily tries to pick up speed. The demon weight causes him to sink more into the ground as he moves due to the pouring rain. Perfect. I leap through the air right as he attempts to catch his balance. Too late. With a leaping, two legged kick, I slam right into the demon's face as hard as I can. He falls backwards hard just as Zara comes up behind me, catching Katsu in the air as I toss her to my vampire. Zara slams my blade into one of the demon's eyes with teeth jarring force. The demon screams in rage. A spilt second later, I feel the force of Selene's magic rip through the air like a bullet, more powerful than I've ever felt it.

I scramble out of the way just as Zara pulls Katsu from the demon. I roll over just in time to watch Selene raise an arm to the sky and slam it down to her side. A powerful, deadly bolt of lightning collides with the demon's body. He screams in his final seconds, drowned out by another clash of thunder.

In seconds, we're left with the stench of a burned body and scorched earth. Elemental magic still electrifies the air. Selene turns wild green eyes on me and then on Zara. I step toward her, shaking from the feeling of the power she just called. I really don't know what Selene is capable of. Before I can ask, Selene slams Zara against the house with a surge of energy. Before Zara can defend herself, Selene strikes again. Blood flows from Zara's lip and nose, but she makes no attempt to defend herself. I stand there, helpless and confused as Selene strides toward her, fingers crackling with another spell prepped.

Chapter Thirteen

Zara stands up, expressionless. I take a step closer to them, shivering from the cold caress of the rain. Not realizing that I'm holding my breath, my heart begins to beat firmly against my chest. Selene raises her glowing hand and releases the spell.

She gets as close as humanly possible to Zara without touching her and then slaps her before grabbing her face tightly.

"Selene, stop-," I begin, but she doesn't hear me.

"She's mine!" she cries. "Don't you dare think that you can take her away from me. She's not yours to claim, vampire. I can feel your energy all over her."

Oh God. She knows. She already knows. I open my mouth to try to explain, to make her understand, but suddenly I am mute, afraid that anything I say will sound like a lie.

"How could you?" Selene spins on me, tears clearly evident in her eyes despite the rain. My heart breaks at her pain. Pain that I put there. "How could you? I've given up nearly everything for you and it takes you all of two seconds to run into her arms. I warned you, Rayne. Did that one omission change everything? Do you not even care about my feelings at all?" Selene is shaking in rage and all I do is stand there and look like an idiot.

"You need to understand," Zara says, reaching out gently, eyes red from the emotions charging the air, but her body language is non-threatening.

"I'm not speaking to you!" Selene screams, lashing out with her power.

This time, Zara blocks it and growls, but doesn't make a move to retaliate. Instead, arms in the air, she walks away, giving us some space.

"Does she speak for you now? Because last I recall, you've always spoken your mind."

Something about her words lights a fire inside of me. I'm not being controlled, at least not in the way that she's thinking. How dare she think so low of me.

"You're judging me now about lies? Fuck you, Selene. I was coming over here to own up to what I've been doing. I was going to be honest and tell you everything because I love you and I need your help. This is hard to explain and it's not what I want. I don't love her. I feel a connection with her that is not entirely of my own doing."

Selene seems to want to walk away from my explanation, but I step in front of her, forcing her

Alanna J. Faison   Killer Rayne

to listen. "We both made a mistake and underestimated the power of the blood-link. Because of that, we've had to deal with consequences. But no, I'm not going to blame it all on that. Part of it is me too. Part of it is attraction to her and her power. But, I want to leave it at that, we both do. She has Sage and I thought that one day, I'd have you again," I respond, pacing back and forth, hands moving wildly as I speak.

I come to a stop back in front of her, fuming. "You kept your brother a secret from me for a very long time. You've had plenty of opportunities to bring him up. It's not like I couldn't handle it. I think I can handle just about anything now, after the murder of my family, don't you think? You told me once that trust is a gift not easily given, but you're full of shit, you know that?"

"And why can't you trust that I know my brother more than you do. You formed judgments based off of what your enemy told you. Your enemy, Rayne! That's all it took for him to divide and nearly destroy one of us. Have you ever thought of that? No! I'm sure you didn't figure that part of the plan did you? There was a reason I never told you about my brother. He was on the run for a very long time. I haven't seen him since I was seventeen. In order for him to be safe, no one could know anything about him, not even you."

"Well, we all see how well that's worked out, right?"

Selene pushes me. "Vai se foder!"

My tattoo comes to life in reaction to the physical action. I push my power back down. "Listen, Selene. I kissed Zara. Twice. The first time was in reaction to me attempting to push back the bond. My power reached out to her and it was like a drug. I asked for it. The second time was right before coming here. I fed her blood because she was pretty banged up. She lost herself and pushed the vamp pheromones really heavily into me. Neither one of us meant for it to happen. You know that I'm not lying because you know how that works. She's probably regrets it more than I. No one is cheering harder for us to be together than her. If you're going to lash out on someone, let it be me. She doesn't deserve it," I sigh.

Selene is silent for a few seconds, then she asks, "So, why is so hard for you to give me the benefit of the doubt? You're standing here in my face, asking me to do the same thing for you, after you've promised to kill my brother. Why, Rayne, must you be the moral citizen of this story? You just became a part of this world. I've lived in it for my entire life. I've protected you as best I can and I've stood by your side, yet, you act like you can't even forgive me." She sobs into her hands. I reach out to touch her, but she pulls away.

Alanna J. Faison   Killer Rayne

"Selene, I-," I hang my head down and choose my next words.

"Selene. I know I don't deserve how good you've been to me. I should have stayed. I should have listened. I didn't and now I have to earn your forgiveness. But, if your brother really had something to do with either my family's or Anubis's pack's murder, I don't know if I can ever forgive him. I will defend myself if he attacks me. You can get the explanation you need from him, tell him to run if you see him, but I can't give you more than that. I'm sorry. I won't lie to you," I say honestly.

My tattoo glows, warning me of a force that I couldn't sense just a couple of seconds ago. "So that's it, huh? You'd kill her only brother, her twin, her best friend, just like that? Have you no heart Rayne Whitmore?" A velvety, deep voice with a hint of an accent steals into the night. He sounds like an actor with that "A plus" performance. Selene freezes like she's just seen a ghost and I turn to find someone I least expect step into view.

"I didn't sense your presence. How long have you been lurking?" I ask the man standing before me. He can only be Santos as I peer into the face of the stranger that looks so much like Selene. He's slightly taller than her, has short, dark, thick, straight hair, alluring green eyes, a diamond shaped jaw structure, neatly trimmed goatee, with a dangerous smirk painting his face.

Santos is just as handsome as Selene is beautiful.

"I have my ways. I came to observe and to show my sister here that this isn't the life that she wants. She should be by my side, where her rightful place is. Selene, you know that I'm right. You'll never reach your true potential without me. We are linked, you know that." He looks at her, completely ignoring me.

"Santos. What are you doing? What is your plan in all this?" Selene asks, physically forcing herself not to run into his arms, wary of her own brother. I watch as she squeezes her hands into fists and sways back and forth.

"Hello to you to irmã," he smiles a hundred watt smile. They are twins alright.

He still ignores me and I take that time to seek out Zara as well as the winged watcher. There is no sign of the demon, but Zara is stalking somewhere close by, waiting for her opening. Good. She's angry that she didn't sense him either.

"I want you to join me on the right side of this war. Make no mistake, Selene, this is war. We need to take our rightful place on top and Namen is the key to doing that. Anyone who opposes us is a threat to our future. Selene, the world is going to find out about us sooner than you realize. We must go on the offensive while we are strong to ensure our survival. You have to understand that," Santos explains. It sounds good, but their intentions aren't that noble.

"Santos, Rayne's family died because of Namen. The people that worked for their family. Her mom, her dad; her sister was only thirteen. What threat was she to have been murdered by a demon? I saw the bodies Santi. I've been here every day helping her pick up the pieces. What happened that night is unforgivable. So... why?" Selene asks, stepping closer to her brother.

I want to stop her, but he's still her brother right? Will he hurt her? Will he see my movement as a threat?

"If Namen made that decision, then there's a reason. He makes sacrifices for all of us. There are no mistakes," he responds like a press secretary. I look at him sideways, pulling Katsu slowly out of her sheath.

"What's in it for you? What has Namen promised you that is worth selling your soul?" I ask.

His face is confused, blinking as if he's never thought of it before. Then, it's gone and he's back to his suave self, shrugging at my question.

I don't like it. I can't put my finger on it, but something doesn't seem all the way together about

Santos. But, it's almost time to make my move. Selene is going to try to stop me. I don't have time to solve this puzzle.

"Did you have anything to do with my family's murder?" I ask, pointing the sword at Santos.

He looks at me in amusement as if I said a corny joke instead of asking him if he helped murder my family. Selene steps in between us in warning. I take a step forward anyway. Zara's deadly energy spins in my head waiting for my command.

"Oh, no Rayne. I had nothing to do with that little incident. I'm just sorry that you weren't in the house too. My sister would probably already be with me by now if she wasn't playing babysitter for you."

"Santos," Selene warns as my rage grows.

Little incident? The pain that my family experienced is a little incident?

"One more question, you miserable piece of shit, did you have anything to do with the deaths of the wolves that were part of Anubis's pack?" My hand shakes as I await his response. I know that he'll tell the truth as long as he continues to flaunt the air of superiority he thinks he rightly deserves. I want to cut him down piece by piece.

He laughs as he turns his green eyes toward me. His power bursts around us like a solar flare. It's as if his power responded to the pleasure of the memory. "You should have heard their screams."

My tattoo explodes as new adrenaline surges through me like a bullet train. I give the word to Zara and do my part to distract Selene by going after Santos. If I can actually reach him, then that's even better. Selene is ready though. She feels my power burst and attempts to throw up a barrier to stop me.

Katsu devours it as I slice down, never missing a step. Her next attack however, hits me head on and I hit the ground rolling backwards. I pop up just as Selene readies another spell with pleading eyes. I force her and Santos to pay attention to my frantic attempts to get to him. As he preps his own spell, I feel their magic attempt to mingle and it almost stops me short. He watches in oblivious pleasure as Selene's hands shimmer with magic, still working to keep herself between us. Then, I feel Zara use the same demon magic that got us here to melt into existence right behind Santos. He sees her in time to turn but Zara grabs his arm and wrenches it back. Finally, Zara wastes no time acting like the monster she warned me that she is.

Chapter Fourteen

Selene screams in rage as she realizes what just happened. I try to grab her but she breaks free and tries to rush to his aide. Santos' eyes go wide in pain as Zara makes no effort to make the bite a pleasant one as she bites into his flesh with the savagery of a lion. Santos pushes his magic into Zara trying to overload her with pain, but she's like a pit bull that's locked onto its prey.

Suddenly, Zara drops Santos to the ground and stands there dumbstruck, blood dripping from her face. Selene doesn't seem to notice the pause in the assault and still sends a blast of solid air right into Zara's midsection. She bounces off of the ground and doesn't get up. I wonder if her ribs are more damaged now.

Selene reaches Santos on the ground, trying to cover his wound as still pouring rain causes the blood to seem to flow more freely. He picks himself up off of the ground and looks at me in rage. He's already plotting his payback. They exchange words in their native language quietly and then he disappears leaving a chill in the air.

Selene turns toward me and a handful of different emotions paint her beautiful face: rage, betrayal, fear, and surprise to say the least. She opens her mouth to speak but Zara beats her to it.

"We may have a bigger problem on our hands. There's something wrong with Santos' blood. There's something strange about it and I think that I've tasted this before. I think that he's being controlled."

◊◊◊

After Selene disposes of the demon's body with a spell that dissolves it back into the earth, we survey the damage to the house. The living room has fared the worst. The flat screen is cracked on the floor and the speakers are in broken bits. There's blood on the upturned cream suede couches and deep gouges in the floor.

Then, we grab some clothes and make a decision to meet up with Jaxson to fill him in on everything that just happened. Luckily, we don't run into any more trouble on the way to the pack's estate because my energy level is now in the negatives. How I'm still standing is a miracle in itself. Zara is trying to hide the extent of the damage to her ribs, but Selene and I both know she's pretty f'ed up.

There are four bathrooms in Anubis's old home, so we all shower, get dried off, fill our bellies, and survey our injuries. They allow me to sleep the rest of the night before we get to business. Between Zara and me, we definitely need the rest. Selene makes a run for some herbs to make a healing potion while I sleep.

Alanna J. Faison   Killer Rayne

The thundering rain doesn't even rouse me from my slumber. After I wake, I meet up with everyone in the dining room. They all seem to have been up for a while now. Even Zara, whose injuries had been worse than mine seems refreshed and alert. Pureblood vampire healing. I don't even want to think about my black eye.

As we all sit at the table, I run my hand over the tiny scar on my face that I received the night that I killed Anubis. It is a constant reminder of my ineptitude. I deserved to have it scar. I'm the only one here that had been born human. This world that I've leaped into has left no room for re-tries or do-overs. I have to do better this instance, or I could cost someone else their life too.

Since this all began, I've had my ankle broken, been impaled, tortured, nearly drowned, broke my nose, thought my arm was sliced off, gotten clawed more than once, been ambushed, bitten, knocked out, and nearly kidnapped. That's not including losing my family and an ally. To top it off, if it wasn't Zara that got to Santos first, I might have just lost the love of my life forever because I would have probably killed her brother. At the very least, I would have died trying. She's still pissed at me for creating a diversion for Zara to even get to him. Boy did I dodge a bullet.

Jaxson, Christopher, a wolf named Phillip, Selene, Zara, and I are all at the table. Zara has already gone over the incident with her police contact and the vampires that we killed. She's sworn on her life to find the other man and get to the bottom of their missing pack member's bodies. As hurt as the werewolves seem, they all understand that this is another casualty of the world that we all live in.

"Taking the bodies seems to be another diversion of Namen's. He's trying to eat away at our emotions and we can't let that happen. We've committed to this and all we can do now is see it through. If we get their bodies back, then so be it, but until then, we must keep our focus on the threats we face," Christopher says firmly.

We all nod in agreement. It says a lot about what kind of man Jaxson is; to let Chris in on our discussion after he tried to fight him for control of the pack. He clearly recognizes what an asset he is and knows that he deserves his place at the table. Or, he could be trying to pacify those in the pack that wanted Christopher to be alpha. Jaxson will be a great leader. I just hope that I don't disappoint him either.

I wanted to ask about Christopher's mate, Rebecca, the one that tried to attack me after their battle for Alpha, but Chris didn't seem to be upset about my presence here, so I left it alone. Hopefully when the time comes, it's not her that has to watch my back. Hopefully, she got the message loud and clear when I ran her through with Katsu.

Then, I talk about my problem with Namen invading my thoughts and how the blood bond with Zara had been affecting my power and our need for each other. It's uncomfortable to talk about but we all agree that both of the issues need to be addressed.

Zara firmly apologizes to Selene.

"Hear me out, Selene. I may be a vampire and it's painfully obvious how you feel about my kind, but when it comes to love, my heart beats just like anyone else's. I won't deny that I had been mischievous in the beginning, but that was all fun and games. I see you and I wouldn't hurt you in that way. People like you don't love quietly; you love with every inch of your being."

The passion and honesty in Zara's voice draws me in. "I see you. I know what it's like to be robbed of your greatest love. I wouldn't do that to you purposefully, I'm not that type of cruel. This damn bond was underestimated. I allowed it to control us and I'm far too old to have made that mistake. Rayne is yours to love. She is mine to protect, even from myself," Zara says quietly, but passionately with glowing red eyes.

The entire room goes silent as we watch Selene's reaction. A tear falls from her eye as she turns to me. Surprisingly, Zara takes a finger and wipes it away. Intimately, Selene grabs her hand before Zara can pull away completely. They stare each other down, each seeking something in each other's eyes. Truth. Validation. Understanding.

"I'm sorry for the pain you've endured. Being immortal can be even more painful than I could imagine," Selene whispers to her, looking down at her small frame.

"You have no idea," Zara responds. I feel her desire for, something, anything, through our bond. Wholeness. Images of her and Sage flash through her mind, deepening her sorrow.

"I understand. Rayne fills a void in you. We each need a piece of her in order to survive. I just don't know what to make of your desire. You can't fight your nature Zara."

"I'm not like other vampires. I don't just want to consume, Selene, I want to complete."

Their powerful energy fills the room and I can't help but let out a gasp as a wave of desire and heady need fills the room. Jaxson and Phillip both look at me with yellow rimmed eyes, breathing in my desire, my craving for power. I ignore the warning look saying 'cool it' that I get as I breathe deeper allowing my tattoo to respond to the wave. I open up attempting to absorb what I can of their power and then I feel it creep into the back of my mind.

I blink twice and shake my head to try to get rid of the invader, but it's too late, he's here.

"I know what you want, Rayne. I can give it to you. I can give it all to you. You want power, you want seduction? It's yours. Just come to me. You will be the most powerful human alive," Namen teases. His voice is smooth, deadly, and magical. I feel his hand caress my arm and I shiver as the power he represents soaks into my skin.

His energy is dark and tainted. Still, I soak it up like a sponge and cry out as it feels as if a knife just cut me deep. I want nothing of his abhorrent power. Why is he here? Why now?

"I don't want what you have to offer. I want to end you," I tell him venomously.

"Oh, are you sure that's what you want? You seem to have issues making up your mind lately. With me, you can have whatever you want, whenever you want, as you see fit."

"Can you reverse time Namen? Can you go back to the time before you decided to have my family killed?" I ask contemptuously.

He laughs. "Of course not. Why would I want to? Your entire family was a threat to me. The only reason that I allowed you to live was because I didn't want the witch girl involved. It would have ruined my plans for her. Even better that she found a way to give you power, now I can use you in my army too," he responds.

"What the hell are you saying?" I question angrily. I don't like what he's insinuating.

"Do you really think that I didn't know your whereabouts that night? Surely, you aren't that dumb. I want the witch. If I killed you, she would never forgive me. Now that she knows I have her brother on my side, it's only a matter of time before I have the high priestess with me. I could live with you coming along too, but frankly, it's her that I want. Plus, she's grown exponentially in power over these last couple of years. Much more than I hoped for."

He laughs and I think I'm going to be sick.

"So, Selene is the only reason that I'm not dead?"

"Let me put it this way: yes," Namen responds smugly. "But, she can't keep you that way anymore if you continue to oppose me. I'm growing tired of your stunts." He speaks to me as if I'm just an unruly child that needs to be put in her place.

"I think you're afraid of me and mine. We have the power to oppose you and you know it. That's why you're here now, I'm a threat to you.

You're going to keep doing any and everything you can to distract us because you know heads up, you'd never win. That's okay though. It won't work," I respond defiantly.

For a split second, Namen's gray eyes burn with fury, but he quickly recovers. "You know Rayne, I can get inside your head whenever you're vulnerable. When you're sleep, when you daydream, when you're upset. You won't even be able to make love to your witch without me getting inside your head and torturing you."

"Screw you," I spit.

"You know why I chose you for this little experiment? Because you're the weakest link on the chain. I break you and I break them all. Here's a little parting gift to show you what you can look forward to. I was watching inside the demon's mind as he destroyed your family. Have a look," Namen waves a hand and disappears.

I try to escape my own mind before the images hit me, but it's like I'm locked in a cage, unable to tear my eyes from the horrid images that flash across the screen. Over and over I watch as the Devourer drags my baby sister, kicking and screaming across the floor. Over and over I watch as he pummels her face, knocking her over, playing with her as he feeds on her fear. Over and over I watch as she begs for her life. Over and over I watch the tears fall as the fight leaves her. Over and over I watch as the demon rips her open, drinking in her pain before slicing her neck. Over and over I watch her fall to the floor, lifeless.

Finally, I can't take it anymore, afraid I'll go insane from what I'm seeing, I scream in rage and disbelief. I wish against reality that I can take her place, pleading with my own mind to free me from this curse.

Chapter Fifteen

𝓐 blow lands on my face and I topple out of the chair I'm sitting in. The stinging sensation is nothing compared to my mental anguish. Forcing myself to look at my attacker, Jaxson is standing over me with wild eyes. He steps back to give me some room and I notice that everyone else is sharing the same look.

"You were screaming bloody murder. What the fuck?" Jaxson asks cautiously.

I look them all over and despite my best efforts, break down into tears. Moments later, I feel Selene's warm energy surround me and pull me in close. Finally, I work up the courage to tell everyone what I've just experienced. It's obvious that I truly am the weakest link.

"No one should have to see that," Phillip speaks quietly.

"He will suffer for this," Selene promises, with venom in her voice.

"We have to get him out of your head. He's not going to let you rest until then."

"I don't know if I can sleep after what I just saw," I admit.

"You will. We need you. You're not weak. If you were, he wouldn't be going to such great lengths to do this to you. In fact, I think he knows something that we don't about your power. What do you think, Zara? You're the only one that has experience with someone being unmade," Selene asks, still holding me tight. I really, truly don't deserve her.

She seemed unfazed by the revelation that Namen wants her, I'm sure she put it together once we found out Santos was working with him. Still, the fact that I'm supposedly only alive because of her has to be unnerving.

Zara sighs and thinks for a few seconds. "Sage was different, or at least that's what I was led to believe. She had shown signs of incredible strength even before her unmaking. With Rayne, there were things that Selene said she noticed, but I don't think this is about her power necessarily. Or should I say physical strength. Each person that becomes unmade displays different qualities of supernaturals. Different abilities."

"When I first fought Rayne, her power exploded when I made her believe that she was going to die then and there. In a matter of minutes I was able to give her a power boost that would have maybe taken years to manifest otherwise. I had suspected that the immortals were not completely invested in making her as strong as possible. I wondered why, but I never truly thought of it."

"So, what are you saying, that even the immortals may be afraid of her power?" Phillip asks. He's thinking deeper into this.

"You know how I feel about them, so I can't say for sure, but something just isn't adding up. I don't know what else to add. I think I should take you to see my grandmother. She might be able to help," Zara offers.

"Your grandmother, the head of the Drake vampire clan? Sounds intriguing," Selene says sarcastically. She left off the 'and dangerous' part.

"You will come too of course, priestess. After all, a show of goodwill between the witches and vampires may be beneficial in the end," Zara tells her.

"I don't speak for the witches," Selene responds.

"Maybe it's about time that you did," Jaxson speaks up, commanding all of our attention. "You are a high priestess by birthright. There is a war coming and sides need to be chosen. Either they will stand with you or they leave this city is what I say. No more fence riding for any of our kind. Lines must be drawn in the sand. Namen wants you on his side because he knows the power you command. Make him fear it. The same goes for you, Rayne. Do not doubt your strength. If you were chosen, you were chosen for a purpose. I saw you that night in the woods, remember. I fought you and I named you my second. You are worthy and we stand with you," Jaxson says passionately.

The two other wolves nod in agreement and Zara bows with one arm across her chest, like a noble. Selene squeezes my hand and smiles. I stand up and hold my head a little higher, grateful to have powerful allies.

This all started as a quest for justice, but it became a battle for freedom. I have to be more than I am in order to do what needs to be done. I have to believe it unwaveringly.

"Okay," I say growing excited. "We will figure this all out one step at a time. From here on out, this is a new world and we will provide the framework based on our success or failure. I assure you, we won't fail," I say with more resolve than I've felt in a very long time.

"Now, that's what I like to hear," Jaxson smiles.

◊◊◊

Last, we talk about our ambush driving to meet with Selene, the two lieutenants that are incredibly dangerous, and Selene's fight. The two lieutenants are going to be a problem.

"Namen is commanding a great demon following, even among high level demons. This does not bode well for us and it will be even worse if we don't get that gate closed," Zara begins. "He has promised the demons something big if they're fighting on his behalf. Chaos, fear, anger; remember that some demons feed off of these. They will only get more powerful in a battle. We have to stop many of them before it gets that far."

"I'm wondering if he's conducting experiments on awakeneds as well," Phillip says. "You said one of the men you fought was almost like a wolf-vampire hybrid. It has to be DNA manipulation. He's taking the best traits of both and using them. Remember that you said that Namen wants to see if he can turn humans into awakeneds, well, it stands to reason that he'd also want his own kind to become stronger."

"You're right. I mean isn't that what he's supposedly been doing for hundreds of years, making deals, learning how to increase his own power by stealing souls and other witch's magic. He's commanding demons and now some weaker vampires. If I was a turned vamp and I knew that someone like Zara existed, I'd want more power too," I admit.

Jaxson looks at me questioningly. He has no idea what she's really capable of. Hell, even his entire pack could be considered monsters among monsters. If I were weak, I definitely would want a power boost. Namen is offering them that and more. I get it, I really do, but the repercussions would be dire.

Selene steps in by saying, "We need to make a move now. The gate is the first thing. Zara and I can go while the rest of you strategize about what to do next. Our power will be enough. We need solid plans that take into account each of our strengths."

"A firm timeline of events is going to keep us on track as well. There will definitely be things that we can't foresee, but you're right, we need to stay in front of Namen's plans as much as possible. I'm also going with you to shut this gate down. I'm the fastest wolf here. I can patrol for threats while you do what needs to be done. I may even be able to sniff out any other demons in the area," Christopher contributes.

"Done," Jaxson says, leaving no room for argument and making us all remember that he is the alpha and this is his territory. "Rayne, you will get some sleep first. No more than a couple hours. It will give us time to call a few more members to keep them on the streets in threes, getting information. We'll have the beginnings of a plan by then."

"I think that it's time that you checked on Damien too," Selene suggests.

I nod in agreement. "When I wake up, I'll call." I yawn. I didn't realize how tired I still am. My body still needs a little more healing. I can now feel that my chakra levels are low. I go back upstairs for a nap with no argument.

◊◊◊

I dream that I go back to my house where this all started. I am standing in a pile of rubble that no one has felt the need to clean. Police tape still hangs around the perimeter in some places. I pick up various items out of the charred ruins. All are unrecognizable. I keep wandering until I notice something shimmering in the sunlight.

Near a wall that is still halfway standing is something sticking out of the trash. I reach down and pull it out of the ruins. It was my mother's. An expensive diamond hair comb that she said was given to her by her mother on her wedding day. I study it. Miraculously, it's still intact. The diamonds are shaped like flowers hanging off of a vine. I touch it for a few more seconds before I put it in the pocket of my black harem pants. The next thing I do is reach out to the sky as if I can reach my family in the afterlife, and then the world disappears.

I open my eyes from the dream and look around. I'm taken aback by the fact that not only am I standing, but I'm definitely not where I was when I went to sleep. This is the living room to my house. The one I share with Selene thanks to Damien, my father's best friend and the man who is like a big brother to me. I step over the broken pieces of furniture, and then without thinking, touch my pocket. Something inside pokes my leg. I pull it out and find the comb from my dream in my hand.

"The hell is going on here?" I ask aloud to no one in particular. I'm definitely freaked out by this and I put the comb on the coffee table as I look around at the destroyed window where Selene knocked the demon through. Katsu is strapped to my back and I pull her from her sheath as I take a few more steps around the house, exploring with my eyes as well as my awakened powers. There's no one here but me.

I try to place what happened, but nothing is coming to mind. Was I really dreaming at all? Was this Namen's doing or my own? Either answer right now is not that comforting. The fact that I traveled to my family's home while I was sleep says a lot about my mental state no matter how much I try to deny it. I'm still hurting. I'm still allowing that pain to rule me.

Suddenly, I hear movement outside. I reach out with my power and feel for intent, and then I open the bond with Zara. She and Selene are still at the gate, but the task seems to be nearly finished. In the distance I can see Christopher's wolf through Zara's eyes. She's on alert at my alarm and also confused by my location. I give her a mental nod that I'm calm and okay, but to stay aware. When I catch a glimpse through the window at the bodies moving closer and surrounding the house, I laugh out loud.

I have half a notion to try to escape and see how far I get. Even if I have to shed a little blood to do so, it might be just the release I need. It was probably the accident in Zara's car that caused them to track me. My damn phone was left there, I forgot. In the back of my mind, I can hear them calling my name, yelling that they know I'm in here and that I have one minute to give myself up before they come in.

I've had plenty of visions of how I'd go out, but getting arrested isn't what I had in mind. I question Zara mentally, wondering if it's worth trying to get away. She firmly tells me no. When Selene finishes, she fills her in. I can feel Selene's fear for me through Zara.

Selene says to leave Katsu there, put the sword in the bathroom under the rug and do what they ask. Do not fight back. I'll find you a lawyer to get you out, today. Don't say anything, Rayne. There will probably be media everywhere. Keep your head down and stay silent.

I close the bond and do as I'm told. One last glance into the bathroom mirror into dead eyes. I drop the sheath on the hallway floor.

"Last chance Rayne Whitmore! Come out with your hands up."

I step closer to the door and turn the nob slowly. The sunlight hits my eyes causing me to tear up, just as red dots paint my chest and my face. I lift my hands slowly as the click of weapons fill my ears.

"Come forward. Now, on your knees!" a man orders.

I comply as I'm forced to the ground on my stomach and cuffed.

"You're under arrest for the murders of Elizabeth Whitmore, Jason Whitmore, Jasmine Whitmore, Raymond Jones, Stephanie Hall...

Incredible. Claiming I'm responsible for it all, that I killed my family.

Chapter Sixteen

The back of the police car feels like hard plastic. The cuffs rub against my wrist bone with every bump. I lean forward slightly for comfort when the female officer in the passenger seat turns to look at me. I look out the window instead, not willing to play this game.

"Look Graves, she knows that she's not getting out of this one. How could a girl like her plot to kill her entire family? You have to be some kind of sadistic bitch," the female officer commentates to her partner. I roll my eyes and continue to look out the window.

"Don't worry, we'll get a confession out of her. Soon, the whole world will know the story of Rayne Whitmore, the rich brat that didn't get her way. What happened girl, did daddy not buy you a Ferrari for your birthday, or was it a beach house? Maybe your mother made you wash your own dishes," the man named Graves says.

They both laugh. When I don't respond, Graves slams on his breaks really hard causing me to slam my face against the Plexiglas partition separating us. I force down a growl and let them play their game.

"Rich uppity bitch. You thought that with money you'd never be found, well, that's the mistake that people like you make. You shouldn't have come back you idiot. Let's see how far money gets you in prison while you're in a dark corner getting taken by a gang that likes pretty girls like you," the female officer is trying her best to scare me. As if I'd have any problems getting attacked in prison. As if it'd ever get that far.

Finally, we reach the headquarters and as Zara predicted, there's media everywhere. Camera lights flash all over the car, reporters with microphones are speaking quickly as they motion their camera people to zoom in. Two officers from another car clear a path as my two wonderful escorts pull me out the car and usher me through my walk of shame. I try to keep my head down as a flurry of questions comes my way.

"Rayne Whitmore,"

"Rayne, you're accused of murdering your family,"

"Where have you been all this time?"

"Do you have any comment on-,"

"Rayne, Rayne, can you tell m-,"

"Rayne, it's been two yea-,"

"Ray-,"

Alanna J. Faison   Killer Rayne

"Rayne Whitmore,"

We continue to push through the crowd when thankfully the doors to the precinct open and I'm met with a less hectic atmosphere. With a jerk, I'm pulled into processing. It's going to be a long day.

◊◊◊

Finally, I'm put in an interrogation room where I'm re-read my Miranda rights. I sit there listening to the buzz of the light above me, gaze fixed on the crack in the wall across from me, barely listening to what the detective is saying. Once the detective finishes, I say, "Lawyer."

The big man with salt and pepper hair and a creepy old school porn mustache looks me over and grins. He leans in close enough for me to smell his cheap cologne and his breath that smells like old soup and horse shit. If I had some breath mints, I'd pop them in his foul mouth. I cough at the combination and lean away. He motions for someone to come in the room. They peek their head in the door and he gives them a nod. A few seconds later, there's a knock on the window that's probably in confirmation to whatever it is that he asked for.

"Now," his gruff voice starts. He sounds like a two pack a day smoker. "The camera's off. Let's cut to the chase, we know you didn't kill them, but see, the world doesn't know that. Our job is to make a statement if you will. Nothing is out of Namen's reach. You see, when the smoke clears, I know what side I'm going to be on and it's never the losing side. I have enough evidence to put you away long enough where you won't be able to make any moves against him. You don't have the resources to take him on. Now, the entire world knows that you're still alive. The media will be hounding you for months."

I think about his words and scrunch my lips to the side. He's right. The media will be watching me now dammit. Will my friends be able to be seen with me? It'll cause too much speculation and attention. To keep my anger in check, I tap my fingers in a slow rhythm.

Namen, this is a bitch move.

"Why are you even talking?" I ask annoyed. The all white room is annoying. These cuffs are annoying. The hard metal chair is hurting my ass. His breath is hurting my nose. I tilt my head to the side, giving the detective an amused look, then I continue tapping on the brown, rickety table.

He reaches over the table and slaps me hard before grapping my cheeks with his big hand. I barely feel the slap, but his hands on me really piss me off. That's how you get pimples, from people who touch your face with dirty ass hands. He doesn't even turn around when the door opens.

"Get your filthy hands off of my client now and uncuff her," my lawyer demands. I feel his power heat up the room and command both of our attention.

The detective releases his grip quickly and he gives me an angry look. I can tell that he's not too happy that he gave in to his demands so quickly. I give him a smirk of satisfaction as he unlocks my oh-so-fashionable iron bracelets.

My lawyer is clad in a dark gray suit with a navy tie. His head is bald but it fits him perfectly. With a clean shaven goatee, he reminds me of Jason Statham. His dark, pupil-less eyes let me know that he's half demon. He lets his dark eyes return to normal then winks at me. Zara sent me a half demon lawyer with the power of persuasion. Brilliant.

"I'll take this seat now so that I can consult with my client. Thank you, you may leave," he tells the detective, dismissing him promptly. The detective gets out of his seat and walks to the door, slamming it like a kid having a tantrum.

"Now," he begins, shaking my hand. "My name is Pierce Brooks and I am now and henceforth your lawyer. Zara Drake has paid me handsomely to represent you whenever you need representation. She told me to do whatever it takes to get you out of here today. Zara was very adamant about that. So, in order for me to do my job, you have to tell me everything. Do not leave out a single detail.

"Okay, well, here goes." I spend the next hour telling Pierce everything that's come to pass. He asks questions here and there as the story goes on, but for the most part remains silent and is actually not surprised by anything. He takes some notes. When I finish, his hand is rubbing his chin hair.

"This is going to be a fun case. I can get you out of here today definitely on some procedural grounds, but moving forward will be a challenge, especially if the police in charge are working with Namen Young. I will definitely work to get the case dropped immediately. Hold tight while I get your paperwork for your release."

I do my best to wait patiently when I feel Zara pulling at our mind-link. I open up to her and a flood of emotions hit me.

You're all over the news. They're nicknaming you Killer Rayne. There's speculation about you murdering your family, why you did it, who you paid. It's on every channel, Zara tells me grimly.

What the hell am I going to do? These bastards are on Namen's payroll. He did this, I growl.

139

We'll figure it out, don't worry. You may have to change your hairstyle and appearance some, maybe invest in a good wig. We can do that. Put a glamour on you or something. Namen's trying to take you out of the game. We won't let him, Zara promises.

Okay, Pierce is getting my paperwork done now. I'll be out soon, I tell her.

Good, good. Selene contacted Damien. He's on his way to get you.

No! He's not supposed to be anywhere near this. They'll come after him. Tell him no, I demand.

Believe me, Selene tried. She knew that he had a right to know before the news broke, and then he insisted that he do what he could. He refused to let anyone stop him. I know this is not ideal Rayne, but Damien is a grown ass man and we can't make choices about his life for him. Men are prideful beings and he's not going to let you take away his honor as a man and as his duty to your father. Accept it for what it is.

She's right and it pisses me off to admit it. Before she closes the bond, I say, *Zara, I don't know how I got to the house. I was dreaming and then I wasn't. Maybe I was never dreaming in the first place. I ended up at my family's home, and then I went to mine. Please tell me that you have an idea as to what the hell is going on.*

Alanna J. Faison   Killer Rayne

As of now, I really don't know. I have an idea, but I'm not ready to share it. I need to check a few things first, but we'll figure it out. We'll figure it all out. After we get you to my grandmother's, you can summon the immortals and get Namen out of your head okay.

Okay. Tell Selene that I love her and not to worry.

Will do.

Ten more minutes pass as I sit alone in this room with my negative thoughts to keep me company. Finally, the detective and Pierce walk in, looks of anger and satisfaction paint their faces, respectively.

"You're free to go, Whitmore," the detective tells me.

"So soon? Just when I was enjoying the feng shui of this place," I say sarcastically as I try to keep my anger in check. This guy pisses me off. To scare him, I release a little bit of my power into the room, just enough so that he can feel the chill creep up his spine as he locks eyes with me.

I've been through more than I've ever imagined I could survive. But, this thing is far from over. Namen has decided to change the whole game. The lawyer leads me out of the interrogation room just as the detective grabs my arm.

I glance at the tall man that interrogated me and despite my anger; I still manage a little smirk at the fact that I'm obviously a true threat to him now.

Namen, you bastard, you played your hand perfectly.

"Namen says to tell you smile for the cameras," the detective whispers smugly. I pull my arm away and tilt my head toward him in defiance.

"You know, I'm going to make sure that you're the first human that I kill," I warn.

"There are too many witnesses now. You won't be able to make a move now that the whole world is looking at you. You think you have friends. This police force belongs to Namen Young."

I brush up against the detective and lift my head so that my lip is touching his ear. I'm close enough that I can smell his cheap cologne mingling with his sweat. He fears me and I like it. "Well then," I whisper softly, "I guess I'll have to kill you all."

Chapter Seventeen

Pierce pulls me close to him to and gives me his suit jacket. "Cover your face. I'll lead you outside to where your guy is waiting. I'm going to stay back and throw the media off of your trail. I will get in touch with you through Zara, okay."

I nod as I cover myself with the jacket. I'm definitely not comfortable with not being able to see my surroundings, but the only danger I should be in right now is of being photographed. Around me, I can hear police officers whispering about me. I want to tell them where they can shove it, but it's best to keep walking.

The commotion grows louder as we reach the front. The clicks of cameras and of reporters drown out the noise of traffic and fill my ears with chatter and speculation. It hurts me to think that people believe that I may have had my family murdered. Now is not the time to set them straight though.

"What really happened the night of the Whitmore massacre?"

"Rayne Whitmore, the lone survivor is walking out a free woman, for now."

"Move back, everyone move back now. Make room, please," Pierce demands.

A car door opens and I am pushed in. It shuts immediately, but I don't dare uncover my face. When we pull off, I wait about thirty more seconds before I reveal myself to Damien.

"So, please tell me that internet and t.v. were destroyed overnight and it'll take months for this to reach the rest of the world by telegram," I joke despite the anger running rampant through my veins.

"It's already been handled Ray Ray. Don't worry," Damien says with a scowl on his face.

The car speeds up as we zoom through traffic. His phone rings and he answers it through the car's system. "We'll be there in two minutes,' he says once he picks up.

"Understood," a female voice responds. The line goes dead.

Damien runs a red light as I stare at him confused. I was in there for a few hours, but based on the amount of reporters, there's no way he could have done anything that quickly. My lawyer didn't even know about it. He would've told me.

"What did you do D? When?" I ask suspiciously. I buckle up, forgetting that I hadn't done it.

"I spoke with my contact at the feds. I went to the department that deals with supernaturals. We made a deal. I did what needed to be done. The F.B.I. was going to get involved. This would've taken years to resolve if I didn't strike a deal," Damien explains.

"That's not telling me jack. What did you do?" I nearly yell. I have a very short fuse right now.

He squeezes the steering wheel tightly as I lean forward in the backseat so that I can get a good look at his face. Before he responds, he pulls up into a neighborhood and into a driveway. The garage opens as we pull up and a black BMW pulls out. D hops out of the car quickly and pulls me out roughly. He's frustrated and hiding something.

He puts me in the back and then slides in the passenger seat. There's a woman in the front. She's dark skinned like Damien, hair pulled back in a ponytail, and a black fitted cap turned to the front. I can't see her features because she's still facing the front, silent.

We reverse and I think it's time to continue this conversation.

"Don't try to get out of this. What the hell did you do?" I snap.

"I told you I made a deal!" he exclaims, turning toward me. He doesn't have on his signature sunglasses and the stress and fear in his eyes worries me.

"Tell her Damien," the woman speaks up. I look at her sideways, wondering just who she is. I'll get to her later.

"I made a deal to give them a few of the weapons that Jason had developed to combat supernaturals. In exchange they are working a story that you were in witness protection all this time. The man responsible for the killings was identified by you and when the U.S. Marshalls went to pick him up, he killed himself. You were getting set up to start your life again and a press conference was to be held, yet someone leaked the information to the police and they were too eager to arrest you without looking at all the facts. That will be the story." Damien stares me down, daring me to argue.

Oh, it's coming. I squeeze my eyes shut willing my power to stay in check. Two deep breaths later, I'm still barely able to hold back.

"You're going to give the government the weapons that you were against? You're going to hand them power to start a war against the awakenends when that's exactly what I'm trying to prevent!"

"I did it to save you!"

"At what cost! Dammit D, you didn't even wait to see if we had another plan. I have a lawyer. He needs to know what the hell is going on."

"He can be notified," he shrugs.

"Do you understand what you're saying? Namen is using any and every excuse to make the first move against the humans, against the government and you may have not only given him one, but you could very well have convinced supernaturals that were undecided that it's time to take action," I am fuming. My tattoo is glowing and I feel the hair on the back of my neck sticking up.

We pull into a parking garage and start to circle through the levels slowly.

"It was a decision that I made. How will they know?"

"They'll know when agents start busting in their homes and killing them."

"Hear him out Ms. Whitmore. He's not as naïve to give them the most dangerous tools." She turns to me, smiling her full lips and batting her long lashes. "He loves you."

I look her over with a frown. "And who might you be?"

"My name is Tamara Owens. I'm the owner of a small security company that Damien just bought out to make a part of Whitmore Industries."

"And what type of security do you do, Ms. Owens?"

She laughs lightly. "We have a fresh concept. We are body guards as well as self-defense instructors. Anyone that asks for our services must be prepared to learn to protect themselves as well should anything happen to our employees. Our client's safety is so vital to us that we will make sure they are as protected as possible." Her smile makes me want to like her, but I can't say for sure if I do.

"She's also my girlfriend; Rayne, play nice," Damien admits.

I nod and roll my eyes as I cross my arms. "So, how much have you told your girlfriend about what's really going on D?"

"He's told me everything Ms. Whitmore. I can assure you, if he is loyal to you, I will be too. My word is everything to me."

We lock eyes and I search for a hint of deception, but I find none. I look back at D who also returns my stare head on. I trust him. I always have. I guess I'll have to trust him on this as well. Still, I can make my position very clear.

"You know that if you betray us, I will kill you," I warn.

"Rayne-," D starts.

"No, she needs to know that I'm serious. I'll rip your throat out and feed you to my wolves. This isn't a game. This is life or death in every aspect. We can't afford loose ends and if you show yourself to be that, you will be killed. That is a promise."

Tamara looks at me with a look that I've seen on Selene's face plenty of times: deadly determination. "Understood."

"Now, how long have you been together?" I smile.

◊◊◊

We keep the conversation light as we enter Tamara's main office. Two security guards are at the front and I can feel the energy of others all around the building. As we wait for Selene, Jaxson, and Zara to arrive, I learn that Tamara learned Dragon Fist Kung Fu in secret for years when her parents were in the military. They were stationed in Burma where an old master taught her. We've made promises to spar with each other in the future. She'll probably be able to expand my skills as well. Strength is good, but technique can always be refined.

In less than three minutes, their arrival is announced. I stand up when Selene dashes toward me, pulling me close and kissing me. Her energy explodes all around me, proof that she was extremely worried.

She speaks softly in Portuguese, rubbing against me. "Oh God, I was so scared. What are we going to do?"

"It seems that Damien has already cleared things up for me," I say pointedly.

He nods toward Zara. "I see that you've been making yourself useful, vampire."

"Get to the point," Jaxson says, giant arms crossed.

"Yes, please do. We have plans to make," Zara adds, smirking at Damien. She likes him.

He let me bite him once, she tells me through our bond. I gasp out loud and she winks at me. Selene gives us both a look.

"I made a deal with the government to make Rayne come out like the victim. The world will think that she was in witness protection the entire time. I'm giving them some weapons that we developed to combat your kind," he says frankly.

Jaxson reacts first, slamming a fist on the table, cracking it. "You did what?!"

Damien continues, doing his best to look unfazed by the massive man in front of him. "They were never field tested and they were minor weapons, more so security enhancements if you will."

Alanna J. Faison   Killer Rayne

"Exactly what were they? You do know that Rayne's girlfriend is a witch or have you forgotten? You gave them something that will be potentially dangerous to her. Rayne must be pissed at you," Zara laughs incredulously.

I frown, I wasn't just thinking of Selene when he told me. I was thinking of all of my friends, but when she puts it like that, it makes it even worse. Ugh. Dumbass.

"Start talking. It better be something that doesn't piss me off," Jaxson warns.

Tamara grabs a remote and stands behind Damien, rubbing his shoulder for reassurance. He squeezes her hand as she turns on the screen. Images float with holographic technology all around us. D steps into place in the middle as we look at the weapons that my father had started developing.

"First we have these vests." He points to the screen right in front of him, turning the image 360 degrees. The vests look like any standard bullet proof vests. "These are anti-magic vests. I don't even know how well they'd hold up against powerful spells, but the concept is for them to absorb the energy."

Selene gives me a look and then steps closer to the image, turning it herself. "I want to see these in person."

"Not a problem. They will all be available for you to check out," Damien assures us.

Jaxson growls and D takes a step back.

Tamara points to the second weapon. "Next is the one that I decided we use."

"I'm sorry, and who are you?" Selene asks. I snicker at her because I pretty much asked the same thing.

"I'm Tamara, Ms. Marquez. I am Damien's girlfriend and the CEO of this office that you're in. I'm also your new friend," she smiles confidently.

Selene and I share a look and I just shrug.

"Oh, is that so? Then call me Selene please, no need for the formalities, friend. Hey friend, may I ask what is your stake in all of this?" Selene smiles back sarcastically while pulling her hair behind her ear. She may look innocent, but her energy tells me that she is very pissed about this deal.

"Well, I am very good at what I do. You're going to need humans on your side doing day to day things that you can't. Do I look like I want to be a slave to anyone? Hell to the no. Our people have been there and done that. I won't. So, let's just say that I have everything to gain by being on your side," Tamara explains.

"Or access to weapons that will hinder us if things don't go your way," Jaxson adds.

"I'm not like that. I have morals. As I told Ms. Whitmore, I live by my word."

Jaxson studies her, then nods at us. He could smell a lie if she told one. She checks out, for now. Apparently, not satisfied, Zara flashes in front of Tamara, startling her. She gasps in surprise as Zara grips her face. The two guards rush in the room but Jaxson stops them with his massive arms. He's waiting to see this play out.

Surprisingly, Selene preps a spell, waiting for any decision from Zara. I don't know what all went on with those two, but Selene seems to have less animosity against her now. Damien pleads with me with his eyes to do something. When I don't, he grabs Zara's free arm. She twists out of his reach and pulls him into a headlock. It's comical really.

"Now," Zara begins. "What else do you want?" She forces Tamara to look into her eyes, becoming a victim of her glamour.

I've never seen this done to this extent. Tamara's eyes dilate and she falls under the spell, completely transfixed only on Zara. She opens her mouth to speak as Damien struggles under my vampire's grasp.

"I want to be like Rayne. I want power. I want to be unmade," Tamara says truthfully.

"Now, that's more like it," Zara says as she releases them both and I stand there stunned.

So that's it huh. She wants to get in good so that she can claim the same power that I have. I watch her shake her head as if clearing a fog and then I turn to Damien who is now rubbing his neck. The security guards too have backed off.

"Did you know about this?" I ask Damien suspiciously. The answer better be the right one.

"The hell? Ray Ray no. She never mentioned that to me. If she did I would've told her that it's not worth the risk. You know that I don't lie to you," he says emphatically.

"Well you definitely have put us all in a bad position. We don't put a lot of trust in humans and I damn sure don't really want humans mixed up in my affairs without my knowledge, using us to gain power. People like that become reckless," Jaxson says matter-of-factly.

"I'm not crazy, a fanatic, or anything like that. I'm skilled and I want to have the power I know I deserve. The world needs more people like you, like us," she argues turning toward me for sympathy.

"People who feel that they deserve the power often are the ones that don't. Keep that in mind," Selene responds.

Tamara clinches her fists then relaxes. "I will do my part. You'll see. I will be an asset."

"There's not enough time. Being unmade is no walk in the park. There's torture involved. Do you want that?" I ask.

"Or maybe I could just turn you right now," Zara stalks playfully around her as she pushes her aura onto Tamara just like she did to me when I fought her. She doesn't have the power that I have, so Tamara falls to her knees, letting out a low moan, and shaking as the power rolls over her. All of us in the room feel it. Jaxson's eyes change, bringing the wolf forth. Selene's hair begins to float in a non-existent wind. I feel Zara's power within me, rolling over my own like waves.

"Please, stop," D pleads. He too has fallen to the floor.

"Oh, lighten up Damien. This is what she wants. I could make it feel good too. The bite will be exquisite. You will be mine, but you will have the power you crave. Is that what you want?" Zara teases, rubbing Tamara's back, speaking softly into her ear.

Zara is dripping sexual energy and no one in the room is immune to its effects, regardless of how powerful we are. Where Tamara stinks of fear, it excites us. Zara laughs and releases the force of her aura like a rubber band snapping back into place.

"I- I don't want that," Tamara whispers. "I don't want to have to die to get it."

"You think being unmade isn't dying Tamara? Death would be welcome after that. Think about it. If you prove that you are worthy, I will speak with the immortals about you. I understand what it's like to be powerless, I sympathize, but you must be certain because there is no going back. You will make more enemies, there will never be a normal life," I say to her as Selene picks her up off of the ground.

Damien gets up too and pulls her closely. They both have a seat. Jaxson just shakes his head and comes forward. He places himself in the center of the room, commanding attention like a true Alpha.

"This can be settled later. I don't feel that her intentions are bad. Let's leave her alone. We have work to do. Just know that we're going to keep an extra eye on you. This is a war that we can't afford to lose. If you want to help, then you need to know that you may not live to realize the dream of becoming unmade. Namen Young will kill any and everyone that stands in his way. Knowing that, if you still want to do your part, no matter how small, that is good enough for me." Jaxson smiles at her and she can't help but smile back.

Her confidence returns in full force and it makes me respect her. Here she is in a room with these powerful awakened beings and she just shakes it off and keeps moving. Most people would have run for cover. I don't even feel any fear in her. D has sure picked a good one.

Chapter Eighteen

Tamara reopens the images that have closed since our interruption. She again points to the second piece of technology. "These are contact lenses that are supposed to keep people from being glamoured. I'm wearing them now and apparently, they don't work so well, so don't worry."

Zara laughs and we share a look. Maybe they just don't work on purebloods.

"The key to these are the reflective lens that keeps the magic from reaching the brain. Or, so I was told," Tamara chuckles, smoothing her hair.

Damien gets up for the last item that was bartered for my freedom. "This is a mixture that if consumed within two hours of a werewolf attack, will negate the effects of the virus. Think of it as a morning after pill."

A weapon, or defense against a witch, vampire, and werewolf. Just great. D has managed to piss off everyone in the room. Am I really worth it? There could have been another way, but we had no time to explore our options.

"Tell them the deal's off. There has to be an alternative. The government will just find a way to improve on these tools. They'll study them and make more," I say, a sick feeling rising in my gut.

"I won't. You could go to prison. There is no other way to explain where you were this entire time, why you never came forward. I'd been working on scenarios for over a year and nothing seemed to fit," Damien explains.

"What about kidnappers?" Selene asks.

"Go on."

"Well, it may be cruel, but we could always pin it on someone else, right Zara," Selene brainstorms.

Zara begins to pace back and forth. "Hmm, it could work. When I worked as an assassin, I used to use other criminals like rapists and murderers to do my job for me. I'd glamour them, have them kill my mark and then they'd be caught at the scene of the crime and dealt with by the human courts, case closed."

"Brilliant," Jaxson states.

We're all equally impressed at Zara's scheming. She kept her hands absolutely clean of it and rid the world of scum too. No trace back to the client either. I work it out in my head as Selene speaks again.

"So, we'll find a big time trafficker, make him take the fall. Glamour him into a confession. They have to say that you were in witness protection this whole time if they want this bust. We'll figure it out." Selene sounds desperate.

"Pierce is a half demon with powers of suggestion. He can get them to write up a plausible statement. This could work, especially if you have something to offer that will be worth their while. I can get a name of a trafficker no problem. We can shut down a whole slave operation as well," Zara agrees.

Jaxson grunts in agreement, as his phone rings. "Work it out," he demands as he takes the call out of the room.

"What will we say about Jason? Why would this trafficker target him and the family?" Damien asks.

"We'll work it out," I snap. It's too risky to give the government these defenses. At least not at this time, not when Namen may start a war sooner because of a threat that he sees.

I'm not going to jail and nobody's reputation is getting destroyed either.

"D, I love you like a brother. I appreciate what you tried to do for me, but you aren't up to date with the situation. I had wanted to keep you out of this, but now I know that you're not going to have any of that. Still, I need you to work behind the scenes. I need you and Tamara to figure out what other humans are in league with Namen. I don't know how, but if the police are in his pocket, then surely there are other influential people riding on his team. I need names and occupations. They will need to be taught a lesson too. Tamara, have you ever killed anyone?"

"No," she responds suspiciously, squinting her brown eyes.

"Well, if you're on our side, that day will come," Selene finishes for me.

"Why don't you take the night to sleep on it. Decide if you're really about that life," I suggest with a raised eyebrow.

She gives me a look that says that she's not used to other women ordering her around, especially not younger women. "Understood," she replies.

"Good. Now, I look forward to our sparring session in the future," I tell her honestly.

That is, if any of us are still alive.

◊◊◊

Zara leaves the room just as Jaxson re-enters. She's getting ready to touch base with Pierce to see if he thinks that he can pull off this ambitious move.

Jaxson tells us that his wolves found a stray lamia tonight on the streets that they killed. He also says that Phillip and Chris have come up with the beginnings of a plan. We will discuss that after I meet with Zara's grandmother of doom.

Finally, Tamara switches on the news. CNN has plenty of speculation, analysts going over my case, psychologists weighing in on my mental state, and replays of me getting out of the police car in cuffs and me leaving covered in Pierce's jacket.

Pierce did make a statement after I left. He kept it vague while sounding extremely confident that this case will come to a conclusion sooner rather than later and that all questions will be answered. After I watch again as I get pulled out of the police car, Damien goes out to see what the word with Zara is. He'll be making a call one way or the other tonight too. I'm just ready to crash now.

This is all utter bullshit. Namen is a scheming, conniving bastard and he'll pay for this. Now, the news will be flooded all over again with my family's murders and I will be forced to continue to relive that pain. There will be questions every time I'm in public, old friends will try to get in touch. Without thinking I punch the wall and my hand goes through it. I blink back a tear before it falls from my frustration.

Warm, soft arms envelope me. The scent of citrus fills my nose as a loving kiss is planted on my cheek. "You're not going through this alone, Rayne. It's going to be okay meu amor," Selene whispers softly.

She tickles my ear with her breath as she chants a calming spell. I turn around so that I'm facing her. Her soft breasts rub against mine and I embrace her. "I know. I don't deserve it, but thank you."

"Yes, you have been an ass lately, but with all the problems we're facing, I'm ready to let it go to the back burner. We're going to figure this thing out with my brother and I'm going to forgive you and Zara for trying to kill him. Besides, Namen is the focus of my rage as well. He's manipulating my family too. He's trying to gain me like a prize. Who knows what else he's been involved in. It frightens me to think about it, merda."

"I know. He's not going to take anyone else away from me and he's not going to tear any of us apart."

"We will get him out of your head," Selene promises, placing a kiss on my forehead.

"Okay, I believe you. And I know that even though you are going to try to forgive me, it's going to take time to build again. I have faith in us because you're where I wanna be."

"Oh, I am still mad, but I don't want to even think about life without you. I'm invested in us," she responds. "But, it'll have to wait. There are much bigger things to worry about."

"Okay." I smile.

"Let's get the official story in order and then we'll go visit your family's graves. I'm sure there will be reporters there and it'll help your image. I also think that it's time for you to reconsider looking into your father's company."

I nod. We're going to need access to these weapons and I might need to step up to shut down some things that may hinder us in the upcoming battles as necessary. The company was supposed to be mine to begin with. I will have to make my way to the top, even if I have to have Zara glamour people to do it. Just as I'm thinking, Jaxson comes inside.

"Believe it or not, I actually still have a job, so I have to handle that. You let me know if anything changes. I'll send someone if you need them. You are my second, you are pack."

"Thanks Jaxson," I say as I hug him, smelling the scent of rain and grass.

When I start, I'm going to put him on the payroll, at least until this is all sorted out. He needs to be able to focus without worrying about clocking in. He can be my personal body guard on paper.

Next, Zara and Damien both come back into the room and get my attention.

"What's up?"

"Tonight, Selene and I will be hunting down Julio Escobar. He's a drug kingpin that also sells young boys and girls to the highest bidder. One of my contacts told me that he is leaving Chicago right now and is traveling on the road. We are going to meet him. Apparently, he never really leaves Mexico, but there was a special sale that he was required to oversee, the rape of his ex-girlfriend was sold to the highest bidder as well as the subsequent execution. I thought you'd approve of this one."

"Damn right. Too bad you and Selene will get to have all the fun with him. Please make him hurt for me. What will I be doing?"

"Pierce is coming here and you will prep for your four p.m. press conference. The U.S. Marshalls agreed to my terms. They've been looking for this son of a bitch for twenty years. He's gotten off twice already from mistrial and missing witnesses, but I assured my contact there that they'd have all they need as long as they pull some strings with the other agencies. They even promised to make the police force here look like a joke. As for your whereabouts this past year, every Marshall will be getting a Christmas bonus to overlook it. I have a hacker on the inside that is creating a paper trail to say that your fake death was authorized as well as placement in witness protection," Zara smirks. She obviously had to call in favors that she's been sitting on. I'm sure this was not how she wanted to cash in.

Damien hands me a coffee that I didn't even know he was holding. "Looks like you're in for a long night."

I grab it and pull it to my chest, like a lover, inhaling the rich fumes. It tingles my nose as it provides just a sliver of comfort. "So it seems."

Chapter Nineteen

Carefully, I replay the scenario in my head, hoping this all adds up, yet there are still pieces missing and I'm not comfortable with all the issues just yet. There are too many holes to be filled and I curse Namen's name once again for slowing us down in this way. He's fighting a psychological battle and he wants me to break. But why? That question will have to wait.

"Zara, how did you get all that done? This all seems too easy. I don't know what to think right now because you just seem to happen to know all the right people at the right time," I say hoping I don't come off as sounding suspicious.

"Well, first, my wealth exceeds your own simply because I've had hundreds of years to accumulate it. When you've been in the business of killing, you tend to make large sums of money, especially when you're good at it. That's something you should know. Your father's company specializes in weapons and weapons are used to kill. It is the primary reason why you father got so rich so fast. Second, the clients that you take tend to do two things: predict how much you will make and tell a friend."

"What does that mean?" Selene asks.

Zara smiles devilishly. It's the look of a sadist that enjoys delivering pain. "Politicians, famous people, those hoping to climb the social ladder tend to need extra help in doing so, in winning, in grasping the spotlight. Many times, they can't do it on their own. Shady deals go down, people flex their muscles. I get called. They pay They pay for discretion. They pay to make things look accidental. They pay for me to not take a hit out on them later on down the line. And 'sometimes,' I tend to remember things that I've done, 'sometimes' I keep records just in case, 'sometimes' I can make people's lives a living hell just for the fuck of it."

"You're a bitch," Damien says as he shakes his head.

"Of course I am," she responds, flashing fang. "Now, as for this particular individual in the agency, let's just say that he accidently leaked government secrets to a woman that was posing as an escort. She was actually selling those secrets to another government. Because he didn't want her traced back to him or the fact that he was dumb enough to fuck up on a national security issue, he needed me to handle it. That's all you need to know."

"Wow. I don't even know what to say. I'm sorry if you enjoyed having him under your thumb. Now I've ruined it."

"Oh, no worries. Secrets are as valuable as jewels and trust me, I have more than a treasure chest of them."

"What did you mean about my father making money off of killing?"

"Damien, would you like to handle this one or shall I?"

"No, you go ahead. I like how you tell stories."

Selene rolls her eyes.

"Now. Your father's name had come up several times for potential hits when he was younger and inexperienced in the business. Oh, he was ruthless in his dealings, but he didn't know how to play the game the way the big boys liked to play. By the way, I do my research thoroughly on all my potential marks, part of the reason why I was the best, being able to glamour information out of people doesn't hurt either," she brags.

"Would you just get on with it?"

"Okay, okay. Now, your father had already had a nice sum of money when he started the business thanks to-,"

"Dealing drugs when he was a teenager. I know that, everybody knows that. A true rags to riches story and the reason why he had to join the military. Grandma and grandpa put all his clothes and stuff outside and told him to do something better with his life or never see them again. The media loved that about him."

"Right. So, he had already been a business man and like any true entrepreneur, he invested. He saved a lot and hid the money with people he could trust. His boys he ran with did their jobs well and flipped that money three times over. Isn't that right Damien?"

"Yes. We ran the neighborhood. We pushed weight, and we did so very well. Catering to those rich white boys up the way too. They were our biggest clients and they liked to talk. Jason learned a lot about their family's businesses, how to manipulate them, so when he came back, money was already stacked. He took care of me and we took care of them. He now had discipline, the brains to get things done, and was a war vet."

"Your father was well versed in the ways of the streets and he took that with him when he went into business. He knew about weapons and he knew that the illusion of security was something that people clung to. In the very beginning, he wasn't selective on who he sold to, he just wanted to make enough profit so he could push other people out of the way. Damien, you should tell her how he did it."

"Alright, fine," he sighs. "First, you should know that he got all of us off the streets and gave us jobs. Think about it. A group of young black men that people only saw as thugs were turning businesses upside down. We did what we did, but after, we were able to clean those same streets up. We gave security systems and cameras to all the stores and houses around where we grew up. We did a lot of good there. We went to college and we paid for many kids from the neighborhood to go too."

"I know, D, you don't have to explain, just tell me what I need to know," I say.

"Alright, so, there was another company that we were competing against. They pretty much had the monopoly on security systems at the time. Jason employed some really intelligent boys that were in trouble for hacking. He paid their bail, for their lawyers, and hired them. Slowly, we installed bugs and viruses into their security systems causing them to malfunction. It was a slow process, but after five years, they went bankrupt. There was no trace. More brilliant people began to become employed and we repeated the process. People lost their jobs, their livelihoods, and some of them committed suicide."

"Wow," says Selene. "There's plenty blood on all of our hands it seems."

"Yeah, well, we justified it by saying that they would do the same if they were in our position. We hired some of their people, made them sign confidentiality statements. We hired misfits, people who never would have had the chance to succeed otherwise, and if we stepped on a few to get to the top, oh well."

"So, plenty of people had already wanted daddy dead. He played the game his own way, and more often than not, did things that were against the law."

"He had his own code. There was a method for everything he did. Your father was a good man," Damien says passionately.

Zara ignores him and continues, "Then, there was the second side to the business, the supernatural research side. The experiments-,"

"Those didn't last long! It was a mistake," Damien growls.

We all turn to Damien, waiting for him to continue.

"For about six months, we attempted to kidnap and experiment on awakeneds. We needed their blood for research, needed to study them in a controlled setting. Zara put an end to that."

She crosses her arms and I look at their exchange.

Alanna J. Faison   Killer Rayne

172

"Explain. Now," I demand.

"Oh, I took that hit. That's when I did my research and I even pretended to be a kidnap victim. Damien came in and talked to me, asked me if I considered myself a bad person. There was no file on me that they could find and all of the other prisoners were guilty of some type of human offense that they felt justified their capture."

"Always judging by human standards," Selene says, surprising me.

I've never heard her separate herself from us like that. I can tell that she's still pissed about the weapons. My father is not really being cast in a favorable light and I can see now why it would be believable that a drug kingpin wanted revenge on my family. I can't believe how oblivious my parents kept us.

"So, I know that you have somewhere to be, just tell me why you didn't kill them then," I say.

"Because Damien and Jason both knew what they doing were doing was wrong and they both were finding a way to make it up to all the people they kidnapped. Even if they didn't agree with the things they had done, they knew treating anyone like a lab rat was not moral. When I escaped, I followed them and listened to their conversation. Because of that, I let them live. I felt that if they were willing to give them a second

Alanna J. Faison   Killer Rayne

chance, they earned one too. I destroyed all the equipment and left a warning for them, but I left them in one piece," Zara says matter-of-factly.

"I get it. My father was not an honest man. Story done. Go get the bastard that is going down for all of this so that we can get on with our lives. It's what my dad would approve of, it's what he'd do," I laugh.

My daddy had been my hero for so long that I'm not too enthused about the destruction of his character, the way I've imagined him since I can remember. I walk out of the room to go to the bathroom so that I can splash water on my face. They don't follow me as I search the hallways until I find it.

My eyes look tired, hollow. I search them for the innocent Rayne that I was lifetimes ago. Nope, not home.

Fuck this.

I'm not throwing myself any more pity parties. I know what I know and now it's time to move on. I have a job to do.

Kill the man that changed my life forever.

That is, after we pull off the scam of the decade. Blackmail, lies, secrets, and more. Cab e t.v. drama at its finest.

Alanna J. Faison   Killer Rayne

Chapter Twenty

My witch and my vampire take their leave once again going on a mission to save my ass. I really hope that this time together brings them just a little bit closer to an understanding. I owe both of them more than I can repay and all I want for now is for them to be able to be friends. It's my fault that Selene really doesn't trust Zara now, but we all need each other.

Pierce, my lawyer, shows up about half an hour after they leave. He's holding a box of pizza and some beer. Clearly, he wants me to be comfortable while we go over all of this.

Damien has also left so that he can prep the execs for my glorious return, or entrance, since I never have been a part of Whitmore Industries. Apparently, there has to be some sort of vote and legal issues to sort out. They'll be worried about stock and company stability and other things that I really give no fucks about.

I just need to get inside so that I can see for myself just what it was that my father had done. I need to get to the bottom of the weapon situation, and to do that, I need as much clearance as possible. I had originally told Damien that I wanted no part of this shit. I should have known that I'd have no choice but to come back home.

Pierce pulls out a chair for me like a perfect gentleman and puts a paper plate in front of me. I open the pizza box and am assaulted by the delicious aroma of baked dough, cheese, and pepperonis. Classic. I haven't had pizza since I've been back and my mouth waters instantly. I inhale the hint of garlic butter sauce on the crust and sigh in content. After I consume two pieces, I crack open a beer and get ready to begin.

"So, do you think we can pull this off?" I ask in between gulps.

"I'm going to Olivia Pope the hell out of this, don't worry," he assures me, however I'm lost on the reference.

"Huh?"

"*Scandal*. Kerry Washington, the show?" he leads me as if I'm supposed to know.

"I know who she is, but I've never seen the show. There wasn't much television watching where I was, remember."

"You have got to catch it. You're missing out. Anyway, she handles situations for very important people. Scandals, murders, elections, you name it. I'm going to do that for you."

"Good, because this is either going to be brilliant or the dumbest thing anyone has ever tried to do."

Alanna J. Faison   Killer Rayne

He laughs as he bites into his pizza, pausing for a second to savor the wonderful taste. "Look, you are allied with people that have a lot of pull. If they are willing to use their power to help you, trust in them that this will work. It's all about who you know. They can make this happen. You'd be surprised at all the shady deals that go down every day."

"Hmm, I'm sure they do, but forgive me if I'm not too optimistic about this. Too much could go wrong. Did they really call me Killer Rayne?" I frown.

"Well, you know how the news likes to give nicknames. You'll be fine. By the end of the week, America will be falling all over you. They'll want to make your story into a movie and I'm going to make sure you can sell it."

"I don't want the publicity. I want to be left alone so I can do what I've been fighting so hard for. Namen wants me to be in the spotlight, I can't allow that to happen," I say rubbing my face in frustration.

"Can you act?"

"What?"

"Can you act? Because, I'm going to need you to sell this with an Oscar winning performance.

Can you do that for me?" Pierce asks seriously, all business.

"I may have picked up on a few things from some friends," I say thoughtfully.

My father often personally installed security systems for his famous friends and I became friends with their kids because he took me with him a lot when he traveled. The movie stars loved to give me pointers and have me play act with them as we pretended to go off into other worlds. Those were fun times.

"Good. Now don't doubt me. Remember, I can persuade people around me and that'll get the fire started. If you can shed a few tears, poke your lip out, and look non-threatening, the story will do the rest. You have people spinning the story for you as we speak. I am great at my job Ms. Whitmore."

He straightens himself in the chair and pushes his power on me. Instantly, I feel calmer, more sure. Damn, this may work.

"Now, let's get this story straight. Julio Escobar tried to blackmail your father because of his past as a drug dealer to run drug shipments for him through Whitmore Industries. He also wanted access to weapons that only your father's company could provide especially since many guns are now outlawed. Your father pretended to agree but was secretly working with the U.S. Marshalls to apprehend him at the drop site. Julio found out about the plan and retaliated by having your family killed. He missed you and before the second hit to take you out could take place, the Marshalls picked you up. How does that sound so far?" he asks.

"So far, it sounds semi plausible. With my dad's past and all that, people just may believe it. Continue."

"Well, you were placed in witness protection and sent to an undisclosed location of course. However, even your girlfriend thought that you had died and after so long apart, you just couldn't deal with her not knowing. You tracked her down and when one of Julio's informants on the force caught wind that you were back in town to see her, he worked up some false documents and had you arrested. They were supposed to have someone on the inside take you out to finish the job. They were going to make it look like a suicide. All of this happened before the Feds could come resolve the situation."

"Well, as long as you fill in the small holes, I think that with Julio actually being arrested and glamoured into believing our story, it will actually work. Which one of the officers will you have go down too?"

"Does it even matter? The whole force should go down. They're trying to find the cop with the most questionable record. It shouldn't take long," he assures me.

"Okay. Now, teach me what to say."

◊◊◊

After three hours of prep, I'm interview ready. Bring on the tough questions; I'll face them like a champ. After we finished, Damien sent me off to sleep at Tamara's house under a four man guard. I was too tired to complain. Right before I'm about to doze off, the new phone that Damien had given me in place of the one that I lost after the accident, begins to ring.

"It's done," Selene's feminine voice says coolly.

"Good to know. Are you guys okay?" I whisper, more from my exhaustion than anything else.

"Yes. We ended up having to kill about four of his men to get to him, but Zara was able to feed the story into his mind before they picked him up for arrest. He was spilling it all before they even got him in cuffs. I almost felt bad for the poor bastard," she responds.

"Yeah, probably before you remembered how he sells kids for a living."

"Oh, I gave him a firm kick in the nuts, not once, but twice," she laughs.

"I wish I could have been there to see it. I'm sure that's not all you did," I reply. I know her well enough.

"We're just going to keep that between me and Zara, okay."

"Fine, hold out on me then." I pause. "How is it being around her for an extended amount of time?" I ask, knowing that Zara is probably within hearing distance.

Selene is silent for a couple seconds before she says, "I want to dislike her, but I really can't. At the end of the day, she will never escape her nature; that is my belief. I grew up untrusting of vampires and I can't say that I really trust the one that has a bond to the woman I love. Yet, for some reason that is still beyond me, she wants to be by your side, helping you become who I knew from the very beginning you are."

With a heavy sigh, she continues. "Rayne, I wish that you were stronger when it came to fighting the power that draws me to her. I wish that you never found her attractive in the first place. You cheated. I didn't tell you the whole truth about my family. And, we are in too much of a mess right now to fix us the way we need."

"Selene,"

"I'm not done. I said that I'd forgive you, but I won't soon forget. Merda, I love you so fucking much it's insane. I'm so angry with you, with this entire situation that somewhere in the back of my mind, I wish that I would have just told you to walk away the night that I met you."

Her words sting. I couldn't imagine not knowing Selene, not feeling this love.

"But, the rest of me knows that I'd be missing out on a love that is worth risking everything for, even my sanity. For you, I will accept Zara and all that comes with her. That includes your bond and this attraction to her and her power. We live by different sets of rules and I know there are some things like this that you weren't really prepared for. How can I fault you for that?"

I wait a few seconds, just listening to her breathe. Her voice is so soft and fragile that I know she was holding back tears as she spoke. I feel like the worst person in the world for causing her even an ounce of pain. I love Selene and all she is: her loyalty, passion, love, strength, and heart. That is what should have shown through when I kissed Zara. I should have remembered that she can't compare to what Selene and I mean to each other, no matter how much of it was out of my control. I should have remembered that before I refused to hear anything but her brother being one of Namen's men.

Selene deserves it all. She deserves the best of me and the benefit of knowing that I won't be looking for anything or anyone else. I love her. Period.

Still, I need to know if there is anything else that she's hiding because I can't continue wondering if there are any more secrets, any more half-truths. I tell her as much.

"Selene. I wish you could really gaze into my heart because you'd see how much of it beats for you. I've loved you from the beginning and I'm not ashamed to say how much you've got me. But baby, I also have to know if there's anything else that you feel that you should tell me. Especially where your family is concerned, I can't have you keeping secrets. We've come too far to hold back. If you don't feel that you can trust me with those things, how can you say that you truly love me?"

"I don't think that's fair. It was a judgment call that I made because I promised my brother that I would keep him safe. I've loved him much longer than I've known you and plenty of what I've done in my life has been to protect him. I refuse to feel bad about that. I will say that I am sorry if you felt that it was about you and me, but it wasn't. I love Santi as much as you loved Jazzy. We are twins. We are bonded in ways that you will never understand," Selene tries to explain.

"I get that. And now, I will help you get answers. You know that they may not be the answers that you want."

"I know. There is nothing else to tell. Meu pai is a cruel, power-hungry man. He made his living by causing other's pain, including his own children. Minha mãe never once fought on our behalf. She's always been too afraid of him to even talk back. They were set up to be married the same way pai tried to set me up with Sergio. You know everything else about my childhood and problems already."

I get it, I really do. When you have a family like that, you are not easily trusting.

"So, your dad had a lot of influence and money like mine, but his traditions and your culture shaped him into a certain kind of person."

"No. He's the type that would be a bad man no matter where he was born. It's inside of him. He makes no apologies for anything he does. He just doesn't care. He regards his values above all else. My father is a narcissist."

Everyone has good and bad qualities about themselves. "What traits do you share with him Selene?"

She laughs at my question. "Well, sometimes I feel that my values hold more weight than others. And I don't necessarily believe that we should be in the business of apologizing to people for things that we do. I honestly have never thought I was like either one of my parents. I don't really know if that's true because mãe never took the time to know me at all. I think that she hates that I look so much like the both of them. She hates my existence because it reminds her that she is stuck with my father forever."

I adjust the phone on my other ear as I turn to get comfortable on the memory foam mattress. Eyes closed, I continue the conversation, smiling at how normal I feel at this moment even though what she's saying is serious.

"Would you ever go back? I want to come with you to meet them."

"I have unfinished business there that I've ran from for so long. Now, it seems that I may not have a choice."

She pauses in thought. "That place, Rayne, has so many terrible memories for me. I wasn't allowed to have too many friends and the ones that I had were spoiled, bratty children from families like mine. They didn't want to be my friend because they knew that I'd take my place ahead of them. It was only me and Santos. When I told him that I was attracted to girls, he knew what that would mean to my family. He was afraid for me."

"I can't ever imagine what you had to go through, just to be who you are. I don't understand why that is so hard for people to get? It makes me so angry," I tell her, clenching my fists.

Her father had allowed someone to do the unspeakable to her, yet she survived. Selene is so brave.

"Rayne, men and women are murdered by their families because of who they are every day. Sometimes people just can't accept differences. They see it as a direct attack on them. I don't get it either, but it's what we're fighting for now in a way. That is what we should focus on. Not my past because it can't be changed. Humans don't want to know us awakeneds. They will destroy themselves trying to destroy us."

"I know. I'm going to deal with these weapons soon. I'm going to take my place in the company. I just wanted to forget about all that for a second," I admit.

"I get that. Tomorrow's going to be a long day, so get some sleep. We'll be there when you wake."

"Okay. Selene..."

"I know, Rayne. I love you too."

Alanna J. Faison   Killer Rayne

"Okay. Bye."

"Bye."

It doesn't take long after that for the world of dreams to claim me.

Chapter Twenty One

They let me sleep until noon. When I wake, my body is really sore and stiff. I yawn and untangle myself from the thick comforter before getting out of bed to stretch. Twenty minutes later, I head to the bathroom that is adjacent to the room I'm in.

The bathroom is pleasantly large with a double headed shower. The tiles are a nice earthy tone. There's a bowl of potpourri on the sink that lends the room a subtle lavender smell. It's calming and as I brush my teeth with the new toothbrush laid out for me, I look at my nearly healed black eye that's an ugly yellowish green color and frown.

Damn vampires.

I give my face a good scrub, remembering that the damn detective put his greasy ass hands all over my face. I do not do well with acne. It's horrifying. Once I turn on the water and get it the right temperature, there's a knock at the door.

I turn to open it, but Selene slips in before I reach the nob.

"Hey," I say as I wrap one arm around her in a side hug. She kisses my cheek and smiles.

"Don't say it. I know I look terrible. I've been telling you to get sleep and yet I've gotten none."

"Well," I start as I look at the dark lines under her eyes and the uncharacteristic state of her hair. "I think we've all seen better days. Somehow, you still manage to look attractive."

She smiles, but it doesn't quite reach her eyes. Together, we stand in silence just watching each other. I almost feel like a stranger to her, afraid to reach out and touch her skin. Then, she touches my hand as if reading my mind.

"Can I shower with you?" Selene asks shyly.

"Of course. There's plenty of room," I say.

We both smile and undress. Selene makes it to the shower first, sliding the glass door open and stepping inside. I follow close behind her, closing the door gently. The hot water stings my back and then numbs it. It feels amazing and I nearly want to fall back asleep.

Selene wets her hair and face before wiping the water from her eyes. She gazes at me with those green depths and says, "I really miss you Rayne."

"I miss you too, Selene. I really do."

"We need to do something about this eye before the press conference," she tells me, gently touching my face. "I have the drink ready for you in the fridge. It should help ease some of your aches. I wanted to do your makeup, but Tamara offered to do it so that I can rest. Zara and I picked you up a business suit and heels."

"Thank you," I say honestly. "I haven't even thought about what I'm going to wear. I just want this done with."

"It will be soon. I'm going to be right there with you okay," she assures me as she turns me so that she can wash my back.

I turn back around slowly and pull her in for a gentle kiss. The soap smells like an ocean breeze as it slides against our naked bodies. For a second, we both deepen the kiss, unspoken need coursing through both of us. Yet, we both know now is not the time. I want her so badly that it hurts, but I still force myself to pull away.

We finish washing each other's bodies in silence.

◊◊◊

Pierce grabs my shoulders firmly and turns me squarely toward him. His black solid tie lies perfectly against his chest. I turn on my game face as he speaks.

"Are you ready?" he asks.

"I don't have any choice but to be," I respond dryly.

"Well, just make sure that you put on an Oscar-worthy performance. The world is watching and I can't persuade them. My reach will only extend to those in the room."

"I'll play my part, don't worry. Was the statement by the Marshalls released yet?" I ask. They were supposed to release a statement about ten minutes before I go up for my press conference stating that all charges against me should be dropped due to the federal involvement in the case and the apprehension and confession of Julio Escobar.

I can hear the reporters speculating in the next room. Their voices sound like a group of hens clucking. It instantly annoys me. Suddenly, I feel Zara's energy sooth me in my mind, taking the edge off. I sigh gratefully. Pierce motions to me that it's time.

As soon as we step to the stage, clicks of cameras go off creating a lightning storm of pictures that will adorn the headlines. I walk up to the microphone solemnly. Reporters stand up holding recording devices and some notepads. I take in the entire room until I see that both Selene and Zara are standing in the back dressed as security.

Men and women in suits await my statement as I step closer, grabbing a chair and stare at the eight microphones in front of me. I look to Pierce, beginning my part as the poor victim in one of America's most recent tragedies. He touches my hand in reassurance and I give him a shy smile.

Then, I begin. "Hi, um, my name is Rayne Whitmore and I know that many of you feel like you're seeing a ghost. Something unspeakable happened at my home and I had to leave behind a life and friends that I always thought that I would have. I took that for granted." I pause, allowing myself to take a deep breath, look down in contemplation, and then into the eyes of the reporters. I feel Pierce work his demon magic, swaying the group into sympathy.

"I lost my family, dedicated employees, my home, my identity, everything because a criminal decided that our lives meant nothing. Then, I had to endure one of the greatest humiliations I've ever known yesterday when I was wrongfully arrested for the unspeakable crime of murder against the people that I cared about the most. I had to sit and listen-," I pause again, this time allowing real tears to fall as I think of my baby sister and what Namen forced me to see.

"I had to sit and listen to a detective tell me that I had my baby sister executed. I had to hear the police tell me that I was the one that planned and hired someone to take away so many loved ones from so many families," I say, voice cracking.

Pierce's magic wraps around the group, tighter. A few shake their head in disbelief and sympathy at what I had to endure and I know they're mine. It's time to drive it home.

"They didn't even know that one of their own had planted evidence and chose to side with a murderer that was trying to use my father's past against him to further his own unspeakable list of crimes. They tried to win. They tried to beat me down, break me, and then finish the job. But I'm here to tell you today that I am a survivor."

My voice rises in confidence as I pull the audience further into my story. "I refuse to hide in the dark anymore and I plan to continue my father's legacy. He wanted me to run his business. I was supposed to be at his side. I was supposed to watch my sister grow up and start a family of her own. I was supposed to go on shopping trips and dinner dates with my mother. I can't do any of that now. I was robbed of future memories, so now, the best I can do is live my life to its potential, to make them proud of the person that stands before you today."

I look to Pierce and he nods.

"I want to start a scholarship fund for victims of violent crimes to be able to attend college, get the counseling they may need, and I also want to begin a mentoring program for young kids that have lost parents or siblings. They shouldn't fall through the cracks. All this can be done once I take my place in Whitmore Industries."

Zara nods. They will look like fools if they try to keep me out of the company now. Making plans as a benefactor as if I'm already a part of the business is a boss move. Selene smiles at me and I wipe my eyes with tissue sitting on the table.

"Now, we're going to spend ten minutes taking questions," Pierce announces once I finish.

Chapter Twenty Two

The press conference was a success. I had the reporters eating out of the palm of my hand. They were also wondering why the local police that arrested me hadn't issued an apology or joined in the conference to clear anything up. The news was going to be looking into their practices for weeks.

I hope that Namen sucks on that for a while. His bitch ass had to be pretty damn angry with me now. Good. Angry people often make mistakes. I know that from experience. I want him good and angry for what he's put me through. Arrested, fingerprinted, and all that. Ugh, just ugh.

Damien, Selene, and I are now on our way to my family's graves. They are going to exhume the body of the girl in my grave and allow her family to bury her properly. Reporters have already caught wind that that's where we're headed and have staked out a distance away. These shots are supposed to seal the deal according to Pierce.

Selene helps me out of the car, firmly holding my hand and walking with me to see them. It's her first time here and I know that she too has many emotions going through her. The first time I came, I had wanted to do so alone, to vow that I'd get justice, to prove that I could survive the pain, to make it reality that they were gone. This time, we are together, united in our heartache. It may not be equal, but there is no doubt that Selene loved Jazzy too.

I touch their names on the headstones one by one, pausing, talking, and gazing up at the sky as the clouds cover us from the sun. A statue of an angel is looking down and embracing the stone as if protecting mine and my sister's while two intertwining hearts make up my parent's. My mother's headstone calls to me and for the first time in a long time, I ache profoundly at the loss of my mom. I think Selene talking about her mother makes me realize how much my mom loved me. I almost forgot about our ice cream dates and how she'd play dress up with me when I was younger. As I got older, she'd stare at me when she thought I hadn't noticed. I'd ask her what she was doing and she'd smile, touch my hair softly and say that it was nothing.

My mom was a great cook and she'd dance with me in the kitchen when she made Thanksgiving meals. We'd sing Christmas songs loudly in the car when we'd go on trips. She was always proud of me and would come to any event I was a part of to support me.

Damn. When did I forget? When did everything change between us? I could never fix it, but I could do better to remember that it wasn't all bad, nor was it as bad as I made it seem.

Alanna J. Faison   Killer Rayne

Tears fall from my face as if racing toward the ground. Selene wipes my eyes with her thumb and pulls me in close before kissing my forehead. For a few minutes, I forget all about the reporters and the plans.

For a few minutes, I just remember that I'm still a girl that lost her family and no matter how strong I become, there will always be something inside me that's missing. There will always be a tiny part of me that remains broken.

Then, I am pulled into a dark void.

"So, you'd use even this time of mourning to get inside my head. What is it that you want Namen? Tell me the truth. Why are you violating my mind?" I ask him, refusing to turn around and look into those cold, gray eyes.

"I want to watch you suffer. I want your inner torment to eat you alive until you no longer have any fight in you. Then, you will either join me or I will kill you." His voice wraps around me like a venomous snake.

"You think this will make Selene run to you? You're wrong and you don't know her at all."

"She will have no choice when this is all said and done. You just wait. I come to you because as I told you before, you are weak. It is easy for my magic to invade the human mind. I

Alanna J. Faison   Killer Rayne

seek something that only your mind can reveal. I am curious about your power and unlocking it will allow me to continue my quest to make an army of human followers."

I force myself to face him even though the thought of looking at him makes my stomach turn.

"You're going to kill millions, you know that right?"

"I'm going to save this world. Our time in secret is running short. I am doing what needs to be done for our continued existence," he tells me, trying to persuade me.

"You are not that genuine. You are doing this to further your own ambitions and you know it. You want to see humans suffer. You want to enslave us and force them to become monsters that do what you please," I say, stepping closer, wishing I could attack him now and be finished with this.

"You simplify things far too much," he says. For the first time, I hear the hints of an old European accent. It makes me wonder just how old he really is.

"Well, why don't you explain since you're in such a sharing mood?"

"Not just yet. The time will come when I will explain it all. I am not the monster you make me out to be," he reasons.

"Fuck you. You are every bit of the monster that I know you to be. You kidnap children to experiment on and you feed them to your demon pets. I don't even know half of the things that you've done, but I know enough. You don't deserve to exist," I snap.

He stares at me for a second and then laughs. Suddenly, I am on my knees and my head feels like it's going to explode. The feeling is horrible even knowing that he's just inside my mind making me believe that he's hurting me.

"As I said, weak," he states, returning to the heartless bastard that I know him to be.

"You keep trying to find a way to break me, but you can't break what's already been broken, Namen. What you seek here, you won't find," I tell him breathlessly as I force myself to stand.

"We shall see about that, Rayne Whitmore. You have plenty of people in your life that I can test that theory with. I will play dirty. You will scramble to keep everyone safe and you won't succeed. Then, I will open a gate and banish you to hell and let the damned have you to do as they please."

He disappears and I am sent back to the land of the conscious. Selene is holding me close to her, whispering for me to wake up. Damien has a hand on my shoulder, concerned.

"I'm okay," I whisper back, remembering the camera crews in the distance.

Hopefully I just looked as if I were crying and not as if I were in some sort of trance.

"What did he do to you this time?" Selene asks, concerned and knowing that I had to have had another mental encounter with Namen.

"We talked. I'm just glad he wasn't in a talking mood during the press conference. He wants to figure out how the immortals unmade me. He must know that the power is inside each human. He hopes to exploit that." His experiments must not be succeeding, so he's trying something new.

"He won't find it," Damien says.

"I truly hope not. Damien," I say, turning to him. "From now on, I need you to have two security guards with you, Tamara, and any others that Namen may come after. In the daytime, they should be werewolves and for night shift, vampires. Namen just threatened your lives and I will take all those threats seriously. I need to get access to Whitmore resources immediately."

"Fine, but I'm not backing out of this. There is no point in running now. If Namen wants me, he'll be able to find me." Damien reaches and grabs his sunglasses from his shirt and puts them on smoothly.

"There is an issue with the board. They are worried about legal problems that you may bring to the Industries," Damien tells me.

Selene shakes her head and rolls her eyes before turning to stand in front of Jasmine's grave. I turn my attention back to Damien who looks a little fidgety. He's scared, but he won't tell me that.

"Then, let me handle it. Tomorrow morning I expect to have a meeting with everyone. I'm not taking no for an answer. You let them know that I have the press advantage right now and if they try to play me, I'll have cameras outside each of their homes, speculating if they could have been involved in the hit that murdered my family. I'm bringing Pierce with me too for some persuasion."

"Fine. I can make that happen. You know that I support you 100 percent. I'm going to go wait in the car until you finish here. Remember that you have some errands to run and documents to sign later," Damien reminds me.

I nod and turn to give my family's resting place one last glance. Once we leave, my grave will become empty and I plan to keep it that way for a long time.

◊◊◊

After I meet with a team of lawyers that have to distribute whatever was left of my family's assets, vacation homes, funds, etc., back to me, I go to meet Jaxson at Obsession, the wolf club where he works. Even during the day, the club is buzzing with activity. It's a different atmosphere compared to the night, but everyone seems to be enjoying themselves.

There is plenty of drinking going on. Many of the small tables are filled and the music is pumping at a low volume. The latest top forty hits hum through the speakers. A group of wolves are playing Poker at a table in the back. In the soundproof room upstairs where I had first spotted Anubis, a group of people are watching a sporting event.

There are only a handful of people on the dance floor and they are talking more than moving. I also notice a few other types of supernatural beings inside this club, some of whom I've never seen in person. I feel the energy of one half demon and another human that has supernatural gifts. They must be clairvoyant or something.

Humans that possess supernatural skills without being unmade never have any physical strength beyond that of a regular human. They have to tread carefully among some awakends that would seek to exploit them for their gifts. Not quite human and not completely supernatural, they are sometimes easy targets.

There's another in here with some weird energy that I can't place. I take a deep breath to feel them out, but they meet my investigation with resistance. Then, I am shut down from their energy completely as if they just disappeared. Strange. I continue on, exploring with my power until I feel Jaxson's werewolf aura surround me. I turn just in time to meet him.

"How are you?" I ask him smiling.

"I'm fine. Just had to handle some things around here. This, however is not a social visit," he says to me. His studded nose ring glistens in the light and his mohawk looks freshly lined up. Jaxson is wearing a brown button up with khaki pants. His broad shoulders fill the shirt nicely.

"So, should we go somewhere more private?" I ask, looking around at all the wolves, knowing that they can hear our conversation.

"No. Everyone that's here is supposed to be in this room. Those that could make it have come."

Most of the group turns to me now and I look upon each individual in wonder. The ones that are in the room upstairs head down to the main level. "Okay," I begin. "These people are not your pack. I see only two that belong to you. There are others that aren't wolves either, so what's going on?"

I begin to open my bond with Zara so that she can give me insight, but then I change my mind. I can handle this just fine on my own.

"They all wanted to see you, Rayne, before they decide what their choice is going to be. They want to know what it is that makes you so special. Will you show them? Prove to them that you have the heart of a wolf inside you." Jaxson looks to me confidently, crossing his large arms.

I run a hand through my hair as my tattoo begins to glow through my baby blue v-neck. I don't really know what is expected of me here, but my power definitely wants to come out and play. Katsu is firmly in my right hand before I even realize that I reached for her. With closed eyes and a deep breath, I point my katana at the crowd. Her serpent's tail design wraps nicely around the blade.

"I don't have to prove a damn thing to anyone," I say.

One wolf coughs up his drink at my words. A few growl in distaste. I raise my eyebrows and sheath my sword. I give no fucks about their feelings.

"I'm not in the business of appeasing cowards," I say straight up.

Out of the corner of my eye, I can feel Jaxson looking at me, surprised.

"What the hell did you just say?" a stocky man asks angrily as he stands. His rough hands grip the table. His beard gives him a ruggedly handsome look, but his eyes show a monster under them. Still, I'm not intimidated.

"You heard me. Now, sit your ass down," I command. For the first time, I feel the pack magic stirring inside me. A few let out gasps as they feel it touch them at my command.

I try to hide my own astonishment. Nothing should surprise me anymore.

"You fight because it's the right thing to do, not because you have someone strong in your corner. You seek out your own values and you follow that code. I could care less if any of you stand with me if that is not what is in your heart to do. Cowards only follow a leader that they can hide behind. We need werewolves, not little bitches." They can get mad if they want to, but frankly I don't care. I meant every word.

There's a slow clap from behind me. I turn to find a tall, long haired, woman of Middle Eastern decent behind me. She's slightly above average looking with flawless makeup that accentuates her beauty without being overbearing. Her smoky eyes make her look mysterious and dangerous. The wolf is just behind her eyes, flashing yellow before disappearing.

Her hair is pulled back into a long ponytail with two French braids on the left side of her head. Her heels can only be designer. They are red with a zipper on the side and a tall heel, adding to her height. She's wearing a ¾ sleeve leather jacket with the collar turned up and with only a black bra underneath and black leather pants as well.

"Well I'll be damned," Jaxson breathes. I don't even think he realized that he said it aloud.

The female wolf breathes alpha energy. She focuses right on Jaxson and smiles with straight, white teeth.

"Well hello to you too, sexy."

Chapter Twenty Three

$\mathcal{S}$tunned at her boldness, I turn to their exchange, forgetting about the wolves in the room that I'm supposed to be appealing to. They feel each other out with their wolf energy and it's obvious that they like what they see. Suddenly growing embarrassed, Jaxson fakes a cough as the female wolf gives him a predator's smirk.

I'll give them two days before they're burning up the sheets. I look at them again. Two hours.

"So, did you like my little speech?" I ask the wolf, now standing to my right, slightly behind me. I turn my body so that I can see as many of the werewolves in the room as possible.

"I did. You took them all by the balls," she laughs in delight. It sounds like sunshine, bright and warm. "I don't know what's going on, but I want in," she declares.

There are many voices of protest from the crowd at the sudden arrival of this newcomer and both of the pack members in the audience come to speak with Jaxson. They regard me with slight wariness, but otherwise are non-confrontational. The rest of the people begin to grow louder.

"Enough," Jaxson cries, bringing his wolf to the front. The pack energy creeps over the place.

Next to me, I feel the female werewolf breathe it in and sigh. Oh, she has it bad. She is wild, I can feel it. Her energy is all over the place, buzzing with delight. Her wolf longs to run free. I've never felt this kind of wolf energy before. It's almost affecting me. I don't know if it's because I now have a connection to the wolves or if my powers are getting clearer.

"What you heard was Rayne's choice. She said she has nothing to prove; rather you all have something you must prove to yourselves. You all have one week to make a decision. Either you join us, or you leave town. I am the alpha and I'm claiming this city as my own. If you don't believe, then I will have my second personally pay you a visit and you can test her power then."

"Choose carefully," I warn.

"Now, as for you," Jaxson states, turning to the she wolf in stiletto heels. Brown eyes to brown eyes, they stare each other down until she finally relents. Still, the amusement is apparent on her face.

"Let's talk privately. You are a stranger to my city at a time when we are not so trusting. Follow us." Jaxson walks forward, expecting us to follow him.

Alanna J. Faison   Killer Rayne

I look back again and try to pinpoint that elusive energy that I had felt earlier, but it's gone. They didn't seem to be an enemy, but I don't think they were one that he invited either. Should I bring it up? Maybe, but not yet.

As I look around, the club seems to have gone back to normal rather quickly. The two members of the pack are quietly observing the crowd and I nod in satisfaction. If anything goes down, they'll handle it. Besides, I'm much more curious about this woman in front of me.

We head back to the office where Jaxson had spoken with me and Selene before. I make myself comfortable in the black leather chair as Jaxson sits at his desk after closing the door for privacy. She remains standing until Jaxson allows her to sit. Amusement paints her face again. The female wolf doesn't seem to take pack etiquette seriously. She is clearly a firecracker. I'm just waiting on the explosion.

Legs crossed, she looks around the room, pretending to care about the empty walls and desk as she waits for Jaxson to speak. I lean back farther in my chair as I stare at her profile. There's something about this wolf that's different, but what is it?

"What's your name?" I ask her.

"It's Jun. Darn, I was hoping he would be the one interrogating me. That is, unless you're the good cop and he's the bad cop," she says, her voice coming out more like a purr.

Jaxson stiffens in his chair and then composes himself. I try not to laugh at his clumsiness. She's going to eat him alive.

"And do you have a last name Jun?" I ask as Jaxson is too stuck on staring.

She ignores me completely and leans closer to Jaxson, giving him a great view of her small, but perky breasts. I don't take offense. When there's attraction, you sometimes are better off going for it.

Especially when tomorrow isn't promised.

"You feel it too don't you?" she breathes.

"We'll talk about it later," he says quietly, gaze flicking to me, frustrated that I'm in the room.

Oh well, he can wait a few more minutes so that I can leave with all the information that we both need. Then, it occurs to me what she meant. It's that werewolf instinct, that click that Anubis told me about the first time he kissed his mate. This isn't ordinary attraction for these two. This is something deeper. Now I feel like I'm intruding on a private moment and as I look into Jaxson eyes, it's almost as if he's hoping that she really is the one.

"Um, the quicker we get on with this, the sooner I can leave you two to discover yourselves."

With that, they both turn to me and I shrug my shoulders. "What?" I ask. "I get it, I really do. Now, Jun, your last name?"

She gives me another wolf smile, feeling me out. I roll my eyes at her and she continues.

"It's Jun Jones."

"Seriously?" I roll my eyes again.

"I chose to change my last name when I left my family behind. I was a witch by birth, but I was partying in the mountains with some friends about six years ago when I was attacked by two werewolves. My magic was enough to kill one of the wolves, but the other one got me good. The only reason why he didn't eat me is because I fell from a cliff. I broke eight ribs, both of my legs, and more. A couple of my friends weren't so lucky. The other one that survived killed herself last year. It's too painful to bear sometimes. Feeling the magic inside you, dying to be released, but knowing you can't use it because the wolf now controls all. Normally, witches don't turn. That wolf turned two of us."

Her eyes gaze off into the distance as she remembers the awful attack. I search her skin for wounds but as usual, werewolves that are turned from an attack usually become healed of all the evidence.

"My family tried to help me deal with the change, but I was too much to handle. I blamed them for not teaching me better magic to defend myself and for not helping me find a way to at least be able to use my magic even though I was now wolf. They feared my temper and that I would expose them as awakeneds out of spite. I was forced to leave my home. So, I changed my last name. After that, I went to seek help in New Mexico where a pack of werewolves live in the forests. Because of them, I was able to accept the wolf as my other half."

"So, why are you here now then instead of going back to your family to make amends?" Jaxson asks suspiciously.

It's good to see that even though they may have a deep need for each other, he still needs to think like an alpha and treat her as an outsider. She knows that she can't lie to another werewolf, but something tells me that she's had plenty of practice at hiding the truth.

"Because honestly, I'm not ready. I may even have a death wish. I understand my wolf a lot better, but she is anxious about something as if she won't rest until she finds it. She wants a fight and I don't think I can deny her much longer. There is a deep rage inside me. I don't know if it's the magic, my true nature that is affecting her, but she's forever pacing, hunting. I ended up here. I don't know why, but I've been traveling a while and I wanted to be around my kind so here I am. I caught your speech and since you don't smell like anything but human, I became curious as to why an alpha would claim a human as his pack. With your words, I see why. You are powerful, I can feel it."

"You don't even know what we're fighting for," I say to her, pulling my sword. She focuses on it but doesn't make any moves. "You come here with this story, this mysterious aura you put out there. You make moves to seduce Jaxson and then tell me you have a death wish. That last part I do believe. Why else are you here?" I ask sharply, putting Katsu's point against her throat.

Jaxson and I share a look. He was wondering the same thing. Running a hand through his mohawk, he watches our exchange with interest.

Unfazed, or just a great actress, she states, "I caught word that there was an alpha here that had special qualities. His pack was growing more powerful and seemed to have some special abilities that other packs lost. I thought that he'd be able to help me too. It sounds to me like he has some magic inside of him as well."

Jaxson nods and I sheath my sword.

Alanna J. Faison   Killer Rayne

"I like you," she tells me.

"I'll withhold my judgment," I respond.

"You've clearly already made some judgments about other aspects of me," she quips.

"Oh, and what does that mean?" I ask, giving her the side eye.

"I notice things, okay. You were staring at my body. Clearly, you appreciate beautiful forms." She leans back in the chair and crosses her arms, feeling triumphant.

Jaxson and I both laugh at her remark.

"Okay, I think I do like you. Cockiness appeals to me. A beautiful form appeals to me, what can I say; I'm spoken for, so don't worry. My eyes will adjust. I was just wondering about your lack of wounds."

"My father is a healer. Along with the healing that the wolf gives me, he was able to fix everything else."

Sounds about right. But, back to business at hand. I let Jaxson take the lead now.

"That alpha you were referring to is not me. He is dead and we are waging a war against the witch that is responsible for his death along with many other crimes against our kind. This man hopes to expose us all to the world so that he can control it, one nation at a time, with his choice of who should rule where. What do you think of that?" Jaxson questions. He narrows his eyes as he watches her reaction intently.

She seems to be in deep thought again. I feel her weird wolf energy buzzing around her, the hair on the back of her neck rises. It's almost like she's consulting with the wolf inside of herself. She very well could be. Jaxson doesn't seem to refer to him and his wolf as two separate entities in such a divided way, as if it is an intruder in his body, but he was also born a werewolf. Maybe it's different for those that have been bitten. Maybe it's the reason why she has issues because she hasn't accepted the wolf as her.

"I think the world is going to find out about us sooner than later and we had better be prepared for that day. Yet, for one man to make that kind of decision for all of us, it doesn't seem right. I don't know. I do know that I want to know more about you," she tells Jaxson, smoothly switching subjects.

Jaxson grunts. "As I said before, you will either fight with us, or you will leave my city. Attraction or not, I don't have time for games woman."

Her eyes flash yellow. "I think I'll stay a while."

"Good. Now, wait outside until you are called on," he dismisses her.

The same amused look paints her face again as she stands. "I guess I'll be seeing you later then, right?" Jun directs the comment to me.

"Oh, but of course. I look forward to working with you." I stand up to shake her hand. She squeezes firmly, but not enough to hurt me. It seems that she's already staking out her territory. Yes, Jaxson is going to have one hell of a night if she has her way.

Jun's hips sway seductively as she exits the room, closing the door gently behind her.

"So, should I start making wedding plans?" I joke.

"Shut the hell up," he growls.

Chapter Twenty Four

I was able to talk to Jaxson about getting guards for Damien and Tamara during the day. He agreed to do the best he could while keeping the wolves protected. I promised that they'd be compensated as well and was able to convince him that this would be a good way for him to find a real enforcer. Then, we talked about Jun.

She is going to stay at the pack's house so that they can keep an eye on her. After I made fun of him for his reactions to her flirting, he reminded me that I had tried to flirt with him to get into the club and it didn't work. That earned him a punch in the chest.

Last, I filled him in on the press conference and my plans to meet with the board at Whitmore Industries. I told him that I wanted him on the payroll so that he could spend less time at the club and not have to worry about money for the time being. Slightly offended, he declined. For now. I apologized and then went on my way, leaving him to get to know Jun in a more intimate capacity.

It felt good to be able to walk out of the club and not be attacked. I guess the third time is the charm. Keeping my head down and not making any stops, I was able to make it back to my home without incident. Just as I get to the door, Zara is pulling up. I wait for her at the front and then walk in with her by my side.

Selene comes from the kitchen wiping her hands as she takes in the two of us.

"What's up?" I ask Zara before kissing Selene on the cheek.

Zara is dressed in loose fitting black jeans, some gray Timberland boots, and a short-sleeved, gray Henley shirt. Her usual jewelry adorns her body and her full sleeve makes her look attractive as usual. From her scent, she's wearing some Calvin Klein fragrance. I take a step closer to Selene just in case my power attempts to reach for her.

Selene touches my hand and waits for Zara's response.

"I've been called away for a couple days by my cousin. It seems that there is urgent business with the nine that we must discuss. I also wanted to let you know in person that I have some vampires that will be watching you guys during the evenings. If you sense them, then they are not mine. These vampires are trained especially for security and assassination so they know how to remain hidden. I have them watching Damien as well," Zara tells us.

"Okay, thanks," Selene says.

"Not a problem. There's something else that I want you to know. That demon that attacked you the other night, the one that flew away; well apparently she is still in town. I think she's searching for something. Namen may have given her the impression that you have it. Be alert and I'll try to be back as soon as possible. When I return, we will meet with my grandmother. Good luck tomorrow. If you need me, call."

"I will. We'll be careful. You do the same," I say.

"And if you need us, you call," Selene adds, surprising me.

Zara smiles warmly at her, flashing fang. "I will priestess." She bows with one arm across her chest. "Now, make sure you both train."

She leaves in a hurry. Her car roars to life outside.

"She's really worried about something," Selene tells me.

"I think so too. I think she has some issues with Apollo that she's not ready to deal with. He scares her for some reason," I respond thoughtfully. Her energy changes whenever he's brought up.

"Well, that may not be a good thing for us. I wonder if he's going to ever be a problem that we'll have to deal with," Selene says.

Alanna J. Faison   Killer Rayne

"I hope not," I say. I change subjects, not wanting to add to my worries. "But, we have some time to ourselves, so what do you want to do? I turned my phone off so I'm not getting any of these exclusive interview offers. I just want to have a semi normal rest of the day. After I tell you about what happened at the club."

"Well, tell me what happened. Then, I'll tell you what I want to do."

"A female wolf came in and stole the show. Jaxson is completely mesmerized by her. Her name is Jun and apparently she was a witch before she was bitten," I say, flopping on the couch and kicking off my shoes.

"Really?" Selene asks, eyes lighting up in curiosity. "What's she like?"

"Well," I start, thinking about the best way to describe her. I pull Selene down to the couch and into my arms. "She's a wild one. Very sexual and very cocky. She's superficial almost, but you can tell that she's seeking something to hold on to. That something may very well be Jaxson. They are extremely attracted to each other. She's pretty; Middle Eastern I think. Tall, maybe an alpha female. She's either going to be a great ally or a giant distraction."

"That sounds a lot like someone I know," Selene states.

"Uh, and whom might that be?"

"Hmm. I'll let you think about that one."

I frown. I'm not like that am I?

"Now, as for what I'd like to do, I'd like to eat this meal I put together first. Then, I'd like a nice massage, and some wine," she tells me after placing a kiss on my cheek.

"Well, take me to your kitchen," I say trying to sound like an alien. It only comes off corny and lame. Selene still laughs at my attempt which makes me happy anyway.

"We eat rib eye steak, broccoli, and garlic mashed potatoes, which is one of my favorite meals. The steak is cooked to medium perfection and fills me with so much joy every single bite I take. I find myself moaning in satisfaction. I had forgotten that Selene is such a great cook. We enjoy a nice red wine after the meal and I pay my compliments to the chef.

Selene smiles like a kid that just got all a's on her report card. That smile ignites something inside me.

"You're just so damn beautiful," I tell her in a whisper. My voice has gone raspy and it's not from a dry throat.

"Thank you," she says quietly. Selene locks her gaze on mine and I can read all her thoughts in that instant.

"Do you want dessert?" I ask, licking my lips seductively.

She tucks her long black hair behind her ear and bites down gently on her lip. Her brown ombre' shines from the light. Her yellow tank top comes off within seconds, leaving her black lace bra there alone. I look at her as if I'm seeing her for the first time. I swallow hard and grip the table with my fingers tightly.

"Do you want me?" she asks in response. Her gaze is uncertain, begging for validation. I'm sure her heart is pounding.

"I always want you," I tell her honestly. My throbbing down below drives the point home.

She proceeds to unbutton her tight blue jeans. Then, she pulls them from around her waist, off her round butt, and down to the floor. I study her flawless tanned skin and imagine the softness of it under my fingers. Instinctively, I begin to breathe heavily in anticipation. I had thought that this moment would come a little later, but I'm grateful that it's now. I have every intention of making it worthwhile.

Selene directs me to clean everything off of the dining room table. I do so, knocking all that unnecessary shit to the floor. She looks at me with a raised eyebrow and then laughs. I love the sound of her voice. I love her body. I stare at it in expectation. I want it all.

As if reading my thoughts, Selene asks me, "What do you want, Rayne?"

With no hesitation, I say, "I want you inside of me." It comes out pleading, desperate, but right now, I don't care.

"Is that all?" she asks, planning her every move. Her green eyes have a fire in them that I intend to quench. They shine with desire and my body gets chills from their depths.

"I want everything that you're willing to give," I say to her, studying every inch of her body. I breathe in her scent. Strawberries.

The sound of her accent caresses my ears. I want her voice, her warm breath, her lips pressed up against my skin. "I can make that happen."

Oh, I know it. Selene is absolutely thorough when it comes to pleasing me. Memories flood my mind and nearly cause me to climax just thinking about her expertise. I want her in the worst way, but I try to be patient, to not give it all away. But, she knows. She always knows.

"Take it off," she demands.

I stand up and start with my own top. It comes off smoothly, followed by my pants. She turns me around to unsnap my bra with a couple fingers, and then leaves me to slide my panties down on my own. I'm already wet and she knows it without even looking at the slickness developing between my thighs. I want to rush things, but I know in this round I am not the one in control. This show is Selene's to run and I am simply at her beck and call.

Selene turns me around so that my hands are flat on the table and my back is to her. I feel her magic gently caress my skin, leaving a line of chills to my center. Her soft lips press against my back and I lean into her, savoring her closeness and warmth. She wastes no time slipping inside me.

I moan into her mouth as I tilt my head back to capture her lips as she begins her skilled assault on my body. Nips there, kisses here, and soon, I'm feeling pleasure from many different places. I push back against her, begging for her to go deeper, but she denies my request and paces herself. Everything is on her terms and that drives me even crazier.

"Get on the table," she demands, slipping out of me. Her fingers are wet with my love and she makes a show of tasting me, turning me on so much more.

Alanna J. Faison   Killer Rayne

I climb onto the table as she requests, knees pressed against the wood. Her mouth replaces her fingers and I am worked into a frenzy. On my lips is her name, over and over again. I cry out for her, but she refuses to grant me the release that I long for. Seconds pass until I turn around and watch her shed herself of the rest of her clothes. In front of me is an angel and I have no doubt that this woman was made just for me. She's so beautiful that I almost cry.

We lock eyes and tears actually do begin to rise. I blink them away as Selene looks at me questioningly. I just shake my head and smile at her, reassuring her that everything really is okay. She smiles back and climbs on top of me on the table. With a spell prepped on her lips, I feel my tattoo glow in response to her power, my energy attempting to meet hers. We collide and gasp in unison as our lips touch. She's inside me physically and spiritually, freeing me of any bonds but ours.

I arch deeper into her as she pushes farther inside my entire being. My cries echo throughout the room as I pull her closer. Tears coat my face and I can't stop their free fall. She kisses each one with delicacy and I love her even more. I don't even feel the surface under us anymore, all I feel is her.

"Don't you ever leave me again," she growls in my ear, her warm breath sending shivers up my spine.

Alanna J. Faison   Killer Rayne

"I won't," I promise. In this moment, I would promise anything.

Soon, we make our way to the bed where we finish the heated session. I am kissing my way down the back of her legs when she says, "I still want that massage."

"I'll give you anything you want," I tell her.

◊◊◊

Once I shower in the morning, I take extra time to make my makeup look extremely well. It will be my armor today when I go to battle with the corporate types that are trying to keep me out of my father's business. The last time I was in the building, I was a naïve little child. Oh, how much has changed.

I re-arch my eyebrows, filling them in with a pencil, double checking to make sure they're even. Next, I use a hint of dark blue eye shadow before going over it with glittery silver shadow. I define it enough where it brings out my eyes, but isn't overpowering. I love makeup, but definitely in moderation. A few more touches to my face make the look complete. I'm glad that this only took me a few times. Since I've been gone, I haven't really had the chance to play in makeup. I missed it, but not as much as I thought I would. I also add some clear, shimmery lip gloss to my lips.

I put on a black, long sleeved, v-neck dress that stops mid thigh. Over that, I layer it with a dark gray vest, a long silver chain, hooped earrings, and a bracelet. Then, I put on my ankle high black leather boots. The heel is the perfect height and I turn around in the mirror satisfied. Finally, I take a few seconds to smooth out my hair. The short length doesn't take much, but it's definitely growing back. Running a comb through the auburn color, I decide that I am going to color my hair black with an autumn ombre' or highlights. Maybe. My mourning phase has come to an end. It's time to make my own identity once more.

I step out of the bathroom to find Selene dressed in dark khaki pants with a small brown belt, a black ¾ sleeved button up tucked into her pants, and closed toe black heels. Her makeup is light. Her lips are a dark red and her eyes have a smoky look. Selene's hair is styled in beautiful loose curls. It's a look that she doesn't wear often, but always looks beautiful. Her shiny, silky hair looks camera-ready.

"You look very nice," Selene tells me.

I smile and give her another once over. "So do you. If all else fails, we'll be ready for job interviews somewhere else," I joke.

"Very funny. As if you need the money," Selene responds shaking her head.

"You never know. I may need to buy an island to hide out on if we don't kill Namen."

"I think hiding would be the least of our worries."

We stare in silence, thoughtful. I don't want to even think of the alternative. My thoughts go to this meeting that I'm about to attend. I'm sure there will be reporters camping out outside of the building. Maybe Selene should go in separately. I doubt that she'll agree to that though. Supernaturals need to do their best to keep a low profile. I really don't want her image splashed all over the news if we can help it. But it's not like it's going to be hard to link her to me anyway.

"Selene, are you okay with being all over the papers and stuff? It may seem like the right thing to do now because you want to be there with me, but what about later on down the line? All this stuff is going to be out there forever," I warn.

Selene laughs and grabs my hand. "If we're going to make an attempt at making this work, we have to actually be together, supporting each other. I can handle some cameras in my face. I'll deal with the rest of the stuff as it comes okay," she assures me.

The doorbell rings and I know that it's Pierce from his energy leaking into the house. Selene opens the door for the half demon lawyer.

Alanna J. Faison   Killer Rayne

He strolls in with an air of confidence and it touches me, strengthening my own resolve. Pierce is wearing a black designer, fitted suit with a white shirt underneath. Three of the buttons are undone on the button up, giving him a rugged look. His shoes are shined to perfection as well as his bald head. He gives us both a look of approval and a nod.

"Are you ready?" he asks, popping a stick of gum in his mouth and then offering us one. We both take a piece as I nod. "Well, let's get to it then, shall we. You have an empire to claim."

Chapter Twenty Five

We pull onto Carner Street, where Whitmore Industries Headquarters resides. The building sits on just the edge of downtown, having its own small park area with a fountain in the back and a large parking garage adjacent to it. Headquarters is not nearly the largest building in the downtown area, but at twenty stories high still finds a way to be impressive. It's ahead of the curve in energy sustainability and its attractive design draws the eye easily. Some of the floors even have balconies for employees to hang out on, with reinforced concrete and high railings so the people don't trip and fall over the sides.

I stare up at the place my father built from hard work and persistence and immediately can't wait to get inside. It's been too long. Why did I say that I wanted nothing to do with this? Outside, the front is buzzing with activity and as I figured, reporters have camped out to hear my statement. Selene squeezes my shoulder and smiles gently.

"Do you want to go through the security entrance Ms. Whitmore?" Pierce asks.

"Nope. They want to see me looking optimistic about coming back to this place. I'm going to sell it. Selene, are you sure?" I ask her, continuing our conversation from earlier.

Alanna J. Faison   Killer Rayne

"My place is at your side. I said that already," she replies once more.

We pull up in front of the building where a man in a suit comes to meet us. He opens our door and helps us out of the car with a hand. Pierce then gives him the keys. He hops inside and pulls off to park it in the garage. Damien must have told him to prepare for our arrival. Good. I grab Selene's soft hand firmly and stride forward into the crowd of sharks, er- reporters.

"Ms. Whitmore, may I have a word?" the first reporter asks, dressed in a tan blazer and black pants.

"Sure," I respond, still holding on to Selene who is still smiling.

"What do you hope to accomplish here today and if it doesn't go according to plan, what will you do next?"

I take a deep breath in contemplation. Word choice is everything. "I just want to do my best to live up to my father's expectations. His dream was for me to push Whitmore Industries into the future, by his side. I want to bring something new to the fold. I don't plan to fail, so there is no next step."

"They may try to fight your return through the courts. There's word that this uncertainty has caused Whitmore's stock to plummet. What do you have to say about that?" a woman asks.

"If I can survive all that I have in the past two years, I'm sure I can hold my own in a legal battle. I was taught how to make smart financial decisions. I won't fail. My father has made it his mission to take care of his people. They owe him their loyalty. They will do the right thing. Jason Whitmore surrounded himself with men and women that needed second and even third chances. All I'm asking for is one."

"Speaking of second chances, the story is that you couldn't bear being apart from your girlfriend for another day. How was your reunion?"

"It was something out of a dream," I say, turning to Selene and smiling at our small reunion that we actually just had. "She couldn't believe that I was alive and that I risked so much to get back to her. We held each other and cried for so long. I was afraid that she had found someone else," I say going for the tears.

"And what about you, Ms,"

"Marquez. The heavens brought us back together. I left town for a while, searching for something to fill the void left by her absence. But only she could fill it," Selene says, gazing lovingly into my eyes.

"Do we hear wedding bells in the future?" someone asks from the back.

"When the time comes, you'll be the first to know. First, Rayne has to claim what is hers. I will be by her side every step of the way. Now, please excuse us. Rayne shouldn't be late," Selene says politely.

We continue to walk into the building with Pierce whispering about a job well done. Duh. Actor friends, remember. I touch the front doors to the headquarters that my mother's architecture firm designed and smile. Jasmine definitely got her artistic side from mom. Without hesitation, I open the large doors and am greeted to smiles and some applause among the bright lights.

The first level is security, information desks, and various meeting rooms and offices available to the public. Welcoming yellow tones with Whitmore Industries signage adorn the walls. The floor is white and pristine with circular yellow designs. There are comfortable cream and white seats with yellow throw pillows in the waiting lounge as well as many flat screens each showing different stations. The bold lighting hangs around areas that have lower ceilings such as above the security desk. Lights also shine brightly from the walls.

Above us, there is a gap where the second floor is missing. The third floor is an open walk way area that leads to the daycare center and cafeteria with six different food choices. My father always said that if you spend the extra money to treat your employees well and offer them things that other places don't, they will reward you with loyalty and better production. There is also a large fitness center and mini theater that plays old movies three times a week. The movie theater was a donation from a prestigious client.

Every other floor has a different color scheme and is home to a different department. Spread throughout are other security offices or small security desks that employees and visitors must check in to. Human resources is purple, upper management is either brown and gold, or silver and black, marketing is blue, etc. The designated colors are reflected in the floor tile, colored signage or accent wall.

I nod and smile to as many people as I can as we are escorted past security, into the elevator, and up the upper management wing. Selene gives me another squeeze on the shoulder and Pierce gives me a sly look. I steel my face to do what I need to do. Neither of them know exactly what I've come to say. I'm sure this will be extremely entertaining. They'll play the game correctly though, I know it.

The man escorting us stops at a large brown door. He turns to me and smiles. "It's good to finally meet you Ms. Whitmore. Many of us are grateful that you are alive. Your father was a kind man that tried to know all of our names. We appreciated him. Just so you know."

I smile back and touch his shoulder. "What is your name?"

"Taylor. Taylor Martin."

"Okay, Taylor. I will do my best to remember that. When I have time, we will talk and you'll tell me what you do and share some memories of my father, if that's okay with you."

"I'd like that, Ms. Whitmore. Now, knock 'em dead," he whispers to me.

I nod. Oh, that's just what I plan to do. I open the door to find five people sitting at a large table. Damien is standing and closes the distance to hug me when I step inside. He sits and motions for us to do the same. I make no move to do so and Pierce and Selene follow my lead. The six of them in the room look at me in astonishment.

I begin before they get a chance to open their mouths. I had thought of being diplomatic with the group originally, but I don't feel like pretending that that is what I even want to do. No, we'll do it this way. Besides, it's much more fun.

"Ladies and gentlemen, I do truly appreciate you taking the time to clear your busy schedules to meet with me. Don't worry; I'll get to the point rather

Alanna J. Faison   Killer Rayne

quickly. I don't need any introductions. I don't really care what your roles here are. What you need to know is that I have every intention in claiming my place. If you try to stop me, I will not be so generous when it comes to preserving your lifestyles. In fact, if you oppose me, I will ruin you."

Gasps fill the air as Pierce and Selene both work their magic. Selene calms the room as Pierce pushes his persuasion upon them. Even Damien's eyes become large as he falls under the thrall.

"I plan to be a fair and even leader, but on this, there is no compromise. Do not stand in my way. I have friends who will be more than happy to clear up any loose ends. If you choose to accept me, I will protect you as much as I can. You few know a little bit about what the world is truly like, but you still have no idea the extent to which you are humorously uninformed. You don't want to know, so let me do my job. I'm going to run this city and if you oppose me, you will no longer be allowed in it."

A few nod and I motion to Selene who steps forward. She whispers something and suddenly all of them remove their hands from the table, blowing them as if they were burning. Her favorite trick.

"This is Selene. She is my girlfriend. She will also get access to any and everything that she asks for. Promptly. No arguments. Treat her with as much respect as you will treat me. Now, I want this arranged quickly. Remember, if I don't get what I want, you will all be removed. Have a nice day and speak upon this to no one or there will be consequences," I smile and head back out of the door. Pierce drops his magic and it snaps back into place like a rubber band. The door shuts behind me and I hear arguing from inside the room.

◊◊◊

"Damn girl," Pierce begins, laughing and dropping all professionalism. "That was unexpected. You plan to claim this city huh? So what's your next plan?"

"I was thinking on the way here that Namen has far too many human allies and resources. They need to be dried up as much as possible and the people that run this city need to know what's in store for them. I think it will work if I play it right. That precinct that is working with Namen, shit most of the force needs to go. I want names and addresses. It's time to send my own message. I need to meet with the mayor."

I walk purposefully out of the building with my thoughtful companions. The news stations are still outside awaiting another statement. I can hear them speculating about the very short meeting. I watch as our car pulls around. Someone in security must have told someone that we were coming out. Good. They are already preparing for my return. I step on the noisy sidewalk as cars honk going past on the street leaving the smell of exhaust blowing in the wind.

Before anyone can ask me any questions, I smile again and say, "A representative of Whitmore Industries will make a statement within an hour, please be patient. I have no further comment." With that, I take Selene's hand, knowing that that message will be relayed to the higher ups in the corporation. They have one hour or I will be adding names to my list.

We slide smoothly into the vehicle as I think about how much my morals have changed over the past couple of years. Here I am already plotting my next move, of who needs to die first. I'm not just a cold-blooded killer though. At least, that's what I want to believe for now. I need to do this. Kill a few to save millions.

I have to do this.

Maybe, maybe I am just like my father.

Chapter Twenty Six

Damien drops a stack of papers on my table and then hands me a pen. He gives me a look that you give a child that has done something bad and clever at the same time. I pretend that I don't see the stare that he's giving me; instead, I just click the pen and sign all the highlighted portions.

"You know, you could have been a little nicer today," he tries to chastise.

"Please. Nice would have had me there for hours going in circles. Nice wouldn't have given me the result that I needed."

"And what do you think you accomplished today Ms. Whitmore?"

"They fear me. I don't want anything else yet. They will grow to respect me, but right now, I need them walking on eggshells, afraid that if they do anything stupid, it will cost them their lives," I explain, still flipping through papers, not caring what they say.

"And will it cost them?" Damien asks, sitting down across from me and forcing me to meet his eyes.

I stare at his designer suit and striped tie, smirking. They had given a statement fifty minutes

Alanna J. Faison   Killer Rayne

after I left and told the reporters that they were absolutely thrilled to have me. No one was going to contest it and legally they felt that there were no issues.

"If they do anything that will hinder me from saving everyone, yes I will kill them Damien. I have no other options. I will keep my word."

"You sound like someone," he warns.

"My father didn't have to deal with what I'm dealing with and those weapons that he started having developed sure as hell aren't helping things. My people are making moves to secure everyone's safety. I don't make these threats lightly and I also know when it's all said and done, there will be far too much blood on my hands. But, this is my life, my duty. I have to do this."

"You have to kill people."

I don't know if it's a statement or a question, so I don't answer. Instead, I change the subject as I stand up.

"Do you want some water?"

"Sure. No ice," he responds.

A minute later, I come back with the water. "How are things with you and Tamara?" I ask.

"They're fine," he responds shortly. Look, I really didn't know that she wanted to be unmade. I can't imagine what she's thinking."

"She's thinking that she wants to be more than she is. There's nothing wrong with that. It's just that she has no idea what it's really like," I tell him.

"Do you still talk to the immortals?" Damien asks, between sips.

"I haven't. I was supposed to talk to them about the Namen in my head problem, but I really wanted to wait and see what could be done. I think Selene has been looking for a solution on her own and Zara's grandmother Zahira may be able to give some insight because it's like a deep compulsion," I reply, sipping my own ice water.

"There are also some issues with my powers that I need to figure out and I plan to take a few days soon working out if my new powers are here to stay. Ever since I fought Zara and my power exploded, my gifts have been changing, growing, or both. I need to figure out what it all means and I wanted to use the immortals as a last resort because they don't want anything to do with the human world." I may not have a choice though and Zahira creeps me out even without meeting her.

241

"You've got a lot on your plate, are you sure you want to help run a company?" Damien asks, concern showing in his dark eyes.

"You're going to do most of the work. I'm going to leave it to you to explain that to everyone. I will come in and be seen, but what I'm doing is much more important. Tell them I'm working from home. Once Selene tells me what she thinks about the weapons, we'll go from there. Also, I need you to find me someone you can trust that works in the technology department. I need to pay the mayor a visit tomorrow night while he's at home and I don't want anyone knowing I was there."

"Just what do you plan to do?" Damien leans forward in his seat, giving me "the look."

"I plan to make a statement. He needs to know that from now on, he's just a figurehead and he'd better be a team player."

"Are you sure you know what you're doing?

"Not at all."

"Well shit, at least you're honest," Damien laughs, finishing his water. He sits there for a second, contemplating something before seemingly deciding to drop it.

I don't let him though. "Just say what's on your mind, D. We don't get to talk a lot."

"Yeah, I know. I was just- I was thinking about what we'd be doing right now if none of this ever happened. What do you think?"

I sit there at a loss for words. Sure, I think about it all the time, but I never really say it aloud. I always imagine if I had gone to college and kept dancing where I would be. But at the same time, those visions seem so unrealistic that I can't even voice it. It's almost as if me even trying to, will rip a hole in the world and swallow up anyone else that I love, just for wishing for a normal life.

Damien frowns. "Sorry. I didn't mean to ask you something hurtful."

"No, it's not that, it's just that I can't even imagine it anymore. I can't even see that life," I admit. "Maybe deep inside it is too hurtful to think about." I sigh.

"And that's okay. You're dealing with it as much as I think anyone can. I think that you feel that you should be over it completely, but that's impossible. You loved your family and they loved you," Damien reaches across to squeeze my hand.

I smile warmly.

"Do you remember when your mom made that cake for your twelfth birthday and when she brought it out to the pool you were jumping in the air and knocked it out of her hand?"

"Uh yeah. I was traumatized and thought that I had ruined everything. I ran to my room crying because she worked so hard on the cake and I knew how excited she was to have me taste it."

"And what happened next?" Damien asks patiently.

"My birthday turned into a cooking party and everyone took turns helping out in the kitchen to make something that we all had to taste."

"If I remember correctly, there was a food fight started by your mom and flour was everywhere. Jasmine looked like a little ghost when it was all done and your dad had frosting in his ear somehow."

"My friends said that it was the best party ever. We all jumped in the pool to get clean and even when we were done, we didn't make any of the employees clean up the mess; we did it ourselves and stayed up all night." I chuckle at how crazy that day was.

"What about when you thought your dad got kidnapped because he hid too well playing hide and seek and you called the police?"

I laugh louder. "Let's leave that alone. I was only like five."

"Okay, how about when you told Jasmine that she could be mailed to China and tried to put her in that box," Damien smirks.

"I poked holes in it and everything. She had food and water too. She woulda made it," I defend my younger self.

"Right. How about your first dance, or your first swim meet?"

"They never missed one."

"What about when you got suspended from school for pushing the little boy that took the girls lunch money?"

"Hey, I should have never been suspended. He stole from her," I argue.

"He did, but you pushed him, after you got the money back."

"My dad got that suspension removed. Then, him and mom sat me down and told me that they were proud of me for standing up for what I believed, but I could have handled it in a different way."

"Then what?" Damien asks.

"Then, they hugged me and asked me what I thought my punishment should be. I told them that I shouldn't get to sleep with my favorite teddy bear

Alanna J. Faison   Killer Rayne

for the night and that I should write an apology letter to the boy. They agreed with my decision." I tear up at the thought of my parents being so patient with me and allowing me to have free thought.

"What do you remember, Rayne?"

"I remember Christmas in different countries, riding on my dad's shoulders or stepping on his feet when we danced. I remember listening to my mom sing while she cooked and me and Jazzy playing dress-up with her clothes. I remember Jazzy slipping into bed with me when she had a nightmare and me eating her vegetables when she didn't want them, or taking the blame when she broke a vase. I remember laughing, a lot. I remember my mom crying on my first day of high school and not understanding why. I also remember treating her like shit and never finding common ground as I got older."

The tears remain unshed somehow, but the pain is evident in my face. I had a million wonderfully amazing memories of my family, but I regret the last few years drifting apart from my mom so much. Yes, I've always been daddy's girl, but there's still nothing like the bond between mother and child. Ours will forever be broken.

"Ray Ray, your mom may have not seen eye to eye with you about what seems to you like many things, you being a lesbian included, but that woman was so proud of the fire you possessed. Things weren't as bad as they seem in your head," Damien promises.

I stand up and touch the only picture I have of us in the house, given to me by Damien. All of our smiles had been real. All of our love had been unwavering for each other. I know that, but I still feel like she didn't see me for who I really am.

"You only saw so much. You didn't live there, you didn't see the look of disappointment on her face every time I made a decision that she didn't like. She wanted me to be great, but I had thought I was just fine in my own way."

"I think that Elizabeth wanted you to take advantage of more things that they worked so hard to give you. You were getting older and growing up into the type of adult that you wanted to be, but she just wanted to hold on. She wanted to protect you from this cruel world. She may have gone about it wrong, but parents aren't perfect," he tells me.

No, they aren't. And they have plenty of secrets of their own.

"Did my mom know about what dad really did? Did she know about awakeneds?" I ask, sitting back down.

"She did. As far as I knew, there weren't secrets between your parents. She didn't always agree with his choices, but she always trusted him. Remember that there were things in your dad's past that had to be discussed."

"So what did she think about supernaturals?"

"I think she was afraid of them. She didn't like to talk about that. When Jason found out that Selene was a witch, he told her. That could be another reason why she didn't want you around her," he finally admits.

I don't know how to feel about that. For a couple seconds, I just listen to the sound of traffic in the distance. Processing.

I finally bring myself to ask, "Why didn't you guys just tell me?"

"You know the answer Ray Ray, we've talked about this. We were preparing to tell you everything."

My power begins to simmer in reaction to my anger. Me knowing sooner wouldn't have kept my parents alive, but I like to believe that it would've made a difference.

"Hey, don't take your anger out on me. I don't think I could survive that," Damien semi-jokes.

Too bad he doesn't know the damage that I'm actually capable of.

"Why is our land still in ruins?" I ask.

"No one wants to go near it. I think the demon energy may have something to do with it. I think I heard about that somewhere," Damien explains, leaning back on the couch.

"Yeah, I've heard about that. I just thought that someone would want to profit and make it into a murder museum or something." I laugh at the thought. In this world, you never know.

"Rebuild if you want. Or, get the land cleared if it's uncomfortable for you."

I contemplate that as Selene unlocks the door and steps inside. She had been going over the weapons for hours and I've been waiting to hear the results of her observations. Damien stands up and gives Selene an awkward side hug. They've never hugged before. We peck on the lips and she plops on the couch next to D.

"Humans love to murder people that they fear and they damn sure can get pretty inventive in doing so. With that said, there are too many things in that place that will kill us if there were a war." Selene gives Damien a pointed look and I frown.

"How many are there?" I ask.

"About twelve. They seem to be working on at least eight more," Selene tells me.

"Should they all be destroyed on just halted?" I ask again, trusting her judgment.

"Is it right for supernaturals to have the unfair advantage with everything? Don't you think that destroying things that people spent their entire careers on is a terrible decision?" Damien asks.

"Aren't there enough weapons in the world already?" Selene responds. I can tell by the way her eye twitches that she's growing irritated.

"You have almost every advantage over us," he says, raising his voice.

"You have numbers. There will always be more regular humans than those of us that are awakened. You also have plenty of weapons that can kill us. I don't feel that you need more," Selene says sharply.

"This is why Namen wants to strike first and in such a dramatic way. If he fails to win and supernaturals are exposed, humans will hunt and hunt until they are extinct. All the more reason to not make any moves that could make him do something stupid or give regular humans any more tools of destruction," I decide.

"Rayne-," Damien begins.

"We will use the technology that's been developed for non-combative situations. The weapons will be destroyed and anyone that has worked on them will have to be glamoured. All I can see is death and destruction and awakends will never forgive us if it is used," I say.

"Don't destroy everything. We have secure locations. Put the prototypes in there. Too much work has gone into it. You know that I agree with you on everything else, but I had made a decision to restart the weapons program just in case. Don't allow all that effort to just be destroyed," Damien pleads.

I sit and think for a few seconds, looking to Selene, but she remains expressionless, allowing me to make the decision on my own. I sigh in defeat after looking into D's eyes, his sincerity overpowering my resolve.

"Fine. The prototypes remain, but all that other shit has to go. We need to decide where we'll go from here. Security. Human security is what we specialize in. Whitmore Industries has been making far too many weapons. Let's branch out. We can get into medical tech, more clean energy solutions, better evidence collection, something. We have the brains to make it happen."

"We'll talk about that at the next meeting. Now, are you sure about the mayor thing?" D asks.

"What mayor thing?" Selene questions.

"We'll talk about it. Yes, I need his schedule for tomorrow and all of his security systems disabled once he gets home for the night," I tell him, working my plan in my head.

"Have you always been this bossy and crazy?" Damien asks shaking his head. He heads to the door, hand on the nob.

"See you later, Damien," I respond smiling.

He waves goodbye and shuts the door behind him. I hear his engine start and then pull away, leaving me to explain what I'm doing tomorrow to Selene.

Chapter Twenty Seven

Jaxson picks up the phone on the third ring. His deep voice fills my ears with his hello and I waste no time getting down to business. Well, after a little bit of teasing of course.

"So did Jun pass the sex test. I mean the breast test. Oops, I mean the stress test?"

"Fuck you, Rayne," he growls playfully.

"No, seriously though, after your intimate encounter, which by the way I heard only lasted like two minutes because you were so excited that you forgot to pace yourself, did you find out if she's trustworthy?"

There's a female laugh in the background. Jun obviously heard my joke. A second later, her soft voice comes on the line. "Actually, it was two and a half minutes. I was highly disappointed. For him to be such a big man, he's actually lacking in the-,"

There's a tussle over the phone and then even more female laughter. I can't help but smile. If she's still around, that means that not only is there something to explore between them, but she's mildly trustworthy. Jaxson finally gets the phone back from Jun and I can hear as he steps outside and shuts the door behind himself.

Alanna J. Faison   Killer Rayne

"For the record, I have the size and the stamina to go the distance, so screw you for playing around about my manhood, and screw you again for allowing her to join in on bashing me. There were no complaints and it's none of your business anyway. As your alpha, I command you to shut the hell up about it." He mutters something else under his breath. It's humorous, really.

"Oh please, that alpha command mojo doesn't work on me. But, I'll leave you alone. If she's still there, then that's a good sign. If she really wants in, I need her to do something with me tonight. It's going to be crazy," I warn.

"I think crazy just may be her middle name. Now, what is it that you intend to do with her?" he inquires.

I relay the same plan to Jaxson that I did to Selene. "I'm going to break into the mayor's house and tell him the truth about awakeneds. I'm going to threaten his life if he doesn't work with me. He needs to know about Namen and what will happen if Namen wins. I then need Jun to come in with the Chief of Police whom I'm going to kill in his house so that he knows I'm not playing."

"You're going to do what now?" Jaxson interrupts.

"Let me finish, don't be rude. Then, I need him to appoint a new leader that can be trusted to look the other way while we clean house of all the humans that are working for Namen."

"First of all, Queen Crazy, you can't kill everyone."

"I know that," I say rolling my eyes.

"Second, you can't kill the chief in the mayor's house."

"Fine, Jun can do it. I want her to shift to wolf anyway. She can do it while she's changed. That'll really get the point across." Scare tactics.

"That's not what I meant."

"It's going to be perfect. I'm going to have someone from my staff go back and hack the phones to make it seem like messages were exchanged to meet the mayor at his house to discuss something. His security system will be down, so it'll be very convenient. He won't be able to spin a story that the people of our great city believe that will exonerate him of the murder if he doesn't cooperate."

"And what if the mayor is already working with Namen?" Jaxson asks.

"Then, when Zara gets back, she glamours him for information before I kill him."

"You aren't the type to champion all this death. What's gotten into you?" he asks quietly.

I pace back and forth in my basement, waiting for Selene to join me so that we can spar.

"These are things that must be done Jaxson. Even when we finish with Namen, the world is still going to be changing. This can be our city. It can be a safe place for us if we do what needs to be done now. That means that we have to get out there and let some of these people in charge know that we're here and their best bet is to work with us. It'll keep us all alive longer in the long run." I have to start thinking three steps ahead of Namen's two.

Selene comes down to the basement a few seconds later and sits in the middle of the floor, getting ready to meditate. I continue to focus on the phone conversation. Jaxson growls but otherwise remains silent as he thinks this over. I stand there patiently, breathing into the phone.

"Someone on the force took Anubis's body. They're not innocent. They arrested you for Namen. They probably helped Namen use that abandoned university building for his experiments on those kids. They're not innocent." His voice now has more resolve.

"I know that you don't want to purposely out yourself to any human, but this will work Jaxson.

Alanna J. Faison   Killer Rayne

We will be in a better position. They have to know that death or enslavement is what awaits them with Namen. Even if we have to kill a few to make our case, it'll be worth the sacrifice. As you said, they're not innocent."

"I trusted you with Anubis's life and now you ask this of me after you did not keep your promise. Please, Rayne, do not make a fool of me this time. I want to trust your judgment, but I am the alpha now and I have more to protect than ever before."

"If I fail you again, Jaxson, you can consider my life forfeit. You may do to me as you see fit. That is my oath," I promise. I learned from the immortals that oaths are not to be given lightly. I mean this one with all that I am. I will not cause him any more pain without paying for it.

"As you speak it, it is done. On your oath as my second, as my pack, as my friend. I accept this," Jaxson responds sadly. He doesn't want to, but he knows now that I mean it.

I glance over to Selene who is sitting there, unmoving. I wonder what's going through her mind right now. She doesn't say a word and I want to take that as her having complete faith in me, not fear of my failure. She'll speak up when she feels that it is necessary.

"Now, tell me, how many wolves have fled the city?" I'm curious if any of them have taken the threat to heart.

"Only two so far. One has come to me saying that he will join. He is a seventeen year old. His birthday was just last week and his father had been keeping him away from all things supernatural until now. Strong boy, not very bright, but ambitious nonetheless. I don't want to bring any of our children into this. There are five of our pack's children that are between fifteen and eighteen. I may have no choice though," Jaxson admits.

"We'll give them other jobs, away from the battle if at all possible. They do need to be ready, but for now, I think we're safe. We need to find them a location to go to, if in the end we fail, for them to hide, to start over or at least get away to find others that may be able to stop Namen if we don't," I say, trying to think ahead some more.

"We have time to think. It won't come to that. What we need to do is find out just what it is Namen has promised the demons that have them working for him. Taking out as many of his most powerful followers will cripple him."

"And we will. I don't think that we need to rush. There hasn't been anything in the recent news about an eclipse coming any time soon, so we have a couple months at least. Let's build up a strategy and our own army," I respond. There has to be a way that I can convince the immortals to help, at the very least, Lawrence, my teacher may change his mind.

"Okay. Do what you have to do. I'll tell Jun that she's going to have to prove herself really soon here," Jaxson declares.

"She had better be up for the task," I say.

"Rayne," Jaxson begins. "I don't know her well, but I think her ass is up for just about anything."

We both laugh and then say our goodbyes. Then, I turn to Selene. Her body is pulsing with energy. Tiny electrical surges dance off of her skin as she focuses on her meditation. It seems that ever since she's seen Santos, her power has been growing. I don't doubt it. Supernatural twin connection and all. Instead of disturbing her trance, I decide to get my stretching out of the way. Minutes tick by and Selene finally stands, her green eyes alight with power. It's awe inspiring watching the magic dance behind her eyes like a tiny flame.

How did I not see her for what she was before I became awakened?

Selene is wearing spandex shorts and a royal blue tank top. Her hair is tied back into a loose ponytail and she looks rather eager to get started. I lift my eyebrows and give her an eager look in return before drawing a three foot circle around her in chalk. She stands in the middle of the circle, arms crossed, waiting.

"We'll start with you, okay. You have to knock me on my ass three times without moving out of the circle. I'm going to be trying to do just that to you while you make sure that it doesn't happen," I explain.

"Fine, but let's up the ante if you will."

"I'm listening."

"You have three minutes to knock me out of the circle. For every minute that you don't, you lose a limb that you can fight with," Selene suggests, smirking.

"Now you know that I can't turn down a challenge, love. Let's do this."

"Good. And after this is over, I'm going to show you how pissed off I am about that oath that you just made to Jaxson," Selene warns, already in a fighting stance.

"It's an oath that I won't break," I swear. I root myself further into the floor as if I am a tree firmly planted into the earth. Two deep breaths later, my tattoo glows in response to my power being stirred awake.

"I will kill him before he ever touches you," Selene snaps before unleashing a wave of water onto the ground. I stand there for a half second before the electricity from her next attack slices through the water, directly toward me.

Jumping against the wall and away from the attack, I say, incredulously, "You're trying to electrocute me, really?"

"Stop being a baby, it wouldn't have hurt that bad. Now, let us continue, meu guerreiro."

"Sure, clock is ticking after all."

I go to my secret box of weapons that I've been keeping on the low and reach inside and pull out my second favorite toy, one that will be perfect for keeping Selene off guard. I pull out the kusarigama, a scythe-like weapon with a weighted chain on the end. The main objective with this weapon is to throw your opponent off-guard, entangle their weapon or limbs, and then get close enough to deliver a finishing blow. I plan to test the speed and defense of my witch. She beat me once and I can't have it happen again. Plus, with her little bet, if I can't get her out of the circle within a minute, the weapon will no longer be effective with just one hand.

Selene eyes my toy and smiles, tilting her head to the side. Quickly, much quicker than I expect, she weaves a spell with her hands. As quickly as I can, I throw the weighted chain at her. It wraps around her arm and I pull hard, attempting to pull her out of the circle, but something grips onto my legs and freezes me in place. I look down and see that the water has crept around me and turned to ice. I didn't even realize that she finished her spell in time. Damn.

Using the scythe, I break the ice only to block a stream of magic just in time. Absorbing the blow pushes me back a few feet. I use my own chakra as I had in the fight with the witches when I was with Zara to volley the magic back to her. The understanding of the power comes naturally and I use that to my advantage.

"What the hell," Selene says as she moves her head just in time to dodge her own attack that I directed right back at her.

"I'm improving, love," I respond, sending an extra amount of chakra flow to my legs so that I gain a burst of speed.

She recovers just like I know she will, and weaves a spell creating a shimmering invisible wall between us. Or so she thinks. A fraction of a second that I gained with my speed burst sends the weight wrapping around her legs just as I pull hard, knocking her off of her feet. Her foot is almost out of the circle when she laughs.

"That's one minute down."

I smirk, but narrow my eyes at her. "Cheater."

"Move faster next time."

I put my left hand behind my back and motion with my right hand to continue. She unwraps her leg and throws my kusarigama across the room. I immediately run and breech the circle. With swings and kicks, I have her on the ropes, so to speak. She's ducking and dodging as best she can, but even with only one hand, I'm the better fighter. A quick sweep knocks Selene off of her feet again, but as she catches herself, still in the circle somehow, I see the look of magic dance in her eyes.

Suddenly, her aura explodes around her and then there are bright green arms and hands whipping out of everywhere. I'm too in awe to properly defend myself as one grabs me and throws me across the room. From my back, I flick Selene off.

"I've improved too," she tells me. Then, she's weaving sign after sign -fingers lacing and unlacing in a specific pattern- and I know that once again, I'm screwed.

I pop up and dive straight in once again, like I did when I fought Jaxson and Zara in the woods. Soon, I'm dodging magical limbs that are giving me a run for my money. My dance background makes for beautiful moves as I weave and spin, blocking and jabbing. I know that my second minute is nearly up, so I try to push my chakra out once again. It gives me the leverage I need, by knocking Selene back just a couple inches. There's a lapse in her spell and with that, I land a solid kick to her midsection, causing her to stumble just over the line.

I feel triumphant for only a second before exhaustion hits me like a bus. I fall to my knees, coughing up a tiny bit of blood. Selene wastes no time in dropping her magical octopus arms and running to my side.

"Baby, are you okay?" she asks, pulling me close and examining my hazel eyes.

"I'm fine, really. I just used too much power at once. Pushing out my chakra like that is a bitch. It's definitely not battle ready yet," I try to joke. I feel like I have a hangover.

"Well, two is your limit for now. Don't exceed it. I'm feeling tired myself. But, I think we should keep going. I want to try to restore some of your energy and then, we need to work on some of my hand to hand, okay. I'm not a healer, but this I think I can do." Selene takes my hands without waiting for a response and whispers something in Latin. "Restaurationem deperditi. Hoc fragmen accipio me." She repeats it three times and finally I feel slightly better.

Alanna J. Faison   Killer Rayne

She lets go of my hands and I observe her breathing. I wipe some sweat off of her forehead and smile. She's pushing herself to become an even greater witch, but I don't know if I'm keeping up with her or if she's keeping up with me. Who knows how long she's going to have to keep spelling in a battle. I know that she's forcing herself to do more complex spells to challenge herself, but what is her skill level compared to Namen's? He inserted himself inside my head with nothing more than a thought and his natural ability is that of a necromancer. I don't even want to know how capable he is with that power.

Then, it hits me and I nearly faint at the thought. Gripping Selene's arm tightly, I pull her closer to me, knowing I probably look frantic. I don't know how we didn't see it before. Maybe we did, but none of us wanted to say it.

"Namen has Anubis and probably the other wolves. He's probably going to bring them back with necromancy to control them," I say, feeling hollow inside.

Chapter Twenty Eight

I did this.

I gave him Anubis.

But why? I thought that it would be just to screw with our morale, to make a point, but he has to have a plan. I don't know how necromancy works, but I was assuming that Namen would just be able to see and speak to ghosts, but now, now I hope to God that he isn't making a zombie army or something like that. What if that werewolf/vampire is what he gets turned into? I gag a little at the thought of rotting bodies marching toward us.

"Maybe he's using his body to host a demon," Selene says.

"That is not good. Not fucking good at all. I need to call Jaxson," I say, standing up.

"Wait," Selene says, pulling me back down. I look at her pointedly, and then sigh in defeat.

"Let's just wait until Zara gets back. She may have news for us first. If not, then we'll tell him. If he does have him and uses his body for whatever reason, there's nothing we can do about it right now," she urges.

"It'll be my fault. I made this happen. We gave Namen everything he wanted."

"No, you didn't make that happen. You chose to do something. You chose to fight and keep those lamia from kidnapping children. Namen felt threatened and he responded. Anubis knew what he was getting into. For the short time that he knew you, I think that you gave him hope. Be proud of that. You've sparked something in us. Anything beyond that is not on you. If we aren't strong enough, then you are not to blame," Selene tells me passionately.

"I know it, but deep inside my heart I don't believe it. I still have doubts."

"Then doubt, but just don't quit trying."

I smile at her. "Okay. Let's get on with this then. I'll worry about what Namen may have done later. There are some things I want to teach you."

"I'm ready," Selene says in her sexy voice. She didn't mean to, but it definitely makes me feel some type of way.

"We'll just go over a few combos. I think that we should create a whole new style so that you don't waste energy between possible close combat situations and magical combat. I can help you begin to get it flowing, but Zara is going to be your best bet. She has the most experience," I tell her.

"Of course it would be her."

"Is... that going to be an issue?" I ask warily.

"No. I couldn't dislike her if I tried. She's just much more amazing than should be allowed."

I sense the insecurity coming from Selene and I pull her close. "If you think for a second that I think that she is better than you, that this is a competition, please stop. It's my fault anyway for kissing her. Diana had been trying to teach me a lesson when I was with the immortals, and I didn't listen."

"Why is it that you didn't feel that pull with Diana the way you did with Zara? Because, she tried to seduce you every step of the way. It's like she wanted you to taste her power."

"She wanted me as property, a collector's item. That's why she tried. She wanted me to be power hungry, to crave what she was offering like a drug addict. I think that my power is driven by balance and pure emotion. Your emotions don't get much more heightened than with great sex. With Diana, I never saw myself as an equal. I knew she wanted to claim me. That's not attractive to me. Zara, she-," I say before Selene interrupts me.

"Do I want to hear this?" Selene laughs jokingly, but I still hear the slight tremor in her voice.

"I think you should. I need to be honest with you, especially about this. Is that alright?"

"I don't like feeling like you don't love me as much as I love you."

"Don't ever worry about that. Please believe me. Zara is deeply intriguing and much more complex than I would have guessed. Her emotions can go from one to ten in half a second, but it's so honest that she makes you question your own existence, the way you see the world. I want to know more about her. I want her in my life; no, I think I need her in my life. Just like you are my greatest love, she could be my greatest friend. Our bond runs deep and I allowed that to be tainted by lust, attraction, hurt, and fear."

Selene leans up against the wall rubbing her arms as goose bumps form against her skin. Her mouth is set in a tiny frown, but I know that as painful as it may be to hear, she needs to. I knew that the conversation would come up again because hey, that's what happens in relationships.

I continue. "I acted on my desire that was amplified by our blood bond. Vampires don't blood bond lightly and never with non-lovers. Our mistake. Zara's mistake. Maybe she did know, but I don't think she really thought it through. We kissed and it was like the world exploded inside of me. It was terrifying, consuming, and not what I expected. It wasn't what my power was expecting either. It was dangerous. Her vampiric nature wanted to claim me. It could've been seeking out something close to how Sage made her feel. It was like she recognized my power and wanted to take it all." I shiver as I remember it.

"Zara is a very powerful being. As much as I don't want to admit it, she is sexy. Vampires know how to pull you in without even trying. It is part of their nature. That's why I can't fault you for the second kiss. If she was out of control when she bit you, then once she pushed those pheromones into you, you were hers. But, it isn't real."

"I figured that out. That's why I pushed her away. It didn't even feel the same as the first kiss. I felt compelled."

"In a way you were. But, any type of power play involving you guys will have to be done in my presence. I don't know if it's really over. Sometimes, things are just out of our control. You may need more of her power one day," Selene warns.

"I'll need you much more," I say.

Selene chuckles. "You may need us both. But I'll tell you what. No more female friends, Rayne."

"What about Jun?" I ask.

Selene narrows her eyes. "I want to meet her by the way."

"That doesn't answer my question."

"I don't think I want you around anyone, ever. Why don't I just lock you up," she suggests.

"The only locking up you better be doing with me is with handcuffs. No, wait, after being unmade, locked in chains, and arrested, I think that fantasy is done for me," I admit.

"Hmm, we can use that as punishment then. Maybe I'll have your 'best friend' Zara compel you into thinking you're in prison."

"Oh, haha, screw you, Selene Marquez."

"Only if you deserve it and definitely not right after you were talking about how amazing your kiss was with another woman."

"Not what I said," I say.

"It didn't have to be said. I was mad, but I'm really not anymore. I'm not mad so much about the kiss as I am about how bonded you two are. That is going to bother me for a while, but not so much that

I'm going to hate her. I owe her a lot too and don't forget that I've been alone with Zara a few times now. She's not the bad guy," Selene tells me.

I think about Zara's own words to me. That she's a vampire first. That I shouldn't assume that she's the good guy. Maybe for Zara that's easier to cope with when you've had lifetimes to do bad things. I'm sure someone like her has been keeping a tally and it's probably far easier to have no remorse than to mourn all the things that you have to do that others are too weak to do themselves. That's where my understanding of who she really is comes into play. Someone has to have blood on their hands. Peace doesn't always happen by peaceful means. Sometimes you have to do one horrible thing to set an example just so you don't end up doing one hundred more horrible things. Exactly why the police chief has got to go.

My phone rings and I pick it up to check the id. Speaking of the devil. I'll call her back. The last thing I want to do is jump on the phone with her when I just had this conversation with Selene. I set it back down knowing that if it's important, she'll just contact me through our mind-link. Well, if distance isn't an issue. There's always voicemail or texting.

"I'll call her later," I tell Selene. "Like I said, she can help you with better technique. I want to get you started."

I pull Selene in for a quick kiss that leaves her breathless before grabbing her waist and putting her into a stance that will help her. She smiles at me and I can't help but smile back. I'm never leaving this woman again.

◊◊◊

I took a long hot shower to relax my muscles after our training. Selene caught on quickly and was able to memorize a few combinations that will come in handy. I'm satisfied with our progress. She's going to train with Zara as soon as she gets back and Jaxson is going to start making sure that the wolves change at least three times a day no matter how painful it may be. He wants the ones that can't undergo the second shift to begin training for it. Phillip has been making a list of the skills that each wolf excels at. Some are showing promise, but none have what Jaxson's looking for in an enforcer.

I sit down on the bed and check my phone to find a text from Zara.

'8390 S. Bower Rd. Midnight.'

I text back, 'Ok.'

That's in a few hours. I don't recognize the address, so this must be another one of her safe houses. I find it interesting that she wants to meet us there instead of just coming over here. No matter, Selene and I are going on a date anyway. Pierce called before my shower and thought that it'd be great publicity for me. He got us a reservation at a steakhouse called Spaulding's. It caters to the rich. Perfect for me apparently.

I finish flat ironing my hair, running a finger through it, wishing that it was long once more. My mom loved my long hair. She would've been so shocked when I cut it.

I push some diamond studs through the holes in my ears. There is no way that I'd be wearing hoops in a potentially dangerous situation, no matter how much I love them. No one is going to rip them out of my ears in a fight.

After my hair and makeup is complete, I drop my towel and stand naked in front of my closet, just as Selene comes into the room wrapped in a robe. She looks at her reflection in the mirror and sighs.

"What?" I ask, still looking at my wardrobe choices.

"We are both two years older. I'm twenty five, you're twenty one and we just haven't had a chance to celebrate anything normal like birthdays or anniversaries. It just kinda sucks. The upside is that I still look twenty three."

"Yeah, I never got to have a big twenty first birthday bash where I got super wasted and passed out in the middle of my front yard where you left me until the sprinklers cut on."

"Have you been watching any movies lately?" Selene asks, laughing at my very specific description.

"Isn't that the American dream?" I smile.

"If it is, then it's a good thing that I wasn't born in America."

"Let's get drunk soon."

"Excuse me?"

"You heard me. Let's get drunk soon," I say.

"Will this be in between trying to fight for our lives and saving the world?"

"Of course. I can hire a security team. We can go to a big non supernatural club where I can shake my ass and take shots off of your sexy body. Namen will let us be for one night. Just as he wanted the cameras to slow me down, it's going to slow him down too. He can't just attack outright. We'll sleep in a hotel where there are lots of people. Let's do it," I urge.

"I'll think about it. Only because I definitely haven't seen you shake your ass in a long while and I really need to find some new music to vibe to," Selene tells me, dropping her own robe and stepping all the way into our walk in closet.

I watch her as she looks over her shoulder and smiles at me. She's beautiful, her body is beautiful and I drink her all in. She turns back around and pulls out her baby blue loose fitting v-neck chiffon dress. The sleeves are long and have slits in them. I nod my approval. She'd look great in it with her hair down, some jewelry, and nude heels. I tell her as much.

Seconds later, Selene pulls out a short, black dress with the back cut out in three places. It looks like a diamond pattern, with the largest cut being at the top of the back. "I want to see you wear this," she orders, handing me the item on a hanger.

"Yes ma'am," I respond, entering the closet so that I can pick out shoes to match. Dressing up is one of my favorite past times as well as eating unhealthy food, so I'm kind of looking forward to our dinner date.

After a short while, we finish getting ready and head to the restaurant. We pull into the lot and up to the front where a valet is waiting. I hand him the keys to my Jag and walk hand in hand with Selene to the front door. Another couple is standing around waiting to be seated. They turn toward us and smile, the guy's eyes lingering slightly longer than his date would like. He doesn't see the look she gives him though until she clears her throat.

Soon, the host takes them to be seated and it's our turn. Selene tells the host the name on our reservation and we are taken to a quiet corner table. As we weave through the other patrons, I can hear their whispers about the news and who I am. I ignore it as Selene squeezes my hand.

"They'll move on to a celebrity wedding or the latest government manufactured outbreak soon enough and they'll forget all about you," Selene whispers.

"Not soon enough," I respond quietly.

"Let's just enjoy tonight. It's been a long time." Selene smiles and thanks the host as we take our seats.

I sit down and look at the menu. It is in fancy cursive writing and has no prices listed. Glancing at the appetizers, I allow the atmosphere to relax me. Soft music plays overhead and the lighting is just enough so that you can read the menu and still feel a sense of privacy. I touch my chair letting my hands feel the soft cushion of my seat. Candles are lit along the ledges of the window sills and the décor is tastefully modern. All in all, it's a nice place. The food had better live up to the hype that Pierce made about it.

Our waiter, Marco, is polite and professional throughout the evening. He's earned a generous tip. When it's time for dessert, Marco comes to us with a dessert wine from Alto Adige. "This is compliments of another table. They wish to remain anonymous. They also wanted to tell you that they think that you two are a beautiful couple and that they wish you many years of happiness."

"Thank you Marco. Tell them that we accept their generous gift and that they are very kind," I respond.

He nods and pours us each a glass leaving the bottle on the table. "Speaking freely, I hope that my boyfriend and I look half as good as you guys when we go on dates."

"I'm sure you guys clean up well," I say.

"Maybe we can double date one day," Selene says, shocking me. I raise an eyebrow at her.

"That would be... amazing," Marco breathes.

"What's your number?" Selene asks, pulling out her phone. He rattles it off quietly and Selene types it in smoothly. Then, with a friendly smile she says, "No promises. We're both extremely busy and it might be a while before we can hang, but don't forget about us okay."

"I won't. I'm sorry Ms. Whitmore if I've overstepped my bounds. It's not very professional of me to talk about my relationship, but you guys seem so confident and loving and I know what it's like to be in a same sex relationship. It can be scary sometimes, but you guys seem to have it all figured out."

"She's my soul mate. I just don't give a damn what anyone else thinks," I admit.

He laughs. "Maybe one day I'll be as confident as you. Now, is there anything else you want for dessert?"

"Just roll out the dessert cart and I'll pick something from it."

After dessert, we actually sit and have a normal conversation. Selene and I talk about all the things that we want to catch up on, the places we want to visit together first, where we'd like to live when all this is over, and other dreams for the future. I feel much better about our state of our relationship when we finish.

Feeling full and happy, I pay the extravagant bill and drop a hundred dollar tip for Marco. Maybe he can take his boyfriend out for a nice date. We walk outside and I tip the valet as well after he pulls up with our vehicle. A couple cameras flash in the distance as we slide in the car.

Selene punches in the address in the GPS for Zara's safe house as I pull into traffic.

I take the interstate and get off after about six exits, checking the entire time to see if we're being followed. After that bullshit with Zara, I don't want to take any more chances when it comes to traffic. Car chases and playing chicken is not fun. I grip my seatbelt tighter at the memory.

We pull on a long street with speed bumps every thirty feet. I hate speed bumps. I also hate houses that have vines growing all up the sides of the house. It gives me the creeps. That's exactly what the house next door to Zara's has. Ew. Just ew.

Selene uses magic to try to sense if anyone dangerous is around before we get out of the car. The coast seems clear, so we get out quickly. The house is plain in every way. The paint is white and chipped, the front yard is small, the windows are old with black trim. As I walk up the steps, my heels clack against the pavement, echoing into the night.

Just as I get ready to ring the doorbell, Zara's inside my mind, startling me. "It's open, come inside," she says, spinning inside my consciousness. Pain hits me, but it's not my own. Alarmed, I push through the door and run down the hall toward the source of the pain. Selene is close behind me after closing the door.

"Zara!" I call out, worried. I stumble into a dark bedroom as the heel of my shoes nearly gives out. I haven't run in heels in forever. Catching my balance against the doorframe, my eyes begin to adjust to the darkness.

"Stop worrying. I'm not dead yet," Zara rasps, holding her middle with a useless arm.

"What the fuck?" I ask, looking at her ragged appearance as Selene switches on a light.

Chapter Twenty Nine

Zara's eyes are completely crimson and her fangs are out as well. The pain is driving her vampire instinct to protect herself from threats. Her hair is no longer braided but in a large, poofy ponytail that makes her look even younger. Her white t-shirt is dirty and torn and her pants are in the same condition. She looks like she's barely remaining conscious and I can't help but go to her as her power calls to my own. I know she needs blood but before I can give her some of mine, Selene steps forward, surprising us both by slicing open her wrist with a spell and forcing it into Zara's mouth. Selene hisses at the contact.

Zara looks up at me with those lava-filled eyes and I can't help but shiver as she consumes the life force of my girlfriend. Seeming satisfied, she grips her good arm around Selene's and sucks more deeply from her vein. Selene's breath catches and she looks back at me and then down to Zara whose eyes are now closed in satisfaction. I stand my ground, afraid that if I come any closer, I'll still want her to bleed me too. I think Selene knows that. Finally, Selene taps Zara for her to close the wound with her vampire saliva and then pulls away.

Zara still doesn't open her eyes and I begin to wonder if she's fighting for control. "I'm fine. I'm in control," she responds to my thought.

"What happened?" I ask. "Why didn't you call me and tell me that you needed me?" I hope my words don't come off wrong to Selene, as if there is some unspoken meaning behind them.

"I wasn't dying, Rayne. I didn't want you to worry. I took care of it. My arm is broken but it will heal in a couple days."

"What about your ribs?" Selene asks.

"They'll be fine in a week," she whispers and I hear her labored breathing. Someone or something really did a number on my pureblood vamp.

"Not if you keep damaging them over and over. Is this something that we should be concerned about? Does this have anything to do with Namen?" Selene asks again.

"Yes and no. Mainly, this is vampire business. We had some house cleaning to do. Then when I brought it up, some of the vampire factions didn't want to be involved in this coming war. They want the nine to remain neutral. Others didn't want their children that have betrayed our clans to be punished. They forget that I am the Blade of the Night. They forget that I am the Princess. I had to remind more than a few why I have that title."

"They must not have approved of your methods."

She chuckles looking as if she's feeling slightly better. "Of course not, but this wouldn't be the first time nor the last."

"The head of one of the nine challenged my authority and stated that he feels that my role as enforcer should be cut short. You see, we normally serve for about sixty years and then get some time off to go do what we want for a decade or two, but I have never really taken more than a few years for myself after I lost Sage. Some think that it's changed me." Zara gazes off into the distance; her memories begin to slip into my mind, but she quickly closes me off.

"Some of the vampires that his son Caleb had sired have joined with Namen, Logan being one of them. I wanted Caleb to call them home and have them answer for their betrayal. The problem is we try not to force the sire authority on our children unless we truly feel it necessary. Even then, we only call upon them and hear their side. They can still make their own choices, but it is still our responsibility to keep our own in line. I argued that Caleb has not done that. He keeps in touch with his own and they know what the rules are."

"It sounds like vampire politics are very complicated," I observe.

"You don't even know the half of it. There are things that only the firsts know even though we are still pureblood. They have rules on top of our laws."

"So what happened that made you injured?"

"My cousin called on all of the nine to convene. I saw my parents for the first time in fifty years. They've been traveling the world. Apparently my mother is pregnant again."

"Wow. That's crazy. How many more years is she fertile?" I ask knowing it's off subject, but curious just the same.

"Probably for about thirty more years. It's very hard for us to become pregnant. She's lucky to have three of us now." Zara looks at Selene and then gets back to the story after getting a "move it along" look. "Antonius, Caleb's father, and Camilla, another one of the nine, attacked me. They don't want to get involved and wanted to stop me from doing any more damage, or so they said."

"Well, you're alive, injured, but alive, so that must mean..."

"No, Apollo forbade me to kill them. I don't know if he would have extended the same courtesy if I had lost. I gave up my grab for the head of our family and the nine to allow him to rise. He wants to

285

make sure I don't change my mind. I love my cousin, but he is dangerous on a good day."

Zara winces as she tries to lean against the headboard. I step over to help her get comfortable.

"You guys look sexy as hell tonight," she compliments as she gets a good look at us both, scanning up and down, grinning with fang and then winking playfully at Selene.

"Continue your story vampire," I demand, smiling. Selene is smiling and shaking her head at the flirty comment. Only Zara would take on two purebloods and make time to flirt. Selene's blood is obviously doing its job.

"The members of the nine have astonishing talents and these two are no exception. Antonius can poison you with his bite and Camilla can actually travel in the shadows. There are a lot of shadows cast when there are many people around. I had a challenging fight. Antonius poisoned his blade with his venom and weakened me enough that Camilla was able to catch me off guard." I see flashes of the fight in my mind. Even through her memories, the fight is almost too fast for me to follow. None of them are amateurs.

The two opposing vamps double team Zara, striking simultaneously, trying to throw her off balance, but she's often too clever as she waits until the very last second before a strike connects and throws them off balance in turn. She definitely takes her share of punches, especially from the tall Roman looking vampire dressed in a very nice suit.

The woman rips a slit in her dress to give her better mobility and vanishes in the shadows as Zara and Antonius clash. His punches are breaking through her defense as his blade manages to cut her in a few places on her body, one just below her eye. With a swift kick, her back slams against the wall. She turns to move when Camilla slips out of the shadows and snaps her bone, nearly causing it to poke through the skin.

"The bitch broke my arm after the poison slowed me down. It was burning through me and my adrenaline was making it pump through my system at a faster rate. It would have killed me if my blood had not been pure, but I've been poisoned before and my body was fighting it off better than I could have hoped. Plus I don't like to lose. I had to show them why I could have the throne if I so chose."

"They should be leaving me alone for now and I'm sure some of the witnesses will pass around that I am out for blood. I couldn't take blood from any of their... donors because it would've been a sign of weakness. I also had to go before any of them decided that it would be a good time to get revenge for some of the wrongs they've felt I may have committed in the past against them."

"Oh like, wiping out those that tried to kill Sage," I say.

"Yeah, something like that." Zara laughs and shakes her head.

"What's so funny?" Selene asks, smoothing out her dress.

"They should know how far I'd go to protect those that I love." Her eyes remain shifted to the color of blood, her smirk cruel and calculated. "Not even the angels themselves would be able to stop me. I'd drink their blood and burn this world to ashes."

"Uh, that's just a figure of speech right?" I ask, looking into her eyes and seeing a monster waiting for its chance to take control.

"Perhaps." She puts her good hand over her face and laughs once more. "If I thought for a second that Sage was actually dead, I'd find a way to rip a hole in reality and slaughter all of those immortals. One hundred plus years is a long time to hold a grudge. Those who are of the blood never forget."

I begin to say something in response when I see a lone tear fall down Zara's cheek. She refuses to wipe it away, a testament of her suffering and strength all in one. Selene looks at her in pity, rocks as if she wants to comfort her, but changes her mind. I can't figure Selene out. She just keeps surprising me when it comes to Zara. Maybe she really is just playing nice for my sake.

"Sorry. I think that I'm just feeling like this because I'm in pain. Let me get to the reason why I asked you two to come." Zara gets up without much effort and motions for us to follow her. She leads us down the dark hallway and down to her basement.

The steps creak slightly as we descend and then Zara clicks on the light to illuminate the grimy basement. She clearly doesn't use this place too often from the unkempt state of the room. I just hope there are no spider webs. I. Hate. Spider. Webs. Hate them. Why do they feel so gross? And they're hell to get off of you.

There's a bookshelf on the far wall and I follow Zara to it as I try to ignore the smell of mold and old basement. Why the hell did she bring me here? I ask her as much, looking around to make sure no spider is waiting to jump in my hair from the ceiling. A glance at Selene shows that she seems slightly more comfortable, but hell no, she can't be cool and collected.

"It's a spell," Zara tells me.

"Huh?"

"It's a spell to keep people out, mainly humans. Apparently it's working on you because it must be showing you things that make you really uncomfortable. In this neighborhood, I have to have something that keeps people out or else I'd have the homeless breaking in all the time. The spell does that for me," Zara explains.

"So how do I break it?"

"Feel for it first, feel the magic, and then imagine it washing off of you like a shower," Selene tells me.

"Okay, I'll try." I take three cleansing breaths as I tell myself the moldy smell is just my imagination. It takes a minute, but finally the spell drops and I see a clean and fairly empty basement. The bookshelf against the wall is still there.

"So, can some witches create glamours like that where I truly think that I'm somewhere else entirely or completely change a room for an extended amount of time?" I ask.

"Of course. There is usually a focus object somewhere that keeps the spell intact, but a powerful telepath can drop a glamour on you without you ever realizing it. Some can even touch half a dozen people without even having a focus," Selene explains as if this is nothing but a conversation about what type of cereal to buy.

"Awakends," I say. Crazy powerful. Unlimited potential. Humans would destroy the earth trying to rid the world of them.

"It can be scary. Witches are probably some of the most powerful beings on the planet," Zara reveals, surprising me.

I could see that. They don't have the speed or strength of vampires or werewolves, but the things they can accomplish with their magic is mind blowing. Namen is definitely a testament of that. The soul stealer.

"Something else happened tonight," Zara begins, bringing my attention back to her and the bookshelf as she pushes it to the side and reveals a wall safe.

"My grandmother gave me a book. It is the book of the luna dasa, the moon's servants. It tells the history of the wolves. It speaks of a certain wolf by the name of Ka'el. Have you heard of this wolf Selene?" Zara asks her, knowing that her knowledge of the supernatural is astounding.

"It sounds familiar, but I can't place him," Selene responds, rubbing her head as if the answer will be massaged right out of her brain.

"Hmm." Zara does the code and as soon as the safe's door opens. She grabs an old book. It looks pretty well preserved for the age of the text. "My grandmother's library is extensive and she allowed me to take it so long as I don't keep it long enough for her to miss it. Knowing Zahira, my grandmother, that's about a week. She doesn't like things to be out of place."

Zara turns to a page and we step forward to look. I step back because I can't read it anyway. Definitely not in English. Duh, I should've guessed that. Whatever it says, Zara has no trouble with it. She clearly knows a few languages.

"Ka'el was called the King. He was an alpha wolf that could make other alphas submit and force the change on them. They could not oppose him because his magic was too powerful. His father was a shaman and his mother was a werewolf. They should not have been able to conceive, but the shaman sacrificed his own tribe to a demon so that they could bear the child. The demon was so pleased with his sacrifice that he allowed them to have two sons. Ka'el ended up uniting wolves from all over into a pack so large that it became a small kingdom over which he ruled. They would massacre any invading armies in werewolf form. Rumor has it that they had the power of what your wolves call the second shift."

I allow the story to take image in my mind. A wolf born of a shaman and a werewolf, one that could control magic. Jun pops into my mind and how she had sought out Anubis. I don't believe in coincidences and my eyes narrow as I wait for Zara to continue, afraid of where this is going.

"Slowly Ka'el became tainted with his lust for power and the luna dasa under him grew more weary and afraid of him. They wanted to go off and start their own packs, but Ka'el refused to release them. His brother was so afraid of what Ka'el would do next that he murdered him in his sleep. Because of the cowardly way that their alpha was killed, even if some agreed with it, his brother was eaten alive by many members of the pack as punishment. His kingdom fell and werewolves spread out among the world forgetting, maybe purposely, about Ka'el and the second shift."

"What else?" I ask.

Selene crosses her arms and tilts her head sideways in contemplation. I wonder if she's on the same track as I am.

"I think that Anubis was the reincarnation of Ka'el and I think that Namen knew that. That's why he wanted him," Zara says grimly. I know where she's going with this.

"Rayne thinks that Namen took his body to resurrect him but I thought he would just use it to host one of his demon followers. None of these scenarios are good," Selene says. It's stating the obvious, but stating it aloud seems to make it more real.

"Namen could be looking to resurrect Ka'el and not even Anubis. We don't know the extent of his necromancy power. His nickname of the soul stealer just got a whole new meaning. He could be asking the demons to go to the otherworld and steal souls for him. He has to be paying a heavy price. They want to walk in our world unbidden. If he can control the wolves, he will have an army like in the old world."

My mind goes in circles at how deep Namen really is in line with the demons, at least the low and medium level ones. He has had hundreds of years to plan this and his execution so far has been thorough. I don't know how the hell we are going to catch up. Our numbers are small. Sure, we're powerful, but there's no way we can do this alone. I have to convince the immortals to take up arms if we are to succeed. I need to contact them soon.

Fear washes over me. Selene and Zara both feel it. They turn, concerned with my response. Selene's eyes flash green with magic as if she's ready to protect me from the thing causing my fear, but she can't. Zara's eyes begin to dilate and bleed from the middle outward. She turns, her eyes begging me to relax, but I can't. I am afraid.

Namen knows it. He can feel it. This time, I feel him slowly and deliberately slip into my mind as if he wants me to know that he can. I don't even try to fight his invasion because right now, I know it'd be useless. I hear Selene's voice calling to me and my body hits the ground, vision going black as I transition into the pit of my mind.

"You're breaking. You are crumbling like I said that you would. This world is too much for you little girl. Shall I show you the death of your father this time?" Namen asks mockingly as he sends me images of my father tied to a chair, slumped over with his white button up bloodied and open, a hole in his chest.

"Please, no," I whisper, the image now seared into my memory, another one to haunt me on my sleepless nights.

"You are so much different from last time, you defiant little bitch," he mocks venomously. "Weaker. The weak link that I know you to be."

I feel a mental slap and I groan in frustration. It's all inside my head. I can fight this. Why am I not trying to? In a matter of moments, I've been reduced to a coward.

"I can bring them all back if you wish. They can be with you once you join me," he tells me patiently, almost lovingly empathetic.

He's referring to my family and the idea of them returning is too much of a lie.

"They'll be wrong, I know it. I've seen enough movies to know that you don't pull people

Alanna J. Faison   Killer Rayne

back from the afterlife, especially when they've been gone a long time. That wouldn't be love, that would be selfish and evil in its own way," I say quietly.

The quickness at which Namen felt my weakness makes me question whether he ever left my mind in the first place. It makes me wonder if he's left a piece of his own subconscious inside me so that it can be triggered at any time. This can't actually be Namen talking to me, just to me. I may be deemed important, but I can't be that special. This is a spell, a compulsion, and I can break it, I just have to think hard enough to figure it out.

"Why don't we play a little game?" Namen suggest, his cold gray eyes scanning me as if I am a science experiment.

"Let's not."

He ignores me and says, "I'm going to give you three weeks to plot against me, to strike, to do whatever you feel is necessary to take me down. My people will only defend themselves if they are attacked, but none of us will strike the first blow. However, once your three weeks are up, there will be no mercy."

I study him for a few moments without saying a word. He looks so serious that it's almost laughable.

"Why?" I mean, what is the point of this game. "How do I know you will keep your word?"

"Because I want you to realize once and for all that there is nothing that you can do to stop me. Once you figure it out for yourself, you can either give in or give up your life. My word is my oath. I shall not break it, Rayne Whitmore. Three weeks," he says before he disappears out of my mind.

Everything goes dark once again as if I am trapped in a void of emptiness.

Chapter Thirty

$\mathcal{M}$y brain begins to slowly bring me back to the land of the living as I hear the buzz of voices in the distance. There is a deep masculine voice speaking in the background along with a few murmurs. My eyes remain closed as I try to listen. I breathe in the scent of clean linen and perfume. This isn't my pillow and it doesn't feel like my bed. I force one eye open as I lie still.

There is a tiny crack in the door that allows just the tiniest hint of light to creep into the room. The bed creaks as I shift and then there's a little chuckle right next to me. I jump up to a sitting position, startled and now woozy from the sudden motion. The laugh is feminine and slightly louder now.

"What the hell," I mutter to Jun.

"Sleeping beauty is finally awake. Now I don't have to play guard dog anymore. I just couldn't bear to leave your side for a second so I layed in bed next to you. You should've sensed me," Jun chastises.

"You know, you are one sarcastic bitch," I grumble, checking my body for clothing.

"Oh, you like it, don't trip. Now, apparently you had a seizure or something. Foaming at the mouth, nose bleeding, and some more bad stuff. You scared the hell out of your crew. They thought that Namen guy fried your brain or something." She props herself up on her elbow and looks me in the eye. It's not a challenge, but I still give her a little stare and her eyes shine in amusement. She looks away with an over the top sigh. She should be an actress.

"They know you're up now. I can hear Jaxson telling them that he hears us talking. Before I escort you to them, I just want to tell you that I think your girlfriend really likes me. Plus she has all this power and I think that's pretty cool. That means I pass the test right?"

"What do you mean?"

"Come on. She has to be a good judge of character, you should trust her judgment."

I laugh. "She probably just likes your outfit. I'm sure you're too sarcastic for her liking."

"Oh, it's part of my charm and you know it. That vampire though, she's a bit scary. Her energy is crazy powerful. She better not try to bite me."

"Oh, Zara? She's harmless. You'll be cracking jokes with her in no time," I say as I wipe the rest of the sleep from my eyes. "How long was I out?"

"A few hours. Jaxson told me what you want me to do with you. You live a very exciting life don't you, Rayne," she observes.

"Yes, it's all fun and games."

"Until we murder a few people."

"Don't think of it as murder, think of it as outsourcing their souls to the afterlife."

She snorts at my comment. "Now that was funny, and bitchy."

"Trust and believe, I can do bitch better than anyone."

"I am sure you can," she winks.

I sit there for a second realizing that she just made my comment sexual. Yep. I think I like her just fine. Too bad Taryn isn't with us anymore. Something tells me that they'd be chilling and slamming shots like no other.

Taryn was a great fighter that was just following her alpha. She didn't deserve to die like that. Neither did those kids.

My mood shifts, catching Jun's attention. She puts a hand on my shoulder. "Jaxson also told me how they lost plenty of pack recently. He didn't give me too many details, but you have that same look on your face as he did when he was talking about them. I can't say that I've really had a pack or somewhere where I've felt that I belonged, but they all love you out there and frankly I'm a little jealous."

Her words shock me. Not what she says, but the look in her eyes as she says it. She's been running for a long time and wants a place to call home. Now, she may have a mate bond with Jaxson if they have time to explore it further. She also has a lot of emotional baggage that we don't have time to sort out. But, don't we all. Aren't I just as broken? Broken people seem to find each other one way or another. It makes me wonder what secrets Jaxson keeps to himself.

Selene, Zara, Jun, Jaxson, and I; we're all putting pieces of ourselves back together. We also all found each other through fate or chance or whatever you want to call it. I can't deny Jun a chance when Anubis gave me one just weeks ago.

"Don't be jealous. You'll find your place. If it's with us, you can say as many sarcastic comments as you want as we go for lunch on the weekends."

"I'm not like you guys. I have this power inside me that I can't use. It's like an explosion that may explode at the wrong time or on the wrong people."

"So you've built this wall. That's okay. Someone here may be able to help you. Everyone here is exceptional and can support you if you deserve it. But, you gotta let your guard down if you want us to do the same with you."

"You sure seem wise for a young thing."

"Ha. I've been through a lot in these twenty one years."

"I've been through a lot in these twenty nine years. Man, after twenty five, it goes so fast." She lies on her back and stares at the ceiling. She doesn't look much older than twenty five, but the werewolf genes are slowing her aging process down.

"I bet. Now, let's get up so we can get out of here and plan so that I can actually live to see twenty five plus."

"Sounds good, and, Rayne?" Jun pops up and stands in front of me.

"Huh?" I ask, stretching as I get up.

"I will deny this conversation under oath do you understand," she growls.

"Yes ma'am. I'll keep it between us. But, I am not above blackmail."

The wolf behind her eyes looks at me playfully. She snorts and walks away, switching and looking back at me just as I walk behind her.

"I wasn't looking," I say sternly.

She flicks her hair and rolls her eyes. "Rayne, everybody looks."

Then, we both laugh as she slips back behind that wall she's built. We walk down the hall to where Selene, Jaxson, Christopher, Phillip, and Zara are waiting. They all turn at once and I give them an awkward smile and wave.

"Your favorite human has decided to join the world of the conscious," Jun declares. "I think that she was disappointed to find that my face was the first one she saw. She just doesn't appreciate a good guard person."

"You went in there to take a nap," Jaxson busts her out.

"That was the cover story. Geeze, you keep it up Jaxson and I'll tell them all about how-,"

"Rayne, are you feeling better?" Jaxson asks, interrupting Jun. She crosses her arms with a fake pout and sits next to Christopher who looks extremely uncomfortable at their proximity in his fitted suit.

"I'm fine now. As you guessed, Namen invaded my mind again. It seems like it's getting worse, more painful. I think I have to get him out for real this time. Well, I don't think that it's really him; I think that it's a spell. Whatever it is, it's making my mind weaker."

"I've been looking into it, with the help of an immortal, I think I can break it," Selene says.

"I may not be able to practice magic, but I am familiar with plenty of spells. I could back you up too," Jun offers.

Selene smiles genuinely at her. "Thanks. I'd like that."

"If the immortals don't help you, we're going to my grandmother's. Your plan for the mayor will just have to wait," Zara tells me. She gives me a look that says that she'll drag me there unwillingly if I try to get out of it.

"I guess I'll have to convince them to help then, won't I."

"Should you be here for this?" Selene directs to Zara. "We still remember what happened last time with Diana."

"Oh, I'm going to stay. I'll be out of sight. Maybe."

"Zara," I warn.

"I'll behave."

"I've heard that one before." Selene gives her a pointed look.

"There's something else. Namen said that he's giving us three weeks to plot against him. He said they will only defend themselves if we attack, but will not retaliate or make any moves against us on their own," I tell them, watching each of their faces carefully. Someone's getting ready to call bullshit.

"Don't tell me that you believe him." It's Phillip that says it first. I didn't expect the quiet, knowledgeable wolf to speak at all.

"No, I can't say that I really do, but he said that he gives his oath."

"And why in the hell would he do that?" Jun speaks up.

"He said because he wants us to see the futility in going against him. We'll realize that we can't stop him," I relay.

"Yeah and that three little weeks isn't going to change shit. He's planning something or he wants to see what our move is going to be," Zara explains.

"So, do we believe him or not? Do we make a move or not?" Selene questions. I know that she's thinking of Santos. It would be the perfect time to try to rescue him or at least figure out what he may know. Namen can't know that we've figured out that Santos is being compelled.

"We need to be cautious. Rayne, can you tell us exactly everything that happened while you spoke with him? Word for word, every detail that you remember." Jaxson's in alpha mode.

Phillip leans forward to listen and Christopher stands up and begins to pace. I think it's more so to get away from Jun. She seems to really annoy him. I glance at Selene and she nods. Then, I take a deep breath and try to relay everything that I remember as best that I can. Sometimes I close my eyes and imagine the words floating past my eyes. When I get to the image of my father, I speak quickly to get through it. Zara comforts me through our bond and I continue.

Once I finish, Jaxson looks between all of us. Before he can speak, Zara steps into the middle of the room. She gathers her power and then pushes it outward enough for it to brush our skin in warning. It's obviously a reminder of her strength as she looks pointedly at Jaxson. She's going to tell him about Anubis and doesn't want him to flip out like he did on me when he discovered that I killed him.

"There's something you should know. It's another reason why we came here tonight and we

Alanna J. Faison   Killer Rayne

wanted to wait until Rayne woke up to tell you this. I have a story to tell you about your history and how it relates to Anubis."

"Go on," Jaxson steps forward, looking giant and menacing over Zara's small frame. Yet, size doesn't matter and we all know it.

"Have you ever heard of Ka'el, the King?"

◊◊◊

There was an argument once Zara finished her story. Punches were thrown between the wolves but Zara, Selene, and I managed to stay out of the physical part. Christopher accused Jun of knowing about Ka'el and Anubis and not saying anything. She yelled that the pack in the forest where she learned to control herself must have known something, but if she was told anything, she didn't remember. Phillip tried to calm everyone down but when Chris was in Jun's face, she kicked him in the nuts.

Chris crouched down and when Jun threw a punch, she ended up connecting with Jaxson's jaw as he bent down to help Chris move out of the way. His wolf came to the surface and he grabbed Jun's arm in anger. That earned him another punch in the face. Good for her. I think. Finally, Selene used the spell to create an invisible wall between everyone until they calmed down.

"You are all hurting and you all feel betrayed in some way or another. It's not your fault that you didn't know your history and even if Jun did know something, it's not like she came here as a spy. They sent her here because Anubis was a wolf with magic and he might be able to help her use her own power that's locked inside of her. She didn't know that he didn't even realize what it was that made him special. She didn't even know about the second shift or that he was dead," Selene reasons.

"I mean really though, you are all werewolves. You can smell a lie. She may be able to lie once, but multiple lies and to keep it up and still continue to lie to you without you even noticing, how unrealistic does that sound?" Zara asks, defending Jun and surprising her in the process.

However, Jun still eyes Zara warily. She's smarter than I realized. Her wolf is not too happy with being in the presence of a pure blood vampire. Her instincts are probably screaming for her to run far away, but she's trying to stand her ground.

"Unless you are too focused on wanting her to be lying that you're forgetting to even use the talents that you have." Zara cocks an eyebrow and leans against the doorframe as if she's bored with it all. Her arm is in a sling, but she still manages to look attractive and deadly. I'm glad that she had time to get her hair in a better ponytail and throw on clothes that hadn't been torn in a fight. Selene had to have helped.

"Pull it together," Selene simply says. Her outfit still looks good, but she's taken the heels off and is standing barefoot and comfortable. "What's important now is what we do with the information that we have. Do we accept that we really may have three weeks to not look over our shoulders and plan something solid, do we rest and train, do we find more allies, do we rescue Santos, or do we do nothing?"

"The time for the wolves to decide is almost up. We will know by the end of the week what allies we have there," Christopher says, sulking. He's unbuttoned the first three buttons of his dress shirt and taken off his suit jacket to have it hang on the couch. It reminds me of my father when he'd come home from a long day and I smile inside.

"I'm not counting on many vampires to be of any assistance. They will either stay neutral or work in the shadows to collect information so that we will remain unscathed no matter which side claims victory."

"And then, they'll just go with the flow, right?" I add sarcastically.

Zara looks at me in regret. "It is as you say. Longevity can sometimes make you a coward. I also still have my own that are watching and protecting. There will be no purebloods among Namen's faction at least."

Yeah, that is a big help. "But there will be genetically engineered vamps that are just as strong," I warn. Plus either Anubis or Ka'el and maybe even hundreds of unwilling wolves. "If he has Anubis and the plan is resurrection, teaching Anubis will be difficult. Ka'el already knows how to force the change on wolves and get them to submit. I see Ka'el or a demon controlling Anubis's body in our future. If Namen controls the wolves and they can shift twice, they can get into buildings, climb, and rip people apart before they know what hit them. We have to do something about that."

"You're right. Also, there are six large covens in the U.S. but they do a poor job of governing the witches. It is more so that if a witch seeks refuge or training, they will assist. If a witch is out of control, they may step in, but they often leave it to other awakeneds to handle. Many covens advocate nonviolence. They probably have known about Namen for hundreds of years but have been far too afraid to do anything. My other guess is that he's taken over more than one coven." Selene bites her lip in contemplation.

"Well, you are a high priestess. They will have to listen to you if you call for a conclave. I don't think a high priestess from America even exists," Jun speaks up. "I may be a werewolf, but I recognize you as my high priestess. I can feel your power calling to mine. There are small towns of witches all along the coast that will fight if you ask that of them."

"There will be no time to call a large conclave to order."

"There's a spell that will be a call to arms to any witch that has the power to listen. I know it well. It's earth magic and actually requires potion and a casting, but any type of witch can do it. It was created after the Salem Witch Trials just in case something of that magnitude ever happened again. My family still lived in Lebanon at the time, but when they moved to America, they discovered a town founded by some other witches that were immigrants or descendants of survivors of the Trials and created the spell just in case people came in and tried to slaughter them." She smiles at Selene, happy to contribute.

"I can teach it to you so you can use it at the right time," Jun says, becoming extremely helpful. I think it's because she's around another witch and is starting to feel like she has a purpose. High priestess. Her high priestess.

"Maybe that's why you're here too," I tell Jun. She turns to me in question. "Maybe you're here as a duty to help Selene. Maybe there are things that you can teach each other."

Jun looks at Selene hopeful, but quickly blinks it away, brown eyes replaced by the wolf. Coping mechanism. Building up walls because she doesn't want to deal with disappointment. But, one look at Selene's sparkling, green eyes and dazzling smile, she allows that wall to crack just a bit.

"I'll, I'll do what I can priestess," Jun assures her.

Selene's eyes reveal the markings of the high priestess only to those that have been awakened and know what to look for. Zara felt Selene's latent power deep inside of her when they first met. Namen also wants Selene for himself because of the power she'll possess with Santos. I think he wants us all. All of us are powerful enough to oppose him, but only if we work together. We have the power to change things forever. We have more power than we can imagine.

"So, Anubis is one priority. That means if we can't rescue him, we must kill him, again. If he is alive, if it's him and not Ka'el or a traveler, demon or whatever you want to call it, we may still have to stop him," Zara says. Jaxson grunts, but I don't know if it's in agreement or dissent.

"I need to try to call Diana," I add. "It's a long shot, but maybe if I beg enough, we can get their help with something, anything.

"I'm calling a pack meeting for the morning. I want you all there. Nine a.m. Phillip, make arrangements and have Rebecca help call people. She needs to pick up groceries for breakfast too. Tell her she's working to get back into my good graces." Jaxson looks at Christopher but he just shrugs, knowing not to argue about his girlfriend. Everything's a test when it comes to werewolves and pack rules.

I need to call Damien too and check in on him. I may need to go to headquarters soon and check on how the weapon situation is moving along. I also need to find out what the hacker has found out about the mayor's schedule. So much to do. Three weeks will definitely help if Namen keeps his word. I guess just because he's a murderer, kidnapper, thief, and crazy person, doesn't mean that he's a liar. He didn't lie to me about Santos. I push that to the back of my mind for processing later.

"If we can get to Anubis, we may be able to get to Santos. We need his strength either on our side or out of Namen's hands," Selene urges.

"First, we need to figure out where they are. I think that they have a glamour blocking the tracking of their location. They could be hiding in plain sight," Zara tells us.

"This is why we need humans on our side too. They can get innocent people out of the way

Alanna J. Faison   Killer Rayne

with a lies about gas leaks or something like that. We'll be able to fight more freely when we need to. We can use them to our advantage. We can get access to blueprints and suspicious activities," I explain.

They seem to contemplate this. I have to get to the mayor first. It will work. This can be our city. We can mold it, protect it, and then watch it grow. There can be an alliance here between all the major races. It can be done once we kill Namen.

"We're going to take our chances. Three weeks to make a dent in his plans. I don't trust Namen, but he knows that. He wants us to do nothing and wait," I say as I pull my rising dress down. "I'm going to go home and try to contact Diana there. I will see you all in the morning," I tell them.

"Fine. See you at nine. Don't be late," Jaxson says, rubbing a hand through his mohawk.

Selene waves at everyone and we head out the door. Zara trails behind us. It looks like we're dropping her off somewhere.

"Are you going to check on your babies?" I ask, referring to her four legged children.

"No, not tonight. They are at a doggie hotel for a few days. I have some things to do," Zara replies searching the area with her eyes as we walk to the car and Selene goes around to the front to drive.

I don't remember it being this cold when we left and I find myself shivering. "Where are you going then? You need to rest," I say gently.

"I'm going to be fine. Just drop me off downtown and then I'll see you in the morning," Zara says quietly. She's so secretive sometimes and I frown at her until she says, "What? I'm going to be fine. I'm not doing anything dangerous."

Selene watches our exchange as she leans on top of the car. "Zara, do you want to come home with us?"

Zara looks at Selene sideways as if trying to ascertain the meaning behind the question. I think she can tell that Selene's making more of an attempt than she probably would have because of me. Selene is genuinely a forgiving person, but Zara is still hesitant and it shows.

"I can't do that Selene, but thank you for your offer," Zara bows formally, slipping into diplomat mode. "You are too kind for words young priestess. Please, just drop me off downtown on third and that will suffice." Sometimes I forget when I look at Zara that she's far older than any of us. This time, her age shows.

Selene looks at me to see if I'm going to argue. When I open the passenger door and climb inside, she quietly does the same and starts the engine. I nudge on Zara's consciousness questioningly as Selene pulls off, but she keeps me locked out. After a couple more tries, I turn my attention to Selene and try to ignore the fact that there's something that Zara isn't saying.

Chapter Thirty One

I've been trying for over an hour to reach Diana. I've gone through everything multiple times. I've meditated, sliced my hand, forced my tattoo to glow, but nothing. My patience is slowly melting into irritation and worry. She should have answered by now. Cursing, I stand up and wipe off my lime green basketball shorts.

Selene fell asleep half an hour ago on the couch. I brush her cheek tenderly with my fingers to gently wake her so that she can get into the bed. Eyes still slightly closed, I lead her into the bedroom and tuck her in. With a kiss on her forehead, she turns to me and smiles sleepily.

"What did she say?" she asks in a whisper.

I whisper back, "She didn't answer my call. No one did." I slip into bed next to her, adjusting my memory foam pillow.

"Huh? That's weird. We'll try again tomorrow."

"Yeah, we have to get up in three hours. Go to sleep, love."

"'Kay. I love you," she mumbles, snuggling closer to me.

Alanna J. Faison   Killer Rayne

"I love you too," I tell her, wrapping an arm around her. Sleep comes easily despite my thoughts circling around on why there is no answer from the immortals. I need rest right now, even if it's for a few hours. Good thing that I had that nap thanks to Namen's invasion turning my brain to mush.

Sleep consists of dreams about me and Selene on a trip to Hawaii together. We jump off of small cliffs into the beautiful water before lazing out on the beach working on our tans. There is no danger, no duty. There's just us. When my alarm goes off to wake us, I feel a deep loss in my heart. It may have been a dream, but it felt like that's what we're supposed to be doing. Still, I'm grateful that despite what I've lost, I still get to wake up next to her. We get to fight by each other's side.

I turn the alarm off and roll onto my back, groaning as my drowsiness begs to take me back under. "I'm going to shower first, you sleep a little longer," I tell Selene as she yawns.

"Mmhmm."

After a twenty minute shower, I wake Selene up and begin to get dressed. Shortly, Selene and I are both clothed and ready to head to this pack meeting. Breakfast better be good. It doesn't take me too long to recover even when I don't get too many hours of sleep. Food does the trick just fine.

Alanna J. Faison   Killer Rayne

When I was training with Lawrence, he'd often make me fight until it was much too dark and then wake me up before dawn to fight again with no food and very little water. Sleep deprivation is another form of torture and he used that too. I trained almost every single day for at least four hours plus the time I studied with Diana. Listening to her yell at me when I didn't catch on to something was also another form of torture.

Still, even if they didn't train me to my potential as Zara had suspected, I wouldn't have gotten this far without them. I owe them more than I can repay and it really bothers me that I can't reach them. Frowning, I lean back in the car and text Damien while Selene drives as I try to take my mind off of my immortal teachers.

Heyyyyy, I text.

Hey urself, he responds shortly after.

How is it without me being present in the building?

Well, lol I think they rather keep u away. U scare them.

I can see Damien's smile as he texts me that. I'm sure he got a kick out of it when they were arguing about what to do with me. No formal business experience, very young, and volatile.

They should have been expecting it though. They knew my father.

I'm gonna come in today. We need to go over some things.

Aight. But don't take all day. I have something to help Tamara out with later.

I have things 2 do 2. I don't plan on taking all day.

Bet. Hit me up when ur on ur way so I can get there in time.

Sure thing.

I put the phone back in my jean pocket and watch the road zip by. Traffic is packed in some areas and it takes us a little longer to reach our destination. Selene parks on the street a little distance away from the house and even as I walk on the sidewalk, I can smell coffee and bacon. My mouth waters instantly. There'd better be some food left for us.

I don't even knock as I get to the front door, pushing it open as if I run the place. Inside, there's laughter that pauses as we step through the threshold, but it quickly picks back up once everyone sees who I am. Most ignore me, but some acknowledge me with a nod or a tilt of their head in submission. I smile at them all, even if they do not give me the same courtesy.

Alanna J. Faison   Killer Rayne

I find Jun sitting alone in a corner, chair pushed all the way to the wall. She holds up a plate in salute and I smile. Although, she seems uncomfortable, her body language shows that she's working to stay. The food has to be a plus. Selene and I both head to the kitchen and grab plates along with a couple other wolves. They both look at Selene and me before moving out of our way to let us get a plate first. Rebecca is standing in the pantry grabbing some more items, but when she sees us, she scowls and leaves the kitchen.

Ignoring her, I motion for the other two people that were ahead of me to get their plates first. They both show their gratitude and fill their plates quickly. I scan the counters and oven to find pancakes, biscuits, bacon, eggs, sausage, hash browns, chopped fruit, jelly, butter, syrup, juice, milk, and even cut up steaks. Damn werewolf metabolism. There's no way I'll be able to shovel down all that food. I'm definitely going to try though.

I fill my plate with bacon, eggs, pancakes, and fruit as I already plan for seconds. Selene gives me a look saying that my eyes are bigger than my stomach, but I don't care. I haven't had half of this food in forever. It's asking to be eaten. Who am I to deny the food its wish?

I pull a chair next to Jun but we eat in silence. She offers me a cup of grapefruit juice when she comes back from getting seconds of her own. I take it gratefully and allow the sour drink to wash down my food. Then, I go back for a biscuit, butter and jelly, and a tiny piece of steak. After I finish eating, I speak loudly, cutting across the other conversations.

"Rebecca, you made all this? It was excellent. Thank you for that."

"You're welcome," she says, surprised by my praise but smiling anyway. She's obviously a girl that takes pride in her cooking. I forgive her now for trying to attack me after Jaxson's fight. Food isn't just a way to a man's heart. Food and I, we're homies and lovers.

Zara walks in twenty minutes later, which makes her over thirty minutes late to the party. She's taken off the sling, but I can tell that her arm is still broken, even though it's nearly healed. Being in a sling and looking weak in front of all these wolves doesn't seem like a good idea. I hope that she doesn't stay long. I also wonder what the hell she did last night, but I won't pry.

I take Jun and Selene's plates as I make my way to the kitchen. There are two people washing dishes and I help for a few minutes, trying to speed the pace along. They sure know how to make as big a mess as possible and as I wipe counters, I admire their werewolf family. Even with all these people and different personalities, it works.

Jaxson's voice carries throughout the house as he calls everyone into the living room. I follow his voice and stand next to the doorway so that my back is against the wall but so that I still can see this room and the kitchen. The side conversations draw to a close as I breathe in the woodsy scent of the wolves. They smell like pine and rain. There is also another scent. Anxiety. Many have no clue why they've been called here.

My eyes scan the room as I look into the faces of the people gathered. Many will die. We have to make sure that many turns into few, but I don't know how that will end. This close to all the pack, I can feel the barest hint of pack bonds pulling at me. I wonder if it feels the same for those that are truly shifters. Pack magic feels wild and carefree. It makes me rock back and forth in excitement.

Jaxson first tells them the story of Ka'el as he heard it told by Zara. He looks to her to fill in any information that he may have left out, but she nods that he's doing just fine. Many of the wolves begin to speak in hushed tones before Jaxson silences them. In deference to their alpha, the talking ceases.

Jaxson then tells them about what Namen may be planning to do when he had Anubis's body stolen. The group stays silent, but their anger begins to boil over. I watch as Zara steps closer to the door and then cracks it slightly in order to release some of the were energy that is bouncing off of the walls. None of them look at me, but I can feel their blame upon me like an anvil. I hang my head low in shame, but Selene catches my eyes and forces me to hold my head back up high.

Next, Jaxson gives his pack members a reminder that staying with them can end in death. He gives them another chance to leave this town, to be released from the pack so that they can find a new life somewhere else. He also reminds them that if Namen succeeds, there may not be somewhere else. There are plenty of stares and unspoken words because of that. I can tell from where I'm at that a few will leave for good.

Last, Jaxson asks the pack to decide to take Jun as one of their own. Jun obviously didn't see this coming because she nearly spits out her drink. She looks around frantically, and then forces her face to be neutral. Everyone sees it though.

"That is, if that's what you want," Jaxson says. His voice remains neutral.

Jun looks around as she contemplates what it is that she really wants. As she studies them, they study her. This is a family but those that are chosen need to understand that pack is life. It isn't used for convenience. I would be the exception. Me being named second was a strategic move and a safety one for Jaxson. He needed someone that could fill that role in these dangerous times.

Jun looks at me, but I don't give her any push either way. This has to be her decision. If she wants to be pack, she has to play by the rules. She can't just up and leave. She has to respect her alpha who could one day be her mate. If she says yes, then she will have to really fight by our sides. It is a huge decision.

I think that Jaxson wanted her to make a decision that felt right in her gut. He put her on the spot so that she couldn't run away physically or dwell on it too long emotionally. He wanted to see the longing in her gaze as she watched all the people in the room. He wanted her to decide quickly.

"I think that I do," Jun replies.

Jaxson crosses his massive arms and waits.

"I know that I do. It's what I want," Jun responds again, more sure of herself. Her composure returns and she smiles at me.

"So, where do my people stand? Do you want to accept Jun as your own?"

Jun stands up at Jaxson's beckoning and comes to the middle of the room. She waits as Jaxson looks one by one at all of the pack and

Alanna J. Faison   Killer Rayne

takes their votes. There are about three no's but the rest are yes's. I give my vote of yes as well. Once everyone votes, Jaxson smiles widely and puts an arm around Jun's shoulder.

"It is done. Give me your hand," he orders. He smiles at her and waits for her to return his grin before shifting his fingers into claws in order to slice his palm and then hers. The flow of pack magic dances gleefully all around us as they merge their blood to solidify the pack bond. "Pack," he states as he did with me.

"Pack," she echoes.

"Pack." Everyone else responds. I can feel the difference of the bond with an actual wolf. The threads seem to wrap around her tighter than they did me. The invisible strings are recognizing Jun as their own. The bond is strong.

"Will we take in all whom wish to join us?" a voice asks from across the room.

"If they are worthy, then yes. I will allow another vote and then we will decide. I will make the final decision, but I want to trust my brother's and sister's judgment, as council," Jaxson says calmly.

"Even those that we barely know?" the voice asks again. I try to seek them out, but my view is blocked.

"If they come seeking shelter, a family, and they choose to fight, then yes. We will not deny them a place. From now on, we will be known as the Moon Reaper Pack. We will become powerful because our survival depends on it. Every werewolf will know the name and they will either beg to be one of us or they will respect us," Jaxson growls. His deep voice is laced with power and no one seems to even breathe as they weigh the weight of his words.

Surprisingly, it is Rebecca that steps up to speak next. "I trust you completely as the alpha and I am with you until the end, Jaxson. I've come to realize that I love this pack more than I could ever comprehend. I will do whatever it takes to earn your trust back and when the time comes, I want to fight the human for the title of second."

"Rebecca," Christopher begins, but Jaxson silences him with a hand.

"You do know that you have at least six people to either convince to submit or fight and win against before you're beta material. One of those people is your mate. Can you do that? Can you do what is necessary, even killing our young if they become out of control?" Jaxson inquires.

Rebecca glances in Christopher's direction, but quickly turns back to Jaxson. "I said whatever it takes," she replies firmly and passionately.

"I look forward to it."

There are murmurs in the group and all eyes are either on Chris or Rebecca. They refuse to look into each other's eyes, but there's tension there. Determination from Rebecca and irritation from Christopher. He knows that the stronger she gets, the more dangerous things will be for her. I wonder if he'll fight her and try to beat her just to keep her from being second.

"Rebecca," Zara says quietly, but still drawing the attention of everyone due to their werewolf hearing. Rebecca turns to Zara with a questioning look. "Don't lose." Zara grins at her and Rebecca stands there in surprise. Zara loves people that have fire inside of them, Rebecca being no exception.

"I won't," she finally replies after getting over the shock of Zara speaking to her in such a kindred manner. "Don't hold back when it's time either," Rebecca warns, the wolf slipping into place behind her eyes, illuminating them to a dark yellow. She's speaking to me and I return her stare with the respect of a warrior.

"I didn't plan to," I tell her.

She nods in approval. It will be a fight for honor. I owe her a great battle.

"Now that we've got someone that has finally shown the fire that I've been waiting on, I need everyone to push themselves to hone their individual skills. We need you to be faster, stronger, and smarter. I know this has been taking a toll on your bodies, but don't let it break you. We are the luna dasa, what we are seeking is already inside us. Anubis began a legacy that we will see completed. All of us will master the conversion. You must shift and you must meditate before and after. Bring your wolf into harmony with yourself. We are one entity." Jaxson paces between the crowd as they hang on to every word. He is a great leader, encouraging and firm.

"We were chosen for this. Us. Because the universe knows that everyone sitting in this room is powerful enough together to oppose someone who is willing to destroy everything. You don't say no to destiny. You rise up and you become more than destiny ever expected."

Selene smirks at the statement and nods in approval. His words are touching her as well. She stands up straighter and her resolve too seems to strengthen. I feel Zara press gently against my mind and I let her in.

The priestess is amazing. Her aura is beautiful. I feel her power rising inside. She has more inside of her than she even realizes. You both do.

It won't mean a thing if we don't figure out how to use it. We have time, but it's not the luxury of years that we need to master our skills, I say.

But you have all of us. Look around. This wolf in front of us speaks these words as he knows that he's not only going to lose some of his pack before the fighting begins, but they may die fighting against even more powerful beings. There is not one hint of fear in his voice or in his soul right now because there is no alternative for him. He doesn't fear death, Zara tells me, eyes on Jaxson, observing him move about the room, touching the shoulders of his family.

I don't fear death either. What I fear are the deaths of those that I love.

Then grow more powerful so that you can protect them always. But remember, as long as you love, you risk the heartache that goes along with it.

Her thoughts go to Sage and I don't know if she purposely allows me to see those memories, but I watch as Zara catches Sage as she leaps into her arms as she finds her after a walk in a field. Then, she embraces her tightly after she turns her into a vampire, crying from the pain of watching her human life slip away. Zara's heart turned bitter and she slaughtered many awakeneds after that, many vampires, those that betrayed her long before I was ever a thought. That rage still festers. It's an eruption waiting to happen regardless of how in control she likes to pretend that she is.

I slip out of her mind just as Jaxson finishes speaking. "The rest of the time is yours if no one has anything else to add." He looks around again and then grunts in dismissal. A couple people leave immediately, but most of them stay to converse.

I yawn as Selene strolls up to me and sits on my lap as I sit in an unoccupied chair. "So, are you ready for a nap or are you going to try the immortals again?" she asks, playing in my hair.

"I'll manage. I can try again. I want you to talk to Jun about her magic. Then, if they still haven't gotten back to me, we will know if I have to go to meet with Zahira, the master vampire that will probably compel me to slit my own throat for her to drink."

Zara snorts and rolls her eyes, clearly having heard me.

Selene looks over her shoulder and chuckles. "If anything, she'll probably compel you to run away screaming so that she can chase you like a game, before she slits your throat herself."

"Now, that sounds like my grandmother," Zara laughs again, eavesdropping on our conversation.

"Not helping. The thought is freaking me out for some reason," I pout.

"Aww, it'll be okay amor," Selene tells me, placing a kiss on my forehead.

"Okay, okay. I'm dragging it, I know. She can't be any worse than Diana when she's pissed off."

"Probably not," Selene laughs at our shared memories.

Once, I accidently sliced off some of Diana's hair with a throwing knife. I was playing around and aiming it at a wall when she came around the corner. It wasn't much, but Diana made it seem as if I'd given her a buzz cut.

Her booming voice damn near shook the house and she ripped me through reality and dropped me from a cliff before catching me at the last second. I damn near shit on myself with that one. Lawrence and Selene seemed to find that especially hilarious seeing that I wouldn't climb up on anything high for days and my legs wouldn't stop shaking. I even almost fell out of the bed and nearly had a heart attack.

That was just one of many of her tantrums. No one pissed her off like her brother Lawrence though. Although he'd take a terrible beating, it seems that he rather enjoyed it. I don't think that she is stronger than him, but she is most definitely crazier and quicker tempered. Diana could be a first class bitch at times, but I am grateful for her marking me so that I could be unmade.

"I'm going to go outside and see if I can contact Diana again. If I can't, we'll go to Zahira's tonight. I'll put off my plans for the mayor until later. I'm going by the headquarters today but after that, I want to do some day drinking."

"Day drinking?" Selene asks as she gets off of my lap. "When did you start saying day drinking?"

"I heard someone say it the other day. Let's do it," I say excitedly. I want to take some shots. "Jun, Zara, hey Rebecca, what do you say? Jaxson? Are you down for some day drinking?"

Zara shrugs. Rebecca lifts an eyebrow at my invitation. But, why not? She could come to like me. Jun gives me a thumbs up. Down for whatever. Eyes turn to Jaxson.

"I need some more testosterone with me if I go. Hey Chris, what time does your flight leave?"

"In three hours," he responds from across the room.

"Shit. Phillip? No, you don't drink. Rashad, Jake, Ethan?" Jaxson asks some of the remaining males.

Alanna J. Faison   Killer Rayne

"Sorry Jax, gotta work."

"Nah man, I don't know," one of the others responds. Jaxson puts his large arm around him and pulls him in close, he looks up into Jaxson's face before sighing in defeat. "Alright, alright man, me and Ethan will come."

"Ha. We're in," Jaxson grins at me.

"Day drinking it is, boys and girls."

Chapter Thirty Two

I head out back and wander out to the trees in the rear of the estate so that I can have a little bit of privacy as I try to contact Diana. One of the males had asked if I wanted him to watch my back while I was out there. I declined, but told him that I'd appreciate if he kept an ear out. It made me smile that he even offered at all. I should at least remember his name.

As I walk, I pull my hair back into a ponytail and allow some of my hair to fall in front of my eyes. I'm coloring my hair back to its normal color today. Maybe I should make it brown. I wish there was a spell to make it grow back out. I need some hair vitamins. Sigh. Rambling to myself.

I find a spot not too far away from the back of the house and I sit down, preparing myself to go through the motions of the summoning. I do everything correctly and for the second time, I get nothing. I wait again and I begin to wonder if my connection with the immortals is severed permanently or if Diana may be mad at me for allying with Zara. Their tumultuous past made Diana very upset that she was in my life and it definitely was not an accident on Zara's part that she got to know me.

Zara had once lived with and trusted the immortals until she and Sage realized that they had to protect the people here on this plane. Killing Blake became something that she's had to pay for every single day.

Diana lost a brother and I'm sure that st ngs deep when you had known him for lifetimes. I know a little about losing a sibling. Maybe Blake was a good person. I'll never know his side of the story. They'll never get their brother back and Zara will never get that time back with Sage. Everyone has lost something. I think that it's time to heal.

I do the summoning correctly, three times to no avail. It's been about forty minutes and I sense nothing. Fear begins to settle in my bones. What if something had happened? I realize how unlikely that is though. Something wouldn't have happened to all of them. Diana is just mad about something. She's just picking a shitty ass time to be acting like this. Our last encounter was pretty heated and she had invaded my mind without a second thought. I'm over it; she needs to be over it too.

Frustrated, I trek back to the house and find Selene still holding a conversation with Jun. Zara is in the corner speaking with the elder wolf and they both look up when I walk past. I shake my head to let Zara know that I had no luck and then I break the news to Selene. She frowns and twists her mouth in thought but doesn't say anything further.

Not really understanding the situation, Jun gives me a warm smile and says, "Selene does interior design huh. She needs to do something with all of this space. It needs some more life in here." She points at the plain walls and the entirely masculine air that the entire house gives off. "Then, she needs to decorate the apartment I'm purchasing. I get a couple months paid with the pack account as a show of goodwill and I want her to come with me to buy some furniture. Looks like I really am going to stay a while."

"Great to hear. If Selene is willing, then I'm all for it. It's been a while since she's been able to show off her skills," I respond, looking at Selene proudly. She made good money doing it too.

When everything went down with my family, she was already on a two week vacation so she didn't have to worry about her clients. She would have never gone on vacation with projects to finish. If she wants to start again, that's her decision. She knows that with me, she'll have all the money she ever needs.

"You guys are cute," Jun says, smiling at us. "I don't know too many real life lesbian couples and looking at you two together, I can understand why women find other women attractive. Plus, no one can deny that you two just seem to fit."

"It's not just about looks. You can't help what you feel or what type of person you're attracted to. Selene is a great person. Her personality alone makes her easy to love," I say.

"I can see that. You can't fight what's meant to be." Jun looks down the hall, presumably where Jaxson went. "I used to think that when two werewolves felt that mate bond that it was fake or forced. It's not like that, however. It seems to grow from whatever type of attraction you've already had and it tells you that this might be it, but it still lets you decide for yourself. Does that make sense?"

"As much sense as it can make. You already were attracted to men like him. It's not going to just push you with someone who is completely not your type and then say hey, this is what fate has decided," Selene tries to explain the way she understands.

"Yes. It's just so heightened and begging to be explored, but I can say no to it. It's hard to, but I'm not under a spell like I was afraid was going to happen. Plenty of people mate without ever feeling that pull."

"Good. It gives you the chance to actually get to know each other. That's a good thing right?" Selene asks gently.

Jun looks back again and speaks softly, "I think so. Damn, I hope so." She stares off into space longingly. When she was sent here, I'm sure this was nothing like she'd ever imagined. She hadn't planned on stepping into the middle of a war, to meet the man that could be her mate, to find a pack that is willing to accept her nature.

Some large cities are simply beacons for supernatural activity and ours is one of them. Because of that, shit can either really blow your mind at the possibilities or it can really hit the fan. There is plenty of power around the area and with Namen being the exception, all awakeneds seem to be civil toward each other. When the smoke clears, I wonder if they'll still feel the same way.

"Look, I have to get to work but I plan on meeting you all at the club for those drinks. Be prepared to get wasted. Bottles are on me," I tell them. Sure it's daytime, sure we probably really shouldn't do this, but I don't care. I want to sip and dance, dance and slam a few shots. Maybe I'll invite Damien and Tamara. Maybe I should ask Jaxson if that's a good idea.

"In that case, I want the most expensive thing at the bar," one of the male pack members says coming out of the kitchen.

"That's fine too. Just come thirsty," I tell him smiling. The tab is going to be outrageous with a bunch of werewolves but who the hell cares. I have plenty of money to spend and people around worth spending it on. This may be their last chance to enjoy something like this. They've lost a lot and if a few drinks will lift their spirits, then I'm down for the cause. "I just hope ya'll like to dance, because I plan on twerking all over everyone."

Everyone in the room laughs at my joke.

"Hey Jax! Come out here will you!" The other man calls.

"Hold up Ethan!" Jaxson calls back from down the hall. A couple minutes later, he comes around the corner carrying some hair clippers and a towel. "Somebody come cut my hair for me. I'm done with this mohawk."

"Aww, but you look so cute with it," Jun whines.

He smiles but still gives her a look. "And now I'll look cute with a haircut."

"I'll do it," the oldest wolf, Caleb says.

"Ah, but before you do, there's something I want to ask you about," I say to Jaxson.

He looks around the room and then back to me. "Is this something you need to ask me in private?"

"Um, not really. I just wanted to know how you felt about me inviting D and Tamara to come out to drink with us at the wolf club. If that's too much, we can go somewhere else."

Jaxson rubs his chin and the small goatee he's sporting. "If you want to invite your friends, maybe we should go somewhere else. I don't want the other people there being even more uncomfortable with humans in their midst. Not yet at least. Some are still deciding what they're going to do."

"I can accept that," I tell him. No one speaks up to disagree and I do understand where he's coming from. "There are plenty of other places to choose from."

"I know a place where we can still have a pretty good time and be ourselves for the most part," Zara says.

We all turn to her.

"It's called Rebel and as long as you have the password they don't care who you are, they'll let you in." She raises an eyebrow at us. "Or, are you afraid it's going to be some sleezy vamp whorehouse?"

"Oh no. I'm just imagining all the fun we're going to have," Jaxson says, grinning. He's looking more forward to this than he was letting on.

Zara pulls out her phone and texts with the speed of a rocket. A few seconds later, a ping comes in.

"So, what's the password?"
Alanna J. Faison   Killer Rayne

"Suicide."

"What the hell kind of password is that?"

"They name their passwords after the signature drink of the day. There's nothing sinister going on here. It's a bar that has a lot of supernaturals that come in, but the human crowd is bigger. The humans don't know that they are partying with us, and the supers just like to be around humans so that they feel like they belong somewhere," Zara explains.

"That sounds good enough for me. Let's all meet there around three. Zara, what's the address?" Selene asks.

Zara rattles off the address and a few directions before taking her own leave. It seems that her arm is pretty much healed or at the very least her mobility has returned. The wonders of being a vampire.

"Well, I've got to go," I say as I text Damien. "But, I can't wait to do this," I say excitedly. Selene smiles and puts a hand on my shoulder. "See you in a bit."

There's a chorus of byes as we head out the door. I mentally try on clothes for the office and then move on to an outfit for the bar. Going more places means that I can wear more things. Wearing more things means that I can shop for even more things. Yay! Selene watches my stupid grin paint my face but doesn't ask. She can't really understand my shopping addiction.

◊◊◊

After dropping Selene off, getting dressed, and heading to the office for an appearance, I try to spend my time getting to know my way around the place and the names of employees. I may not have gone to business school, but I did grow up learning the etiquette of being a great boss as well as how to deal with a certain type of business person.

I paid attention to the lessons that I was taught and I also listened in when my dad and Damien were talking about important business stuff while I sat by the door and pretended to do homework. Forget the homework; I passed all of my tests anyway. Right now, I just need to know enough to keep them in their place and for me to make sure nothing like what happened with my dad happens again with Namen around.

I ask questions and am legitimately interested in how things have been flowing. There's a lot that I have to learn but there seems to be a great team of people here that know just what they're doing. A well oiled machine, this is. My father built this.

But, he had help. He knew that he needed a strong group of like-minded individuals by his side.

Alanna J. Faison   Killer Rayne

I'm not so different. I have help too. I have a team that is down to ride until the very end. Loyalty is everything. Without loyalty, my father's empire would've crumbled long ago. Without loyalty, I won't even come close to winning. Namen's followers seem to be very loyal to him. Maybe it's fear. People often mistake the two when it comes to their motivations.

Damien agreed to come with us to the bar and said that he'd have to ask Tamara when she got out of her meeting. Our company bought hers, but she still gets to remain in leadership. She had to make a few financial and branding changes, but for the most part, her company has stayed the same. I'll have to look into where we can expand next.

On the way home, I spot a hair salon and decide that now's the time to get this hair colored back to my dark locks. When it's all said and done, I end up with some wavy clip-ins that give me back some of my original length. It didn't take long to complete once I flashed them a promise of a hundred dollar tip if I could do a walk in appointment. It also helped that I promised to pay for the lady who had the actual appointment too. She was grateful and in no big hurry.

I eye my hair in the mirror, styled and looking sexy, then head out with a new attitude. Long hair, don't care, bitches. I slide in the car and send Selene a selfie. Man, when's the last time that I did that? What a wonderfully normal feeling.

As I'm driving home, I slow down to stop at the light and glance to see that Selene's sent me lots of heart emojis and kissy faces. I send her some back and tell her *omw* so that she knows I'm headed straight to the house.

K, is her response as I set the phone down and focus on the road.

Looking into my rearview, I notice that a police officer is following closely behind me. I check my speedometer to find that I'm comfortably driving the speed limit. I keep checking the rearview and the car keeps getting closer. There are plenty of other cars on the road and I merge carefully in the right lane as I get closer to the exit for the interstate. The officer begins to get over as well, but suddenly veers back in the original lane and keeps going.

That was suspect. They better not be trying to mess with me because of Namen. They'll soon be in for a rude awakening. Forget about the police chief, I want that detective that questioned me. He's going to get it first. Maybe I'll still have Zara glamour the chief while Jun kidnaps the detective. Then, we'll all meet at the mayor's house for the party. That sounds even more promising. We'll talk about it later. I almost forgot to tell the hacker that we're not doing this tonight.

Alanna J. Faison   Killer Rayne

Once I hit the interstate, I speed home and pull into my garage. I allow myself a couple minutes to feel any intent that may be harmful. When I sense none, I get out of the car and walk inside. Selene is asleep in the bedroom and I lie behind her, pulling her into me. She fell asleep pretty fast. My baby's worn out and I don't blame her. Still, she is ready to do the next crazy thing with me with no complaint. She is the best.

There's about thirty minutes left to get to the bar and I'm almost willing to let Selene just stay home. She wouldn't be happy about it so I shake her gently. "Hey you, if you want to still come you have to get up."

"Okay. I'm getting up," she mumbles.

"I'm sorry I'm so impulsive. I know you need sleep," I tell her remorsefully.

"I'm okay really, Rayne," she says stretching and yawning. "I want to have a little fun with you too."

"It'll be just like old times."

"But, this time, you don't have to worry about trying to get on with me with any weak lines," Selene jokes as she combs her hair and pulls in into a ponytail.

"My weak lines got you, didn't they?"

Alanna J. Faison   Killer Rayne

"Nope, it was the money. I plan to drain you dry," she retorts.

"Ha. Good luck with that. You're in this too deep now."

"I'm a good actor. When I'm finished, I'll write a tell-all and get it made into a movie."

"You're cold blooded, you know that," I say, crossing my arms at her and pouting like I'm really hurt by her fake revelation. "You won't get a dime from me, you hear."

"Too late, I've already transferred all the money into my accounts and my real lover is waiting for me somewhere on a beach," Selene looks at me through the mirror with an all too straight face. She should be a poker champ.

"I will haunt the shit out of you," I warn her as I throw a shirt at her.

"Haunt?"

"Yeah, because the only way you're getting rid of me is if I die."

"Now you sound crazy," she smiles.

"Oh, but I am. My ghost head will be popping up at all the wrong times."

"Stop it," she laughs imagining it.

"You started it you asshole."

"As if I could ever do you that way."

I dig through the closet to find some booty hugging joggers and a belly shirt. Then, I put on some black sandals and spray on a little perfume.

"Damn," Selene says, looking at me through the mirror as I emerge.

"What?" I inquire smirking. Even though I already know the answer, I still love to hear it.

"Can I have your number?" she asks, licking her lips.

I spin around so that she can get a good look. "As if you could handle this."

"Baby, there's nothing about you I can't handle," she says, voice low, sincere. With a flick of her hand, my temperature rises just a little bit, her magic caressing me lovingly. We smile at each other as she gets up and closes the distance between us.

Hands wrapped around my waist, she kisses my neck, chin, and cheek. "I love you, Selene. I'm glad that you still look at me that way."

"Kiss me," she demands.

I waste no time crushing her lips against mine. Scooping me up so that my legs wrap around her waist, her soft hands caress my lower back and ass. I deepen the kiss as heat arches between us. Her green eyes are alight with power and dominance. I delight in the feel of her strength.

Her power balances out my own until I feel a surge of calm, of clarity, of truth. This is how it's meant to be. She's my kite string, my peace. It's like my power recognizes it in certainty for the first time and my tattoo glows so bright that it nearly burns. White hot energy rushes through all of my synapses as I gasp as my awareness of her becomes like a magnifying glass.

I need Selene more than I ever have and I won't be denied it for anything. I motion for her to put me down. The second my feet touch the floor, I rip her shirt from her body. She gasps in surprise, but my lips collide with hers once again. She unbuttons her own pants as I unsnap her bra. The panties, I rip away too. I know that she's probably going to be mad about it later, but I don't care. I'm going to take her, mark her, and love her harder than I ever have before.

"What about... the bar?" she asks, voice raspy with passion. My hands are all over her, touching wherever I feel skin. I breathe her in. Her sweet natural smell driving me even more wild.

"Fuck them. They can wait," I say as I nip her neck, licking and tasting the sensitive flesh. I push her to the bed and plan my seduction. My

349

eyes are hooded with desire and she meets my gaze with her own lust-filled one.

"Whatever you decide," she tells me shivering as I pull my shirt back over my head.

"I love you so damn much," I say to her as I dive in between her legs, tongue darting out to press against her wetness. The heat she's giving off makes me moan into her.

I grip her thighs and pull her into me. With a final look into her shimmering emerald eyes, I dive in, tongue exploring, fingers piercing. I wish that she could enter my mind so that she could see just how much I feel connected to her right now.

"Oh God, Rayne," she cries as her head falls back against the bed. Out of the corner of my eye, her hand claws at the sheets as the other one locks into my hair. "I love you too," she says, barely above a whisper.

Alanna J. Faison   Killer Rayne

Chapter Thirty Three

Jaxson gives us both a knowing smile as he waves us over to their seats. "You're late." He states the obvious as we were supposed to be here an hour ago. "Everyone thought they'd have to pay for their own drinks."

"I'm here, I'm here, buy the bar if you want," I say as I wave at the group.

Selene looks embarrassed as she holds my hand. Everyone knows why we're late. They just don't know that we spent a good ten extra minutes holding each other because we both felt the same sort of clarity about us. I almost didn't leave at all.

Your aura is glowing. It matches Selene's, Zara tells me through our bond. She holds up a tray of shots as she comes from the bar. Everyone grabs one and we all clink glasses.

It's glowing? Weird.

"We're really sorry," Selene apologizes, playing in her hair nervously.

"You don't have to apologize to us. It seems like it was worth it," Jun says.

"Yeah, I'll get over it. Your human and his girlfriend are ordering food for everyone. Pull up a seat guys," Jaxson says.

Selene and I grab seats and I look around the bar. It has two small bar areas on opposite sides of the room and a small dance floor in between. There's even a DJ here at this time of day which is pretty surprising. Then again, the place has a nice crowd. It's pretty clean with good lighting and the chairs spin so that you can get in and out of your seat easily. They're comfortable and I relax as I take in the atmosphere. A waiter comes over shortly to check on us and take more drink orders.

It seems that they've already been putting a few away, but werewolf metabolism will make it a long while before they are drunk. Lucky people. I give the man my card and tell him to bring three bottles of their choice to the table. He nods and asks around. After they agree on three, he leaves, returning shortly with bottles and chasers. Now, the party begins.

"To day drinking," I toast after everyone gets a drink and Damien returns. I side hug Tamara and D kisses me on my cheek.

Selene laughs as they return my toast. "To day drinking. Saúde."

Soon, six large pizzas arrive at our table and everyone cheers. I pour up some more before

Alanna J. Faison   Killer Rayne

352

grabbing a slice. There's a nice beat pumping through the speakers and I find myself rocking to it. Rebecca looks over at me, laughs and shakes her head. She looks prettier when she's relaxed. It seems like most of the tension that everyone had been feeling has been temporarily erased. That makes me happier and I grab another slice of cheesy goodness.

Soon, Jaxson and his boys are telling stories from their college days playing football and keeping their strength in check. They had to take a lot of hits for the sake of maintaining a sense of non-superhumaness. Their words not mine. Jake tells us about a hazing incident where all the towels in the locker room got pissed on by the veteran players. He could smell it and slipped out before all the others got slapped with pissy towels.

Now that's nasty. Men can be so gross sometimes.

Keeping the college stories going, Tamara tells a story about how she snuck into the men's locker room to get back at a coach that tried to hit on her at a party. She inserted a virus on his computer that played animal porn every time he clicked on something. Then, she left chicken feathers all around his office. It made the local paper in her town.

We all crack up at that one and I begin to really feel the buzz of the bottled elixir hit my

Alanna J. Faison   Killer Rayne

system. "Zara," I say, turning to her. "Give me a song. I need some music to dance to."

"Uh, let me think. There's a song called *I Don't Mind* you might like. Or, *Post To Be.* You know what; I'll give him a few. Let's go to the booth."

She pulls me up and I pull Selene up. "Come on guys, we have to dance," I say excitedly.

"Uh, I don't dance," Jaxson says. Figures.

"Well, I'm coming," says D. He grabs Tamara who finishes her fruity drink and sets it down.

"I have got to see you twerk," Jun tells me, hopping up and taking my arm from Zara.

"What about the rest of you?" I ask.

They all look at each other and then to Jaxson as if asking for permission.

"Oh, come on," Tamara demands.

"Fine," Ethan sighs and gets up.

"Turn up!" I yell.

Another group of people respond to my call with hoots and cheers. I blow them a kiss. Selene rolls her eyes and bumps me. The DJ looks at Zara and then the rest of our group and nods. He fades his current song out and begins to play something I've never heard with a smooth beat. I put my hands in the air and sway to the center of the dance floor.

I absolutely love to dance and I show it with every step. They all watch me for a few moments before joining me on the floor. Soon, the crowd gets bigger and I spin through the mass of bodies thoroughly enjoying myself. The beat fills me in a way that's almost rejuvenating and I laugh in delight as Selene slides behind me so that I can grind against her front. We put on a show for a while as a few songs switch. After a while, the dance floor thins back out and we head back to our table.

"Okay, wow. That was way too much fun. I really like hanging around with you," Tamara says. She's tipsy; I can tell by the way she falls back into the chair.

Rebecca, Jaxson, and Jake slam down two more shots after one another and I motion the waiter to bring more bottles. "We have to make this a regular thing," I say in agreement.

"I'll come, but you guys are going to make me into an alcoholic," D says, taking the last slice of pizza.

"You can handle one more, Damien. Don't be a quitter," Zara teases. Her poofy ponytail makes her look innocent despite the mischievous grin that she's sporting.

"Fine," he snaps. Picking up a shot glass and accepting her challenge. She raises an eyebrow in interest. "Let's do this, vampire."

"Oh, I want in on this," says Rebecca. Then, she looks at me. "Come on, Ms. Enforcer. Slam one with me."

"Fine. I'm down. But, now, every time one of us drinks the other has to." I glare at her, raising the stakes.

Jun laughs and grabs a shot glass of her own. "Oh, Ethan," she sings. "You want in?" She chooses him as her mate for this drinking game.

"Why the hell not," he says, shrugging.

I look over to Selene, but she raises her hands in defeat. "Hell to the no. I still have the metabolism of a human. I'm not trying to die from alcohol poisoning. No thank you."

"Pussy." I hear someone whisper and then we all snicker.

In revenge, Selene busts one of the shot glasses with her magic. We all jump back and she laughs. "Pussy who?"

"Okay, I'm in. Jake, are you going to let your alpha down?" Jaxson asks, sliding an extra shot glass his way.

"No sir," Jakes replies saluting. "Ready when you are."

I glare at Rebecca and she growls at me in response. Her straight dark hair falls over her eyes. "That sword hurt like a bitch," she tells me, referring to when I ran her through with Katsu.

"Well, you started it. I'm glad I didn't kill you. You're pretty fun to play with."

"Get used to it. I don't plan on going anywhere for a while," she warns.

"Good to know. Now," I start, raising my glass once more. "To us."

"To us."

The slam of shot glasses hitting the table echoes in my ears.

◊◊◊

"I told you to slow down, but nope, you have to be super stubborn. Now look at you," Selene chastises through the bathroom door.

I ignore her nagging as I hurl my guts out. Rebecca definitely won, the smug freaking werewolf. I can't out drink a werewolf. I get it. Now,

I'm paying the price and I do not need Selene's ass thinking it's just so funny.

"You know Selene, we might have to pump her stomach if this continues. I think she did it to get out of seeing Zahira. Maybe I should compel her to think that she's not sick." Zara makes her way to the door too.

"Go away!"

"Not on your life. You're not going to live this down," Zara says loudly. She and Selene laugh through the door.

"Rayne, let me rub your back," Selene says condescendingly.

"You two are ruthless," I mutter in between coughs. My poor stomach.

"Well, I'm going to help Selene with a few things while you stick your head in the toilet," Zara reveals.

"Call me if you need me," Selene says.

"Uh huh." This time, I almost miss the toilet.

After I clean myself up, I begin to feel slightly better once a lot of that alcohol is out of my system. It's about time for me to meet with Zara's vampire queen. The plan is for her to try to assist Selene with releasing Namen's hold on my mind.

Since Diana isn't responding to my call, it's going to take some compulsion with her magic to do so. Since it would probably be better if a healer assisted Selene because their magic is better tailored for this type of thing, it may not work.

Selene and Zara are both waiting at the front door for me. Selene nods and laughs at my face as I roll my eyes at her and the short vampire. I walk to Zara's new car, a white Ford Fusion. I know that she's still pissed about her Challenger, but I have a feeling that that wasn't the first time she's had a car totaled.

I stand by the back seat, allowing Selene, the turncoat, to ride up front so that they can continue to make fun of me in peace. Zara unlocks the car and we all get in. She makes a show of buckling up, just for me before starting the car.

"Baby, are you still pouting?" Selene asks, turning to face me.

"No. I'm fine now. I'm not trippin."

"Are you really okay?" Selene asks, as we pull off.

"I really am. Thanks," I say honestly.

"That's good baby, because you've got to know your limits. That was not sexy."

"Ugh. I know Selene."

She smiles at me. "Zara brought you a barf bag."

Zara laughs, speeding up and weaving through traffic. "It's in the seat pocket. You know, just in case."

"I can't believe that you're getting so much pleasure from my pain. You guys ain't shit." I turn to look out the window, irritated at how they're double teaming me. They can bond all they want, but not over my post drinking issues.

"Aw, Rayne. I love you. Don't be like that."

"I know stuff about you too, remember," I warn. Not that I can come up with anything right now, but she doesn't need to know that.

"Like what?" Zara asks curious about what stories I could share about Selene.

"Yes, please tell me what you could possibly have on me," Selene says, testing my words.

"Oh, just wait. When you least expect it, I'll bring that time up," I reply mysteriously.

"You're full of it, but I love you, so I'll leave you alone," Selene tells me.

"You'd better."

"So, we've got an hour drive. You guys want to hear me sing?" Zara asks.

"Sing? You? Sure, why not."

It turns out that the vampire has the voice of an angel. Well, you learn something new every day. Selene's voice isn't so bad either and they enjoy their duets throughout the ride. I just spend my time enjoying the view and clutching my seatbelt at her moronic driving. I have to mentally prepare myself to meet Zahira.

Damn vampires.

Chapter Thirty Four

Zahira's home is a white, contemporary style, Mediterranean home. Its smooth brick design with a paved driveway covers the ground all the way up to the door. Large windows add elegance but are so dark that you can't peer inside. A rounded roof and columns add to the beauty of the home. The landscaping is well maintained. I can tell even from the dark. I just know that she has a large pool in the backyard. Very opulent is the entire set up. I'm impressed.

"Well, here we are. This is where I spent a lot of my last thirty years. This is probably the best home I've ever had," Zara tells us, turning off the car.

"It's very nice," Selene says, looking on at the beautiful piece of architecture.

"Thanks. Now, remember, my grandmother isn't like me. She can and will be ruthless if you give her a reason to feel threatened. She's very old and her sense of humanity doesn't really exist that often. Still, she loves me and she'll go above and beyond to make me happy. Just don't let your guard down around her the way you do me," Zara warns us before we step to the door.

I pull at my black leather jacket as a sudden chill creeps over me. It takes a second for me to realize it's the energy of a dozen vampires, mostly powerful, under the same roof. Selene notices it too and slides closer to me.

"No one will touch you while I'm around. They wouldn't dare piss me off," Zara promises.

"Good to know," I say. I let go of my jacket. Then, I allow myself to calm down as the door is opened and we step inside.

"Princess," a male vampire bows low in deference to Zara. A group of other vampires line the hall, bowing with their arm across their chest.

She touches the shoulder of the man who spoke and continues on. No one dare lift their head until she is completely past. The hallway is dark and whatever light there is, is extremely dim. It creates a vampire-like atmosphere that I already expected. I can sense more of the vampires in the house, but no others make their presence known. They seem to have removed themselves once Zara came into the house.

We move so quickly through the house that I don't get to check out all of the rooms, but I can tell that many of the things around are extremely old and very expensive. Zahira must be a collector. The open floor plan lends to the feel of vastness and gives you room to admire the art. If you had time to stop and look.

We make our way around one corner and then another. There, we walk down another hallway where the temperature drops even more. I finally become aware of Zara's grandmother as she touches my aura lightly with her own power. It's not invading, simply curious and a look at Selene tells me that she's doing the same with her. Inside the room that we're heading into, I hear some type of classical music playing low.

I step through a thick, gold trimmed door into darkness after Zara. The music stops. Vampire essence washes over me as it attempts to drown me, no longer just a slight touch on my aura. Zara's grandmother is unquestionably powerful and old. Zara takes two steps forward and then crouches into a bow, one knee touching the ground, head down, and one hand touching the floor.

Unsure, Selene and I stop in our tracks and wait.

"My blade runs crimson, bleeding into the shadows," a soft voice states. It is the source of power coursing through the house.

"I am your blade, to yield as you see fit grandmother," Zara responds softly.

Her submission startles me. I would think that for someone as powerful as she, there would be a hint of animosity, but there is none. In fact, there is nothing. No joy, no anger. She is empty, like a weapon. A tool. Exactly what I never want to be. I guess after hundreds of years, you get used to it.

Her grandmother is next to Zara in an instant. Both of us jump back, unprepared for the movement. She ignores us as she pulls Zara up into an embrace. That is the only semblance of humanity inside of the older vampire. Her movements are inhuman, and her eyes burn an endless pool of blood.

I don't know what I expected, but she absolutely is not it. Her frame is only about an inch taller than Zara's, but they could pass for sisters. Like Zara, she looks to be about twenty three years old with shoulder length dark hair and full lips. Her body is covered in shiny jewels, her feet bare, toes painted with white tips. She's sporting a form fitting dress. She looks like an African queen of old, the ones that I read about when the motherland was in its glory days.

Besides all that, she's totally scary. I can't pinpoint just what it is, but it's unnerving and I know that my instincts were right to be wary in the first place. There's a monster sleeping underneath this beautiful skin and nobody can convince me otherwise. I don't want to stay here longer than necessary.

I swallow hard, forcing my heart beat to remain even. She catches it anyway since vampires are in tune with heartbeats, and smirks like a hungry crocodile.

"I've never understood why my grandchild prefers the company of humans so much, but at least they always make things much more interesting," she says, attention on me.

"Grandmother, this is Selene Marquez. She is the high priestess that I was telling you about."

"Oh, so you are the daughter of Luiz Marquez."

"You know my father?" Selene asks, surprised and uncomfortable.

"When you were young, he tried to move in on vampire territory in that area, Manaus, I believe is where you're from. He thought with the coming of age of the high priestess that he'd be strong enough to push us out. The nine has been keeping an eye on him ever since." Zahira studies Selene carefully and then dismisses her as if she can't believe that her father thought she'd be a threat to the vampires in that region.

"I'm surprised that you remember," Selene responds.

"I make it a point to know all potential threats. The nine have survived as long as we have because we never forget. You'd do well to use that advice if you want to live a long life too," she says cryptically.

"Now, grandmother, this is Rayne. Signum Immortales."

Something about the immortals.

"Ah. I also feel your blood inside of her." She ushers us deeper into the room and into seats so soft that I feel that I'm being swallowed. "Have you given up on the girl then?"

"Never," Zara answers, voice low.

"I just don't understand. She will be the ruin of you."

"Zahira, please," Zara begs.

She ignores Zara and again looks at me. The same vampire from the front door brings in a tray of drinks. Two of them contain blood, the other two wine. It's the last thing I need, but I accept it while ignoring Selene and Zara's looks.

"You don't even know the power you possess. You fear it," she says to me. Her red eyes pierce my own hazel orbs.

"That is not true. I do not fear strength." I set the drink down.

"You fear failure. Therefore, you fear your strength. You are but an infant. Children fear the dark," she chastises.

"Say you're right. Can you blame me for being afraid? This entire world is changing and we are supposed to be the wind that chooses the course. That is a lot of pressure," I admit.

"The world spins every second. Change is a constant reminder that we live. If you want to keep living, you must consume that fear with the flames of your power. That is why you have the problem that you have now. You allowed the witch's power to take hold of the fear that you possess and you trigger him inside of your mind without even realizing it," Zahira explains.

"What else can you tell us?" Selene asks as I contemplate her words.

Her grandmother looks at Selene and then Zara, an unspoken conversation taking place between them. Zara remains firm as Zahira tests her resolve.

"Zara promised us help," Selene tells the older vampire. I beam inside. She looks like a true high priestess as she returns with her own steely gaze.

Zahira's legs are crossed and she sits up in her chair as if it is a throne. The only thing that would make her look more queen-like is if she was a few steps above us with a crown on her head. I thought that my mom was high maintenance. She probably has servants that allow her to use them as foot rests while she drinks from the vein of the pool boy.

"Yes, grandmother, they are powerful. They may become our enemies one day, but today is not that day. We need their power if we are to survive. I will not serve anyone but my family. I will not kneel to him," Zara growls.

"Apollo will not be pleased that you are spending so much time teaching and protecting them," her grandmother warns as she studies her face. She sips the red liquid and licks her lips in appreciation.

1965 virgin blood kept preserved by the best witches money has to offer. I'm sure she really has a bottle of that somewhere.

"I can deal with Apollo. He is practical when it comes to these things."

"Fine. You are the one that chose to yield control to him. You will be punished for this."

Why would she be punished? What is really going on? I know that it isn't my place to ask, but it's really hard biting my tongue. I have to trust that Zara knows what she's doing and she doesn't need me opening my mouth to try and save her.

"That, I accept, as always," Zara replies. Her voice is emotionless.

"Why do you fear him so?" Zahira asks, leaning forward. "He may have more power, but his mind is weak. You surround yourself with powerful allies and he with slaves. You used to want what you have freely given him."

"It is not mine to claim, Zahira, please!" Zara yells. The emotion that was erased just seconds ago flares to life instantly. I feel her sorrow through our bond. "I do not wish to continue this conversation. Please, let us help Rayne."

Her grandmother pouts, an awkward sight with her lava filled eyes. "Fine. This will be on you then, child. Let us go into the library."

We all leave the room and trek downstairs to another dark room. Figures. Mercifully, motion lights click on. This one is filled with the smell of old books. We take our seats among the literature as Selene scans the cases in awe.

"Before the library of Alexandria was destroyed, my grandfather was able to save some of the texts that were hidden in a secret room. A seer had warned him that they would be important and he spent months sneaking out as many documents as he could. The nine possesses more knowledge than any other race. Remember that well," her grandmother tells us proudly. No wonder Zara seems to always know so much.

That was around 332 BC and people don't actually agree how the library was actually destroyed. Wow. That certainly puts in perspective how old these vampires are. I wonder how old the oldest vampire is.

"May I?" Selene asks.

"If you give your word that you will not reveal this to anyone," Zara responds.

"On my honor," Selene replies and Zara nods.

We all patiently sit in silence as Selene picks up document after document and skims through it the way a teenager does the latest gossip magazine. She is truly in her element right now and I'm happy for her. She's always prided herself on her knowledge of supernatural history and now she gets to touch pieces that she didn't even know existed.

As she's skimming, Zara and her grandmother begin to have a conversation in French. They talk and laugh occasionally, clearly not wanting us to know what they're talking about. I think they just want to show off their expertise at speaking another language. Good for them.

"You would love to spend time with Zara's eldest brother, Dante. He is truly a scholar among scholars." Zahira addresses Selene with suspicious kindness.

"Maybe one day I'll have the pleasure of meeting him." Selene eyes her warily. She notices it too.

"I've never tasted the blood of a high priestess before."

"And you won't today either. Please, these are my friends. Stop trying to cause mischief."

"You've gotten too soft. When is the last time that you've had a good hunt?" Her inquiry stirs some emotions inside Zara. I feel her fighting the thought.

"You take blood from those that are willing, but when was the last time that someone begged you to stop before they begged you to take it all?"

Zara's fangs protrude as her grandmother forces her aura on her.

"Stop trying to make me lose control. I am fine."

"I just worry about you. You sometimes forget who you are."

"As if you'd ever let me forget," Zara snaps and Zahira laughs.

"My favorite granddaughter. I love you more than you'll ever know. I just want you to enjoy life. Between you playing with the humans and brooding over the loss of your mate, I have to make sure that you know when it's time to move on and come back to reality."

"I will get her back and I like who I am now. Just be happy for me. This is who I am," Zara tries to explain.

"And I want a great grandchild."

"Grandmother!"

I chuckle despite myself. She may be a vampire, but with that, she just reminded me of plenty of other families. Their worries may be slightly different, but they love each other all the same. It makes me a little jealous. I don't have that anymore.

"Fine. For now, I will leave you be. Priestess, as you search those documents, why don't you tell me why you haven't claimed your birthright."

"I guess I can tell you the story since you've been kind enough to allow me to have access to this." Selene smiles.

I sit back as I wait for her story.

"I was the first born of twins. Witchborn twins that were birthed in a great storm. The storm is said to have been called upon by our magic. As the prophesy goes, that first twin will gain the power to call on the magic of the second twin. Santos was treated as a tool and second class citizen by my father because of that. He was told that his life belonged only to me."

Selene comes to sit down as she tells the rest of the story. She looks to me for hope that I understand her relationship with Santos and the burden of her power little better. I sit quietly and wait.

"Santos was forced to learn to fight so that he would always be able to protect me and so that I would have even more power when I ripped it through him. If he wasn't strong enough, I could kill him by taking too much of his chakra. Santos and I both rejected that notion. I didn't want to use my little brother. I love him. When he made a mistake, he was beaten. I tried to protect him as much as I could, but we often didn't train together and I wasn't around."

I give her a sad smile. I do understand the love of a sibling.

"Because my father pushed him so much, Santos finally snapped. He planned for us to run away together a month before we turned eighteen. I was supposed to claim my birthright. He would essentially have been a slave in his own eyes. So, he resented me on some level. Without him, I'd still be a high priestess because of the circumstances of my birth, my green eyes possessing the pattern that only some awakeneds can read. But without Santos, I don't have my true power. The night we were going to run away together, the plan broke down and I allowed myself to be caught so that he could run and lead a normal life."

"How noble of you," Zahira comments.

Selene shrugs her shoulders as if saying that it was only the right thing to do. To her, I'm sure it was.

"He ended up crashing the car when he was running from my father's guards. An innocent driver was killed and I was unable to go many places without heavy guard after that. I hadn't seen Santos since."

"And now, Namen has him and he wants you too," I say, shaking my head. "In terms of strength or magical power, you may be the most important to him. Even if he uses Ka'el or Anubis to force the werewolves to change or submit, he can't force all of their loyalty. He can however, use Santos against you."

"He can try. The very thing my brother fought against was being used as a tool. I will save him from that fate. No matter what it takes." Selene's voice is full of cold resolve.

"You do understand what you're saying, right? You don't even know to what extent he's being controlled, or why," I say.

Selene gives me a death stare and I leave it alone.

"That's interesting. Do you think you have the focus to help me delve inside Rayne's mind without causing damage?" Zahira asks. She stands up, walks up to me and brushes a cold hand against my cheek.

I don't move, even though I want to. I think that's the reaction that she expects.

"I've been working on something. I can do it," Selene assures her.

"Good." She snaps her fingers and about twenty seconds later, a vampire flashes to her side with another glass of dark red brew. She downs it like a trooper. "Let us not delay."

"Thank you Zahira," I say honestly.

Alanna J. Faison   Killer Rayne

She pulls me up by my jacket, fangs gleaming with left over blood. "Don't thank me just yet."

◊◊◊

Zara holds me down by the arms as I lie on the table. Selene takes my blood from the tiny bite that Zara makes on my neck. Zahira takes some as well, tasting it with pleasure. Ugh. Selene marks my forehead with it and then my palms. I have no clue what she's doing, but I trust her.

"I don't know how deep Namen's compulsion runs, so you're going to have to remain still. It's going to hurt. I'm going to get inside of your mind and then allow the magic to guide Zahira where she needs to go. You have to let her or it won't work. Chances are Namen will see what we're doing and try to stop it. He may show you things that will break your will. Don't let it," Selene warns me. She's concerned, but I try to give her a look of reassurance. I can do this.

"Come on love. It'll be just like a brain freeze," I joke.

Zara snorts and shakes her head. "Open our bond. It'll make it easier. Good. Now, close your eyes."

I close my eyes, but just as quickly, they snap open as I scream from the pain. Zara grips me tighter as Selene works her spell. I beg her to stop as I feel Namen's magic inside of me fighting off the invasion. It feels as if I was thrown into a fiery volcano as my brain heats up to temperatures that are not possible. I know that it's not real, but when it feels this real, you can't help but think that you're dying.

"Selene can't stop. You have to let her in. Once you do, the pain will stop," Zara coaxes me.

I'm aware of Zahira waiting patiently to enter my mind as Selene tears at the gates of my sanity, but I can't let her in if this feeling will get worse. I won't survive it.

"You won't survive Namen breaking you from the inside. Let her in, Rayne," Zara orders. "I'm going to compel her. This isn't working."

She forces my eyes open and speaks some words to me, but I can't remember just what it is. A second later, I'm standing at a window overlooking the ocean. The view is beautiful and I want to leave the room so that I can walk to the shore and put my feet in the water. But, I think I have to stay here. I have to watch for something. If I move, I'll miss it.

There's a flash of light and then I'm chained to the wall of a dark room. The chains eat into my skin. I pull on them in panic. Another flash. I'm standing on the diving board for the first time, my friends all encouraging me to jump. The images flash before me as if I'm skimming the channels. It's too fast for me to keep up, but since they're my own memories, I recognize them anyway.

Reality snaps back into place and I watch in my own mind as the older vampire searches for something. She seems to find it but is knocked back and I'm completely powerless to assist her. Zahira growls and attacks as I am pushed deeper into my mind and away from the action. Here, there is only darkness.

Chapter Thirty Five

I am awakened by a bright light. No, that's not true. The darkness of my mind that was threatening to swallow me has been pushed back by a bright light. I can't explain it, except to compare it to staring directly at the sun and unable to turn away, to blink, or anything. It's a painful experience and I know that I'm not completely conscious yet. Perhaps Zahira has done more damage than Namen had.

Maybe I'll be forever broken.

"Don't think like that," a painfully familiar voice tells me. Yet, for some reason, I can't quite remember who it is.

"I know you," I say, reaching into the darkness, searching.

"You do. But, I am breaking the rules here with the help of a friend and because of that, I have to make sure that you don't completely remember. You won't even recall this conversation when this is done," the voice explains.

I grow frustrated. "Then what is the point?"

"Because I love you so much and even if it's just a little bit, I want to help you. For you, I'll always break the rules."

Alanna J. Faison   Killer Rayne

There's searing pain and longing in my soul from those words. That voice, why can't I remember?

"You are not broken, Rayne. You may not be whole, but you are definitely not broken. I am so proud of you for trying so hard to remain strong, for not giving in. I need you to know that. Now, I need you to listen carefully because even though you won't remember what I'm going to say, somewhere, instinctually, you'll understand when the time comes."

"I'll listen," I say.

"I don't think that I'll ever be able to do this again," the voice says, filled with sorrow. Again, my heart aches. "Namen Young has a very large weakness. There are others that will seek to exploit this for their own gain. Where I'm at, things are… never mind. I'm forbidden to speak on it. Rayne, you must remember who you are. Never forget. Now, listen."

I do as I am told.

◊◊◊

The man in front of me has a sword to my throat. The sharp blade digs into my neck and draws blood. The pain feels real and it takes me a second to realize that this is not me; I'm an invisible bystander inside of Namen's mind.

Who knows how long ago this memory is from. There isn't enough for me to go on to guess and I was never really good at history. So, I simply watch and wait. The memory seems to flicker in and out as if it is simply bad TV reception. Slowly, it clears again.

"You refused my order, Namen. No one refuses me," the big blonde man with the sword says. His European accent is filled with rage.

"We promised those people relief. We cannot just break the treaty on a whim. I will not kill those people, brother. I will die before you make me," Namen warns.

"If that is your wish," his brother responds before pulling his sword away from Namen's throat. With a smooth motion, the big man chants and spells his sword with a touch to the blade.

The steel glows and he swings just as Namen pulls out his own sword, ready to battle his brother. Then, the memory cuts to Namen standing over his brother's body. He howls in pain at his own actions even as he clutches the sword in one hand and bends down to rock his brother's broken body back and forth.

The memory fades again to Namen walking into a village, blood still staining his clothes from the murder of his brother. Inside the town square, villagers are waiting for him, eyes glowing in hate, arrows pointed at his chest. He hesitates, fearful.

"Witch!" they cry. The chorus of voices growing ever louder.

He tries to escape, but one shoots an arrow through his leg, dropping him. Hands grab and beat him.

"I saved your lives," he screams. "I killed my brother to save you!"

They gag him.

He is pulled into the middle of the square where numerous people take turns, kicking, punching, and spitting on him. Even as a memory, the pain as well as his fear overwhelms me. *I don't want to die. I'll do anything. Lord, please don't let them take me,* he begs.

However, it isn't the heavenly divine that answers his plea. A dark spirit takes over Namen's consciousness. Demon. The sinister energy can still be felt through this memory and I shiver. I swear that I feel the demon laugh at my own wariness as if he's cutting through time itself.

Hopefully, I just imagined that.

His attention is now on Namen, the rest of the world put on pause as he brokers a deal with the young witch. "Do you want to live or are you ready to travel through the world of the dead?" The voice is everywhere and nowhere.

"I'm not ready, I'll do anything. There are still some things that I must do," he cries, gray eyes overflowing with tears as he remains restrained

"I can free you, if that is your wish."

He knows that you never make a deal with a demon. He just killed his own brother to ensure his survival. There is no telling how far he'll go; even if that means that he will have to go against everything that he believes in.

But, for what? What is Namen's mission? It is the piece that I'm missing.

"Help me," he pleads.

The demon wraps tighter around his soul, tasting him, contemplating, and then laughing. "It will be done."

There's an explosion of light that knocks Namen off of his feet. When he rises some time later, the stench of hundreds of dead, decaying bodies fills the air. Namen looks about in horror as every man, woman, and child in sight is dead and mutilated. He vomits over and over again, realizing that his plea to be freed is the cause of this massacre. The demon took his payment.

Alanna J. Faison   Killer Rayne

"I take it back!" he calls as loudly as he can, falling to his knees, defeated. "Take me. I cannot have this on my conscience."

He looks out into the distance, angry ghosts are standing over their bodies, their attention turned to him. As a necromancer, he can commune with the dead and with that much death, his powers are heightened. They assault him all at once, screaming, slipping through him, pushing his sanity to the limit.

Namen falls to the ground, hands covering his ears, eyes closed as he begs for the demon to take it back. Yet, the demon never does. Instead, he just chuckles and pulls Namen through a void and back to reality, to his home. Once Namen realizes where he's at, he bursts through the door, calling out for a woman.

"Helen! Helen, where are you!" he calls. There is no answer. "Amelia!" he calls again.

"Namen runs into a room that holds a crib. He rushes up to it so fast that he doesn't even realize that he's stumbled over a body. Falling to the floor, he ends up face to face with a woman. On her forehead is the word 'witch' carved. Blood trickles from her mouth as her dead eyes stare at him.

Before he allows himself to process this loss, Namen is up again, searching the crib. He finds nothing and he lets out the saddest sound of despair I've ever heard. Then, he's running about the house, searching, pleading with himself, calling out to the demon to help, to no avail.

The humans, he thinks. *They did this. They stole my daughter. They killed my wife. I protected them. I murdered my brother for them.* Hate grows in his heart. More determined, he calls for the demon once more. This time, he gets a response and an unexpected surprise.

◊◊◊

I am ripped away from the memory as I regain consciousness. There is no more darkness, no more bright lights, no more flickering memories. Selene is standing next to me, holding my hand and Zara has her grandmother, unconscious in her arms. I guess it worked. I groan as I turn. A migraine sets in immediately. It's to be expected I guess.

"I was inside Namen's memories. I was learning about him. I got pulled away too soon. There was something that I was supposed to see," I tell them as I ignore the tiny jackhammer in my brain.

"We can't send you back. Zahira already broke the compulsion," Selene explains.

I try to sit up as a wave of nausea hits me. Somehow, I'm able to force it back down. "Is she going to be okay, Zara?" I ask. I hope that her helping me didn't cause any permanent damage to her own psyche. Even if she is scary as hell, she's Zara's family.

Zara lays her gently on the couch. "She'll be fine. It was just exhausting." She turns to us and frowns before flashing over to Selene and catching her as she is hit with a dizzy spell.

Zara guides her to a chair and I get up to go to her side. Selene has been working herself far too much lately and I haven't been taking care of her the way I should. I immediately feel guilty.

"I'm sorry Selene. You've been having to push yourself too much," I say regretfully as I squeeze her hand.

She smiles at me and replies, "I can handle more than you think; just give me a few moments to rest, amor."

But, there is no time to rest. My tattoo glows so brightly that this time, it feels as if I'm being dipped into a scalding pot of water. I cry out in pain as I double over, clutching Zara's hand and Selene's shoulder. I don't think that this is supposed to happen. It's painfully obvious, no pun intended, that there is something wrong.

Somewhere in the distance I feel the world being ripped apart with the savagery one would use to rip someone's limbs from their body. The wrongness of the act doesn't disappear even as it's mended over again. Wariness lingers in my core. I try to voice it, but sound won't come out. Fear ices me as I have no idea what to expect next. If it is a confrontation, I don't know if we could survive it.

Right in front of us, there's a tear in the fabric of reality as if someone took a jagged pair of scissors and began cutting. The vibrant colors of another plane bleeds into our existence until the two meld looking like a runny mess of paint. Then, a female form crashes through the void with such force that the entire house shakes and knocks us all off of our feet. It's like a concussion grenade has gone off in front of us; the sheer force of this person's chakra is deafening.

From my back, I look up and meet black, souless eyes. Looking into them is like being thrown into a pit of endless darkness. Emptiness to which there is no escape. My head is throbbing with more intensity and as I touch the back of it, it comes away wet with blood. I'm sure that I have a concussion and I know that Selene and Zara are faring no better, from the sounds of their groans. Even Zahira will not be of any help since she's still unconscious.

The mysterious female fixes her gaze on me and I know then that this is what hell is like. Her presence seems to suck all the light from the room. It takes me a minute to register that she's holding onto an injured, glowing form.

There's movement to my left as well as banging on the door behind me. Yet, the vampires are unable to enter and I'm sure it has everything to do with this monster in front of me. Another second ticks by and we are now all on our feet, hesitant, unsure. I don't look at my allies, refusing to tear my eyes away from the woman in front of me.

She's holding an immortal with a very ugly stomach wound. It's bleeding profusely and I wonder why the wound isn't even starting to heal. Immortals healed like vampires, faster, and this one doesn't even seem to have begun restoration. Jet black hair, beautiful face, I still don't recognize this one in front of me.

She isn't unconscious as I thought. The immortal puts a hand on the woman's cheek and whispers something so quietly that all I see is her lips move. Hesitantly, the monster places her on the floor and disappears. Her vanishing energy leaves the room cold and creepy, like a haunted house. What in the hell is she?

Selene is the first to take a step forward, the glow from the immortal diminishing, showing that she's close to dying. If she dies without the performing the ritual to ascend, she'll be dead for good. Immortals are reborn once they reach a certain age. Their souls repeat the cycle, making them look to be about five or six years old. They retain all of their memories, but have to re-grow into their strength as they age. She doesn't seem as if she'll be lucky to make it more than ten more minutes.

I'd be able to help if I could contact Diana, but I've tried each time with no luck. Why is this one here now? What could have happened? Maybe there is something going on with the immortals. Maybe the actual reason why I can't contact Diana is because she's passed on. My heart drops at the possibility.

Selene is now by the immortal's side. She looks to be about seventeen. She could pass as a junior in high school, not the eons that she actually is. I watch as Selene's eyes go wide in surprise as she reaches out a hand. Then, she stops as if touching the injured immortal will kill her.

"Kaede?" she whispers, fearful and confused.

I frown in puzzlement. Kaede looks like a little girl. This can't be her, can it? But, I know. Kaede was Selene's magical instructor while we were on the plane of the immortals. If anyone would recognize her, it'd be Selene.

The door breaks down behind me, but Zara orders the vampires to stand down and remain close. They leave, but a couple stand near the door in protection. Zara slides to Kaede's side as well and the fondness for this particular immortal is evident from Zara's expression as she takes in her mangled form. She wastes no more time and bites her wrist, bringing it to Kaede's mouth.

I stand there trying to piece it all together, but nothing seems to make sense. My tattoo was trying to warn me. Something is most definitely not right.

Kaede drinks Zara's blood, but it does little more than slows the flow of blood. There is no magical stitching of her skin or anything and worried, Selene looks at me for help, but I'm powerless. I may have been marked by the immortals, but I don't have their type of power.

Or do I?

"Rayne," Kaede's soft voice whispers to me. I step closer and fall to my knees to hear. "There is something that you must know. We've all been betrayed."

My blood runs cold as I can only guess what she's truly telling me. "Who did this to you?" I ask forcefully. My tattoo burns once more as if it too is in fear of something.

"You can't trust them," she mouths almost silently before passing out.

Selene, Zara, and I all share a look of horror as gentle Kaede's wound continues to spill scarlet blood on the floor of Zahira's home.

Be sure not to miss the new Young Adult Urban Fantasy novel by Alanna J. Faison:

The Edge of Awakening

The Soul Tamer Series Book I

A horrible monster killed me.

Not just me. There were so many bodies. There was so much blood. The screams, I can still hear the screams. Why can I still hear the screams? I open my mouth to speak, but I can't. I don't remember how.

Why can't I?

I'm floating. There is no wind, there is no cold, no heat, it just is. A vacuum of endless confusion. The screams. Where am I? Why are there screams? I try to awaken from this dream, but there is no shift in my consciousness. I forget again why I'm here. I forget who I am.

Then, I remember. My name. My name is Jasmine. Jasmine Marie Whitmore. But, I died. I died on the floor of my parent's room, my throat cut open by a horrible monster. I ran as fast as I could. I punched in the code to the panic room, but I wasn't fast enough. The door didn't shut fast enough.

What was that thing? Why did it come for us? Why am I here? Who am I?

Jasmine. My name is Jasmine.